WASIM AND WAQAR
Imran's Inheritors

WASIM AND WAQAR

Imran's Inheritors

By John Crace

Foreword by Imran Khan

B🖤XTREE

FOR JILL

This edition first published in the UK 1993
by BOXTREE LIMITED, Broadwall House,
21 Broadwall, London SE1 9PL

Hardback edition first published in the UK, 1992

1 3 5 7 9 10 8 6 4 2

1-85283-833-7

Cover Design by Design 23
Typesetting by DP Photosetting, Aylesbury, Bucks
Printed and bound in Great Britain by Cox & Wyman,
Reading, Berkshire

A catalogue record for this book is available from the British Library

Contents

Acknowledgements

I would like to express my appreciation to all those who have directly and indirectly helped me write this book. Without their knowledge, time, and support, it could not have been written.

Special thanks are due to:

Wasim and Waqar.

Imran Khan, Javed Miandad, Javed Burki, Wasim Bari, Asif Iqbal, Intikhab Alam, Salim Malik, Rameez Raja, Ijaz Ahmed, Aaqib Javed, Mushtaq Ahmed, Aamir Sohail, Moin Khan, Zahid Fazal, Inzamam-ul-Haq, Wasim Haider, Iqbal Sikander, and Nadeem Abassi.

Mohammad Azharuddin, Neil Fairbrother, Graeme Fowler, David Hughes, Ian Greig, Gehan Mendis, Alec Stewart, and Graham Thorpe.

Omar Kureishi, Iftikhar Ahmed, Munir Hussein, Qamar Ahmed, Inayat Baloch, Imtiaz Sipra, and Iqbal Munir.

Huma, Naeem Quyoum, Jonathan Barnett and John Holder.

Terry Blake and Stephen Green.

David Munden, Ben Radford, Raj Chengappa, Tom Butler, Tim Coleman, Brian Murgatroyd, and Geoff & Lina Denman.

Mum & Dad, Caroline Taylor-Thomas, and Liz Good.

Last, but not least, to Adrian Sington and Rod Green at Boxtree.

Foreword by Imran Khan

I take great pride and great pleasure in seeing Pakistan cricket reach its current level of success. When I went to England with the Pakistan team in 1971, it was with a team full of talented players, but from the moment the plane landed at Heathrow, nobody in the team believed we could win. Most of the players considered it far more important to return to Pakistan with personal glory, than with team success. The tour was seen as a place for personal enhancement, and there was no sign of any team spirit on or off the pitch. I will never forget the last Test at Leeds when we stood to win the series. During the match I heard a number of our players saying that they hoped that one of our best players did badly, because otherwise he would be unbearable. The result of the game didn't seem to concern them; in fact, we lost by about 25 runs.

There was a better team spirit for the 1974 tour, but even so I felt our team was disjointed, and had no real cohesion. When we arrived in Australia in 1976, the desire to win was there, but somehow we never clicked as a team. We had some superb batsmen. Asif, Majid and Zaheer were great players;

Mushtaq and Sadiq were fine players with solid techniques; Javed Miandad joined the side in the late seventies, and we had strong reserves in Wasim Raja, Mohsin Khan, and Mudassar. Yet we never even won one one-day competition. With that sort of batting you would expect to do well in the limited overs game, but even there we were struggling.

We would often go into games with a negative attitude. It's bowlers that win Test matches for the most part, yet even though our bowling attack was very weak, with Sarfraz and myself as the only two main bowlers, captains used to pack the side with batting rather than choose bowlers who could support us. We would go into games hoping to get a draw rather than a win.

I feel that the transition to a winning side came when I became captain. The key was that I never felt it necessary to hang on to my captaincy at all costs, and I could take risks. I wanted results, and I could play for them. I told the Pakistan authorities that I no longer wanted pitches to be prepared that would guarantee a draw. If we under-prepared a pitch to produce a spinning wicket, it was to get a result. When we had our greatest successes we did not have all the big names of the seventies, but we began to play as a team, and in the process played some outstanding cricket.

However, we still lacked quick bowling, and it was the arrival of Wasim in 1985 that gave me some extra help. From 1976 to 1982/3, when I got my stress fracture, I was the lone bowler, and the pressure was always on me. I had support from Sarfraz, but he wasn't a strike bowler. Wasim was genuinely fast, and he came on to the scene at just the right moment, for by then I was the wrong side of thirty, and I don't know how long I could have sustained the attack single-handedly.

It was wonderful to have a bowler of Wasim's ability to bowl with for so long, and my one regret is that by the time Waqar came into the side in 1989, I had almost given up bowling, and that I never had the chance to bowl along side them both when I was at my best. I now wish that I had maintained my bowling, but I kept dilly-dallying over whether to play or not. I had long periods when I didn't play; I gave up county cricket after the West Indies tour of 1988; and so staying fit enough to bowl fast became very difficult. Consequently, I haven't been able to help Wasim and Waqar in the way that I could have, or indeed, should have.

Wasim and Waqar, along with Aaqib, who is very underrated by most people, will be the mainstays of the Pakistan bowling attack for some time. The reason why I take extra pride in their achievement is because in Pakistan we do not have a first-class cricket structure. If we had a structure like Australia, England, or South Africa, the system would have thrown these players up, and I could take no credit. I was very fortunate to see these players and give them a chance in the national team, and now Pakistan is very fortunate to have them. The standard of regional cricket in Pakistan is worse than club level in Australia, and so really it is remarkable that we can produce cricketers of their talent.

Wasim is one of the most talented cricketers that I've ever seen. He has so much potential that it can be very frustrating at times when he doesn't perform as well as I know he can. On his day he's unplayable when he runs in and bowls fast, but God hasn't gifted him with natural fitness; he's fragile, and still needs to work on his strength. He hasn't developed as quickly as a batsman of his ability might have done, but he's still young and has plenty of time. When he does reach his potential, there won't be a player in the world to come close to him.

Waqar doesn't have the natural talent of Wasim, but he's more athletic and even hungrier. I've never seen a cricketer rise so quickly from nowhere to become the best in the world. Sadly, he's had a stress fracture in his back, but when he's fit again he and Wasim can take Pakistan cricket to the pinnacles of achievement.

Christchurch, New Zealand
March 1992.

1

Imran's Legacy

A dull, overcast June day in Edgbaston in 1971, with only a few thousand spectators foolhardy enough to brave the cold, is hardly the setting one would picture for the Test baptism of Imran Khan. A full house at Lord's or Lahore would have seemed more appropriate for the man who was to become the most successful player in Pakistani cricket history.

The performance was as prosaic as the location. As Pakistan amassed a total in excess of 600, with Zaheer Abbas making 274 and Mushtaq Mohammad and Asif Iqbal both helping themselves to centuries, Imran's contribution was a mere 5 before he was run out. And that was the highlight of his debut. Entrusted to open the bowling with Asif Masood, his first 4 deliveries to Colin Cowdrey were all wild inswinging full tosses, and after 5 erratic overs he was taken off. Although he came back later to bowl some tidier spells, he failed to take a wicket in conditions that were ideal for swing bowling.

Unsurprisingly, with Sarfraz Nawaz and Salim Altaf recovered from injury, Imran wasn't selected for the final two Test matches. Indeed it would have been no great shock to anyone in Pakistan, or England, if he had joined the ranks of those cricketers famous only for playing one Test, since he had shown few signs of having the temperament or technique for the five-day game.

The 1971 tour to England was a chastening experience for Imran. He had arrived in the country with an absurdly inflated opinion of his cricketing capabilities considering he didn't even have a measured run-up to the wicket for his bowling. By the end of the summer he was left in no doubt, both by his performances, and his team mates, that he was an inexperienced teenager with a great deal to learn about the game. Fortunately for Imran, and for Pakistan, he was given the ideal opportunity to develop his potential when Worcestershire signed him to play county cricket for the following season.

His career thereafter is well documented. After a number of years playing both for the county and Oxford University, where he was elected captain in his second year, his form had sufficiently improved for him to be included in the Pakistani touring team to England in 1974. If his performances on this tour weren't exactly earth shattering, they at least indicated that he was worth his place in the side.

It was the 1976–7 Pakistan tour to Australia that brought Imran world-wide recognition. His 12 for 165 in the final Test at Sydney not only gave Pakistan their first ever Test match victory in Australia, but also squared a series they were widely expected to lose. 25 wickets in the series that followed against the West Indies in the Caribbean confirmed his new found status, and this was further cemented when he was one of only three Pakistanis, the others being Asif Iqbal and Majid Khan, who were initially invited to play for the World XI in World Series Cricket.

Since his re-admission into Test cricket for the home series against India in 1978–9, he has been a virtual ever-present in the Pakistan side, injury and personal whim permitting. He was made captain for the 1982 tour to England, and apart from the Sri Lanka tour to Pakistan in 1985–6, has been reappointed for every series for which he has declared himself available. He was even forced out of retirement to resume the mantle for the Pakistan tour to the West Indies in 1988 at the personal request of General Zia, the then ruler of Pakistan.

Imran's Test record is unparalleled in Pakistan's history, and it bears comparison with any of the great all-rounders. He has taken over 350 wickets, and for many years had to shoulder the responsibility of being Pakistan's only strike bowler. He has scored over 3500 runs, including 6 centuries. Not as many as one might expect, perhaps, but for many years he was regarded primarily as a bowler, and a batting line-up that often included Sadiq Mohammad, Majid, Mushtaq, Javed Miandad, Asif, Wasim Raja, and Intikhab Alam did not give him many chances to build an innings early in his career. It is surely no coincidence that 4 of his centuries have come in the last five years as his own bowling has declined and Wasim Akram, and latterly Waqar Younis and Aaqib Javed, have come forward to spearhead the attack.

His personal Test record notwithstanding, what makes Imran's career truly remarkable is his record as captain. Many all-rounders have found it impossible to maintain their own performances when given the extra responsibility; Imran appears to relish the extra pressure, and both his batting and his bowling have improved greatly since his appointment. It is a very special quality, and one that only Richie Benaud and Gary Sobers, in recent years, have had. Under Imran's leadership Pakistan have drawn series against the West Indies, home and away, defeated India and England in their own countries, and defeated India and Australia at home. This record of success in the last decade can only be matched by the West Indians, and one is left to wonder what might have happened if Imran had had the battery of fast bowlers at the disposal of Clive Lloyd and Viv Richards.

To say that Imran Khan enjoys a god-like status in Pakistan would be flattering some of the minor deities. Anything he says or does is news. A visit to Ascot, or an evening with someone who has royal connections, may rate an item in the gossip columns over here on a slow news day, but in Pakistan you can rest assured that it will be front-page material.

It is easy to get waylaid by all the tittle-tattle of Imran's 'haughty good looks' and his 'playboy image' and forget the real reason that he is so revered. His following is not restricted in Pakistan, as it is in England, to a few cricket aficionados and adoring hordes of women, but is truly nationwide. He is loved every bit as much by the men of the country, as by the women. Pakistan is a relatively young country that has for a long time felt patronized by the West. Respect is a very important part of Islamic culture, and it is this that Pakistanis seek from the rest of the world. When Imran is reported as hobnobbing with royalty it is a symbol that not just Imran but the whole of Pakistan is being treated with respect and equality.

Imran's activities on and off the pitch have made him the most widely recognized Pakistani in the world, even in non-cricket playing countries. For a while, Benazir Bhutto equalled Imran for popularity, but since her return to Pakistan and her political discrediting amidst allegations of corruption, he has been unrivalled. His appointment as UNICEF's special representative for sport, and his globe-trotting fundraising in support of the Cancer Research Hospital in Lahore, have further consolidated his appeal. As a Pakistani woman living in London put it, 'If you showed anyone in the West a picture of Imran, or Pakistan's Prime Minister, Nawaz Sharif, there is no doubt who would be recognized more often. I am sure that if Imran were to stand for political office he would be elected.'

However, there is no disputing that his cricketing success is the basis of his appeal in Pakistan. Since Imran, cricket has replaced hockey as the national game. In any park, or on any street corner of Lahore or Karachi, children will be playing cricket, oblivious to the surrounding traffic. Success on the cricket field is a reflection of the success of the whole country, and therefore an important source of national pride. Winning the 1987 series in England was much more than a mere victory on the cricket field, as Imran relates. 'The Pakistani community in Britain faces a lot of racial harassment. If anyone tries to deny that, they are fooling themselves. There is racial tension. Pakistanis feel looked down upon, and so the team doing well is a way of them saying they are equals.'

In a country notorious for its selectorial machinations, Imran's Test career has spanned an unprecedented twenty years. He has become the symbol, and the father, of modern Pakistani cricket. Two stories are told that illustrate this. At the 1987 World Cup semi-final in Lahore, when Pakistan met Australia, the press were keen to know the composition of the Pakistani side. Imran was out on the field doing his usual warm-up routine, and the selectors were reduced to begging him to release details of the team, which Imran refused to give until the training session was over. Likewise, on the West Indies tour to Pakistan, one of the West Indian batsmen suspected that Imran was picking at the seam of the ball. He mentioned this to the umpire and asked him to tell Imran to stop. A few deliveries later, the batsman noticed that the same thing appeared to be happening; again, he went to the umpire and said, 'I thought that you had asked Imran to stop.' Back came the reply, 'I did, but he said that he didn't want to.'

Both these anecdotes may well be apocryphal, or at the very least highly exaggerated, but to an extent that is irrelevant. Most people believe they could be true. Such is Imran's charisma and pre-eminence in Pakistan that he is considered of far more importance than any selector or umpire.

That Imran has changed the complexion of Pakistani cricket is no accident of fate. He has worked hard at it, and has always been prepared to stand up and be counted. Intikhab remembers captaining the 1974 touring team to England and asking the players if anyone was willing to open the innings as the nominated openers had been failing. Imran was the only person to volunteer.

The willingness to take a risk for the sake of the team was previously unheard of in Pakistani teams of the seventies. As Asif Iqbal says, 'We were basically a team of individuals. We had some class players, but the emphasis was that if you were a middle-order batsman, that's all you were. No one was willing to be adaptable.'

Imran puts it a great deal more strongly. 'When I started playing for Pakistan there was no team spirit, and it was basically every man for himself. There were times when a bowler had worked out how to use conditions to his advantage, and he would deliberately not tell the others what was going on so that they should not be successful. I've known strike bowlers in the Pakistan team who hated each other and never spoke to each other throughout their careers. They positively enjoyed it when one of the others got thrashed around the field. That's why I've never given any credit to any of the Pakistani bowlers for helping me that much. Sarfraz did occasionally, but that was much later on, when I was already a superior bowler to him; before that, he rarely told me anything. This failure to pass on help is undoubtedly one reason why it took me ten years to develop my potential as a fast bowler.'

Imran may have had to learn his craft by trial and error, but he has gone out of his way to ensure that his successors do not have to. The rapid rise to world class of bowlers such as Wasim Akram and Waqar Younis is testament to that, and both players acknowledge the assistance that Imran has given to all aspects of their bowling from the run-up to psyching out the batsman. But the help has not been restricted to the cricket field. 'When I started bowling I knew nothing about fitness. I had to develop my own training programme for my body. I have been able to tell them which muscles will come under pressure, and which they will have to build, to help them avoid injury.'

Apart from the obvious consequence of improving other players' abilities, this willingness to impart his knowledge has helped to create a team spirit that had hitherto been missing. Players began to trust one another and to play for each other rather than for themselves. The whole dressing-room atmosphere underwent a metamorphosis. Where previously senior players had regarded newcomers to the team with barely veiled disdain, and treated them as servants, the juniors are now welcomed and made to feel a valuable part of the team. It may seem a grandiose claim to attribute this change of attitude to one man in particular, but it is one that holds good. Imran has led from the front with his performances on the field and his behaviour off it, and he has created a team that has learnt how to win. He asks of his team only what he asks of himself, and the players respect him for it. If he calls for an extra practice session, they know he too will be there.

If one considers the amount of talent in the Pakistan teams of the seventies it is almost criminal that they achieved so little success. Imran has changed this, and has produced the ideal cricketing milieu in which youngsters like Wasim and Waqar have been able to thrive.

Like A.H. Kardar, Pakistan's first-ever captain, Imran has always tried to take a firm line on team selection. 'The captain is the one with his head on the chopping block. When a team does badly, the first finger is always pointed at the captain. Therefore, I have always tried to play the team in which I have confidence,' Imran explains. One of the guidelines to which he adheres is that selection should be on merit, rather than on nepotism and regional bias, and it is a precept that has won him a loyal following among the team.

Nepotism has been and still is to a great extent, endemic within the Pakistani cricket structure. Indeed there is a gentle irony that Imran owed his introduction to first-class cricket to nepotism. The chairman of selectors for Lahore was his uncle, and the captain and the senior player were cousins. Javed Burki, the former Test player, captained Imran so well, shielding him from the better batsmen when things were going badly, that he finished the season as the second highest wicket taker in first-class cricket. The allegations of nepotism did not end there, for many felt that his inclusion in the 1971 touring party to England owed much to his cousin Majid, and it was not till some years later that it was unanimously considered that Imran was worth his place on merit.

It is easy for Western critics to take a high moral stance over nepotism, and forget that the role of the family is fundamentally different in Islamic culture. In Pakistan, family ties come before all others; the family is the essential economic and social unit, and its interests come first, and members are expected to give support to the family when needed. Everything is done with the family in mind. As Javed Burki explains, 'It is part of our culture. Abuses do take place. We even had a situation whereby a Prime Minister's mother was the Senior Minister, and father-in-law was Chairman of the Public Accounts Committee. The positive aspect is that family life in countries like ours is very strong, and there is little social disintegration. We have no old people's homes because the old are looked after within the family.'

Nevertheless, Imran remains opposed to nepotism, and sees the roots of its main excesses in the structure of first-class cricket in Pakistan. 'At present, we have a system where there is department cricket, the banks and airlines, etc., competing for the Wills Cup and BCCP Patrons Trophy, and regional cricket competing for the Quaid-e-Azam Trophy. What we really need is to reorganize the structure wholly on a regional basis, like the County Championship in England and the Sheffield Shield in Australia.' He is unmoved by protestations that economic considerations preclude any change. Before the departments came into the game in the seventies there was no money in first-class cricket, and there were no employed professionals. There is so little money in regional cricket, that apart from Karachi, there is not a single local or regional association that owns its own ground or office, and there are no signs that sponsors are willing to come forward.

'We have to change, but sadly there is vested interest which is trying to prevent it. The officials of the departments do not want a diminution of their power. The selectors are immensely influential, and they are answerable to no one. They can choose whoever they like, from anywhere in Pakistan, and providing the team does reasonably well, nobody will question them. Consequently, favourites get picked. The same thing is going on in the regions, because the selectors there are unaccountable too. Lahore is a city of five million inhabitants, the strongest cricketing centre in Pakistan, and its team was actually relegated to the second division. The captain himself said to me, "I was told by the selectors that there were five players whose places I could not challenge; the other six I could pick on merit." This sort of thing goes on all the time, and until we change the structure it will continue to do so.'

The intrigues that accompany the current organization are dizzying in their complexity. A captain's priority in a game is often not to win, but to ensure a certain player can score a half century or grab a 5-wicket haul. Conversely, bowlers who are out of favour are taken off if they look like they are beating the bat regularly, and batsmen are told that they must score quickly. Players learn that a dinner with a selector who will then indulge in *sifarish*, putting in a good word for them, is often time better spent than practice in the nets. For many regional players their primary purpose is to be noticed by a departmental side so that he will have a job, and so there is a premium on fighting and plotting to advance his own prospects and retard the others. Both Lahore and Karachi have two regional teams each. However, because of a shortage of funds or an unwillingness to spend them, these are selected in such a way as to ensure that one is knocked out of the competition early on. Inevitably, a talented player without connections will find himself in the weaker team.

Selection at Test level is not nearly so random as it takes

place in a more public arena, but an odd anomaly comes to mind. Anwar Miandad, Javed's younger brother, was made twelfth man for a game in which he wasn't even included in the original fourteen, and Shakeel Khan, was picked for the one-day international against England at Peshawar in 1987, when he had only played a single game for Habib Bank that season. Even Imran has not escaped such criticism in the Pakistani media. He has been taken to task by the Karachi press for giving preferential treatment to Punjabis. He was once criticized for his championing of Abdul Qadir, which now seems laughable, but there seems to be more substance to these claims with regard to his handling of Zakir Khan, the fast bowler. Zakir was taken to India, Sri Lanka, Sharjah, England, and the West Indies, yet has only two Tests and a handful of one-day internationals to show for his travels.

These sort of accusations are levelled at Test captains the world over; after all, Graham Gooch dropped David Gower, a player with over 8000 Test runs and with three hundreds in his last six matches, merely because he couldn't get on with him. Imran himself is characteristically unrepentant. 'Sometimes you make mistakes. I did with Mansoor Akhtar. He had so much talent, and I gave him every chance, but he just didn't have the temperament. The problem again stems from our domestic cricket structure. I stopped playing in 1981 because I found it so unsatisfying; there would be pitches where there were piles of sand half-way through my run-up to ensure that I bowled off a short run, or else there would be endless crowd disruptions. Worse still, because none of the departments have their own ground, the same pitches get hired from the municipality every time. The result is that the wickets are over-used; they are either completely dead or underprepared, and spinners take a disproportionate number of wickets. Likewise, teams play all their games on the same ground; it's not the same as in other countries where you play half your matches at home, and the other half away. This season, the Karachi wicket is tailor-made for batting, whilst in Lahore the pitches are much greener. It makes it almost impossible to assess form. A batsman playing in Karachi will score hundreds of runs, but he is not necessarily better than someone who only scores a few in Lahore.

'In the end you can only choose those players who you believe to have the ability, and give them an extended run in the team to let them show they have the temperament. You just don't know how they're going to cope with different sorts of wickets and crowd pressure, because they've never had to contend with them. What is of most concern is that so much talent in this country is being wasted through not being given the right opportunities, and this is being ignored because the national team has been so successful. The BCCP even tries to claim credit for the success, which is absurd. Some players are simply so talented that they could not be overlooked, and others like Zahid Fazal have come up straight from the Under-19 side and have by-passed the first-class structure altogether.'

Imran's outspokenness on nepotism and corruption in Pakistani domestic cricket has won him the loyalty of his team, and is seen as further evidence of the fair-mindedness he has demonstrated throughout his career. In the mid-seventies he joined the players rebellion against the Test match fees paid by the BCCP on principle, as he was wealthy enough not to need the extra money, and it is widely recognized that it was within his ambit to use the first-class system to his own advantage had he been so minded. That he hasn't, has proved to players at all levels that he has their and Pakistan's future at heart.

Moreover, Imran has actively gone out of his way to enable his players to develop their talent. Recognizing the limitations of cricket in Pakistan, he has used his contacts to find openings for players overseas where they can experience a variety of conditions and wickets. He has been instrumental in finding Wasim Akram, Waqar Younis, and Aaqib Javed English counties, but the lengths to which he will go are no better illustrated than his attempt to get Abdul Qadir to Sussex. Imran had come to an arrangement with Garth Le Roux, the South African pace bowler who was also signed to Sussex at the time, that the two of them would split their salaries three ways with Abdul Qadir if Sussex would sign him. Imran was going to let him stay in his flat in Brighton as he wasn't using it because he was commuting from London. It was a brilliant idea that would have cost Sussex nothing. The only drawback was that Imran, Qadir, and Le Roux could not have played at the same time. Sussex declined the offer. It is a refusal that seems at best unimaginative; one can only speculate on how effective Qadir might have been on a bouncy Hove wicket.

Umpiring in Pakistan has always provoked controversy. Just three years after Pakistan had been given test status the first row erupted, with the MCC touring team taking exception to the conduct of Idries Beg in Peshawar. Since then, numerous umpiring disputes have flared up culminating in the nadir of the Shakoor Rana – Mike Gatting affair at Faisalabad, and the bad-tempered Australian tour the year after.

There is no doubt that the umpiring has often been neither honest nor fair. Sport in Pakistan is more obviously directly linked to politics than in many other countries. Governments have tended to view success in sport as a fundamental part of maintaining their popularity, and have been prepared to go to some lengths to achieve it. Appointment to the Cricket Board of Control comes directly under the auspices of central government, and knowledge of the game has never been a primary requirement for selection. A Test match defeat has frequently led to Board members being given the sack, which in turn has meant that the Board has succumbed to putting pressure on the umpires who are in their employ. It is hard for umpires to resist; they are not professional and failure to comply will merely mean they are never asked to stand again.

One Pakistani umpire described pressure as, 'Pakistan in trouble at 25 for 4 at Karachi, with a loud appeal for leg before against Javed Miandad.' The same can be said for different parts of the world. Substitute Allan Border in Sydney, Martin Crowe in Auckland, or Viv Richards in Antigua, in a similar position and it is not surprising that there have been so many complaints from touring teams of umpires giving so-called 'home' decisions. What is problematic is that it is almost impossible to distinguish between incompetence and bias on many occasions. Players will tolerate the former, but not the latter.

This issue has caused much bad blood amongst the cricket-playing nations. Pakistan feels that it is never given the benefit of the doubt even when genuine errors are made, whilst what they consider glaring examples of bias, in New Zealand in particular, over a long period of time are excused. The waters are further muddied because Pakistan attributes this apparent double standard to a racist, colonial attitude on the part of the white cricket playing countries.

Throughout this quagmire of accusation and counter-accusation, Imran has remained untainted and indeed has done much to give Pakistan the moral high ground with his constant advocacy for neutral umpires. 'The only umpires who are consistently better than ours are the English because they are professional and umpire regularly, and even not all of them are good. All over the world I have encountered umpiring that was incompetent and biased, and the only solution is to have neutral umpires which would remove the inflammatory half of the problem. I cannot see why the International Cricket Council does not make this mandatory. It has just passed a new ruling on the code of conduct whereby anyone who shows dissent may be banned for three Tests, but tell me one time when a major incident of indiscipline has taken place on the cricket field where umpiring wasn't the root cause? It happens when the touring team loses faith in the home umpires.'

On Imran's urging, Pakistan became the first country to appoint neutral umpires for a home series when P.D. Reporter and V.K. Ramaswamy of India were chosen to officiate in the Test matches against the West Indies in 1986–7. The experiment was repeated for the Indian tour of 1989, with the appointment of John Holder and John Hampshire, and negotiations were in progress for the New Zealand tour of 1990 until Martin Crowe's tactless comment, 'We don't know anything about the two guys appointed, but we believe they will be better than having two Pakistani umpires,' scuppered them. That sort of a remark from a New Zealander was considered too much!

Even when Pakistani officials have been standing, there have been few controversies whilst Imran has been skipper. All of Pakistan's umpires unofficially admit that Imran has been the one captain who has never asked them to 'help him out'. On one occasion the umpires walked into the Pakistani dressing-room and asked him for instructions. 'You do your job, and we'll do ours,' was the reply. Astonishingly, Imran has even come under attack for his views on neutral umpires. Tony Lewis wrote in the Sunday Telegraph of May 1989 that Imran was 'so intent on pushing his belief in neutral umpires ... he will be satisfied with none and passes on his lack of respect to the whole team'. This is a harsh judgement on someone who is respected throughout the world for fair play, and has often recalled a player who he did not believe to be out, most notably when he called back Desmond Haynes who had been given out to a bump-ball catch in a match that Haynes went on to win for the West Indies.

Apart from the intrinsic injustice of partial umpiring, Imran realized that the structure was doing a disservice to the players themselves. They were being given assistance in games in which they had no need of it, thereby devaluing the performance; even if they were not being helped out it was generally assumed that they were, and the team failed to get the true credit it deserved. Amidst the bitterness of England's tour in 1987 it is generally overlooked that the England batsmen were unable to read Abdul Qadir and would have comfortably lost the game in Lahore even without Shakeel Khan's intervention.

Imran's approach has ensured that the Pakistani players receive due recognition for their efforts world wide. In turn, they have found that they can compete, and indeed defeat, the other Test playing countries on equal terms, and their confidence to play attractive cricket has increased commensurately. In the process, Pakistan have changed from a team whose first objective was to avoid defeat, into one of the most attacking in the world.

For many years it was a widely held cricket axiom that Pakistan could never produce genuinely quick bowlers, a belief based largely on the supposition that the pitches in Pakistan rendered fast bowling redundant, and that spinners were the key to success. Sure, there had been Khan Mohammad and Mahmood Hussain in the fifties and sixties, Sarfraz in the seventies but, effective as they were, they could only be described as fast-medium. Before Imran, Pakistan had never had a bowler to compare with the likes of Larwood, Tyson, Lillee, Thomson, or Holding and Roberts.

Although Imran had always wanted to bowl fast, it took him some time to develop into Pakistan's fastest bowler. On his first tour in 1971, he was medium-fast with a Jeff Thomson-like slinging delivery, which was inaccurate and ineffective. The following year at Worcester, he changed his action but lost his speed completely and for a few seasons became a medium pacer. Gradually his speed increased but his open-chestedness necessitated another change in his action. With help from Mike Proctor and John Snow during the Packer years, Imran sorted out his run-up, incorporated a jump in his delivery stride to get side on, and began to bowl some genuinely quick spells.

By the early eighties Imran had mastered the art of bowling with the new ball, and was fast enough to be ranked alongside any of the West Indian pacemen. He was by now so confident of his abilities that he could nominate which balls would take wickets, as Javed Miandad relates. 'Against India on their tour to Pakistan in 1982/3, he would bowl a succession of inswingers, and then shout to the slip fielders in Urdu to get ready for a catch, as he was about to bowl an outswinger. More often than not, the edge would come.'

The story of Imran's development into a fast bowler sounds rather matter-of-fact when it is relayed in black and white. It is worth bearing in mind, though, the self-confidence and imagination that is required to be the first person in a country to break through barriers of belief and prejudice. India have still not produced any out and out quickies. Kapil Dev has taken over 370 Test wickets, but he has rarely bowled quicker than fast-medium, and he acknowledges that the lack of pacemen is a problem for India. He attributes this to a number of factors, notably that the Indian media build up their cricketers to super-star status so quickly, that there is little incentive for newcomers to work hard at their game, and develop from fast-medium to fast. So worried have the Indians become, that they have established a camp specifically for fast bowlers, under the watchful guidance of Dennis Lillee.

Whatever the successes of this camp, and one of its protégés Javagal Srinath made his Test debut against Australia in 1991, the obvious question is raised of how India's sub-continental neighbour have managed to produce three of four quality fast bowlers since the mid-eighties. Quite simply, inadvertently or not, Imran has created a tradition of fast bowling in Pakistan. Ask Wasim Akram, Waqar Younis, Aaqib Javed, or Wasim Haider who provided them with the inspiration and motivation to bowl fast, and they will all reply, 'Imran'. Imran proved that fast, swing bowling could take wickets in Pakistan, and slowly but surely the ground authorities recognized this, and began to occasionally prepare faster Test pitches. This has accelerated the progress of the young fast bowlers, and Pakistan now has a pace attack to equal any in the world.

One doesn't need to have much insight to realize that the key to success in Test cricket in the eighties was to have a string of fast bowlers. Astute captains as Clive Lloyd and Viv Richards were, they didn't need much tactical genius for many of their victories. Bowling Ambrose and Bishop for an hour, and then with metronomic precision, replacing them with

Patterson and Walsh, was Viv Richards' key to countless wins. And who can knock it if it works? Wasim Akram is only twenty-five, whilst Waqar and Aaqib are barely twenty. If all can stay fit, it is likely that Imran has created a tradition that will see Pakistan become the most successful team of the nineties.

Unlike many captains, Imran has always had one eye on the future. He has an almost dynastic, patriarchal attitude towards his team. His retirement has been heralded almost as often as an operatic diva's, but it is likely that the World Cup in Australia, and the tour of England really will be his swansong. After a career which spanned three decades, and which has helped change the character of Pakistani cricket, he will leave the stage to his successors; the inheritors of his legacy.

2

Wasim Learns His Trade

Wasim Akram's rise to international recognition was nothing short of bewildering. After just one first-class game of cricket he was selected for the Pakistan tour of New Zealand in 1985; by the end of that tour he was the youngest player ever to take 10 wickets in a Test match, and he's never looked back since.

It is one of the contradictions of cricket in Pakistan, that a country infamous for anomalies in the selection procedure is one of the few that would countenance the idea of playing an untried youngster at international level. The very idea is anathema to the English and Australian system. It wasn't even as if Wasim was well-connected in the cricket world. 'I've no idea why I was so lucky. Some people slog away for years without being given a chance, and yet I was chosen without even having represented a department side.'

Wasim was born in Lahore on 3 June 1966. His father, Choudhry Mohammad Akram, ran a large spare parts business and the family lived in the affluent area of Model Town. However, while his brothers, Naeem and Nadeem, tended to spend more of their time in the company of their

father, Wasim and his younger sister, Sofia, were undoubtedly closer to their mother, Irshaad Kausar. Close friends have
observed that, even nowadays, Wasim can be somewhat
formal and reserved with his father.

Certainly, it was Wasim's mother who was the most
influential in his education. 'She tried to be really strict with
me, insisting that academic success should be my priority. She
was always trying to make me study. My father was more
relaxed, and often gave me whatever I wanted.'

Like many children from a similar background, Wasim
attended a fee-paying English medium school. Such schools
were founded in the days of the Raj for the education of
British children living in the sub-continent, but continue to
thrive even today, with some of the colonial traditions intact.
Cathedral School in Lahore, to which Wasim was sent, had an
English headmaster and all lessons other than Urdu were
conducted in English.

'I wasn't very academically gifted, and neither was I very
conscientious. I was always missing lessons. Often I would
take my sister to school, leave her there, and arrange to meet
a few of my classmates in the canteen outside the school gates.
Then, still in uniform, we'd spend hours riding, sometimes
four to a bike, around the city. The night before my tenth-
grade matriculation exam in English, I chose to play in a
tennis-ball cricket tournament rather than study. Luckily, I
still passed, but my mother went mad when she found out.'

Most of Wasim's enthusiasm and energy was channelled
into sport. While he may not have devoted much time to
academia, he was truly diligent where games, especially
cricket, were concerned. 'I always loved cricket. When I was
about ten; I had this bat with the names of Imran, Asif, Majid,
Mushtaq, and Zaheer, the big five of Pakistani cricket who

played for Kerry Packer written on it; I used to fantasize about having my name added to that list. Imran was always a big hero of mine. I went to see him playing for PIA once, when he still played domestic cricket, and I queued up for his autograph. I treasured it, and I've still got it at home somewhere.'

He was chosen for the school team when he was twelve. From the start he used to open the bowling and batting, taking a few wickets and scoring useful runs on the small college ground. By the time he left Cathedral School three years later he was captain of cricket, and beginning to make a name for himself. 'I used to play the whole time. I would play at home in the garage with my brother Naeem. Once, I bounced him with a tennis ball and hit him on the head. He lost his temper with me, and threw the cricket bat at me. I would play at home in the nets between three and six in the afternoon, and at night I would play in a tennis-ball tournament.'

These games were a nightly attraction in the lanes and streets of Mazang Adda in the old part of Lahore. Teams would come from all over town to play. Each would put up a few hundred rupees to compete, and the winner would take the pool. Sometimes there were as many as twenty teams playing a six-over a side tournament, and the competition would go on for hours. Wasim quickly developed a strong reputation for this form of limited overs cricket, and many different teams tried to acquire his services. He also came to the attention of a few talent scouts who lived near by. One, a man named Khalid, was so convinced that Wasim had the makings of a great bowler, that he took him on the back of his bicycle to the Ludhiana Gymkhana cricket club.

Whilst Wasim's new school, Islamia college, did not consider him worth a full-time place in the cricket team during his first year, two coaches, Sadiq and Saood Khan, at Ludhiana realized that in Wasim they had a rare find. They gave him a great deal of coaching with his bowling, and Wasim was soon an ever-present for the club. They were sufficiently impressed after one game against Lahore Gymkhana in which he took 4 wickets, including those of Rameez Raja whom he clean bowled, and Intikhab, who he had caught behind off a bouncer, that they put his name forward to Khan Moham-mad, the ex-Pakistan fast bowler, for inclusion in the summer 'Talent Hunt' camp for the hundred best cricketers in Lahore.

Wasim remembers the camp well. 'I felt overwhelmed. It was June 1984, and I was only just eighteen. Mohsin Kamal and Rameez who had both played Test cricket, and Ijaz Ahmed, who had played for Pakistan Under-19 were all there. I used to hang around and watch, as the older players never used to give me a chance. Eventually, the camp commandant Agha Saadat threw me the ball, and said "Why don't you have a bowl". I took a few wickets bowling big inswingers from around the wicket, and when the national selectors came to watch a few days later, I again performed quite well.'

The selectors clearly liked what they saw, and Wasim was soon invited to join the Under-19 national camp in Karachi. 'It was another big shock. Suddenly my name was in the papers, and everybody was talking about me. My father bought me an air ticket, so I wouldn't have to travel down to Karachi by train, but I was still very nervous when I arrived. At the camp I was given a lot of help and encouragement by Khan Mohammad. I altered my action, keeping my right arm higher in my delivery stride and started to bowl very well.'

One person who was particularly impressed by Wasim was Javed Miandad who was captaining the national side, while Imran was in Australia recovering from a stress fracture. 'I decided to have a bat in the Under-19 nets, and Akram bowled to me. I immediately realized he had a very special talent. He had wonderful command of swing, line and length, and he was very sharp to go with it. Such a naturally gifted bowler was a rare find in the Under-19s and I decided there and then that I wanted to play him in the three-day game against New Zealand in Rawalpindi the following month.'

Wasim's ascent up the cricket ladder has dream-like qualities. It is every Pakistani boy's ambition to represent his country, and Wasim was about to play his first first-class game in the same team as many of his childhood heroes, representing BCCP Patron's XI against a visiting national side. Yet, it's easy to get lost in the seemingly effortless inevitability of Wasim's career, and overlook the determination he needed to accompany his undoubted talent. For all his boisterous and rebellious exterior, Wasim was at heart a shy and naïve teenager, of whom his father said at the time, 'he is so simple and straightforward, that I sometimes wonder when he will understand the harsh realities of life.' Being plunged into an adult world, where, for every person willing him to succeed, there were many who would be happy to see him do badly, was a severe test of character, and had he failed, his career could have ended barely before it had begun.

Wasim was not even certain he would play against New Zealand. 'I was included in the squad of fourteen, but Sarfraz and Tahir Naqqash were the senior bowlers, and I didn't think I'd get a game.' Some mystery surrounds Tahir's eventual exclusion from the eleven. The reason given in the papers was that he was injured, yet Javed is adamant that he dropped him. Whatever the reason, Wasim fully justified his selection.

'I took my first wicket before lunch. John Wright edged to slip where Rameez fumbled the catch, but Salim Malik grabbed it at the second attempt. After lunch, I took 6 more, including Bruce Edgar, and John Reid, to finish with 7–50. I took 2 more wickets in the second innings, and the following day the papers were full of stories about "the new fast bowling sensation".'

Wasim was not chosen for any of the Test matches, but he was picked for a one-day gate at Faisalabad. He didn't perform very well in a rain-affected match, but Javed had already decided that he wanted to take him on the forthcoming tour to New Zealand. 'I came up against a great deal of opposition to his selection. People were saying that Wasim was too young, that the tour would ruin him, and that he should get more experience at home first. But I said that he was going to be our best bowler, and that if he didn't go, I wouldn't either. In the end, the selectors said, "If you want him, take him." '

It was certainly a shock for Wasim to be picked, and Javed remembers that he quickly phoned for advice. 'He wanted to know how much money he should take with him on tour. I jokingly said 50,000 dollars, and he panicked. He didn't even know that the Pakistan Board paid the players.'

Javed soon became a surrogate father figure. Wasim knew nothing of the vagaries of international cricket, and was the original innocent abroad. 'I'd never been out of Pakistan before, and I was very homesick at first. I was very shy about talking in English, and Javed helped me out a lot. He even gave me his food on the aeroplane when I was hungry. I hardly ever went out in the evenings; usually, I would eat supper in my room, maybe have a game of cards with Salim Malik, my room-mate, and go to sleep. The senior players never invited me out, and I just wanted to create a good impression.'

The tour itself was not a great success, with Pakistan losing the three match series 2–0, and with an internal quarrel between Zaheer and Abdul Qadir resulting in the latter being sent home. But for Wasim it was a triumph. After playing in a three-day game against Canterbury, he was not selected again until the second Test match in Auckland, where he made his Test debut. 'I'd never even seen a green wicket before, let alone played on one. We were put into bat, and I came in at 147–8; I was absolutely terrified, and I was just praying that I'd score at least one. I got hit on the knee by Hadlee, and it swelled up very badly. I was out without scoring shortly after. When we fielded, my knee was still giving me trouble and I didn't bowl very well at the start. I took a couple of wickets, but we let them make too many, and we ended up losing by an innings.'

After the game, Javed again helped out, negotiating some free shoes and kit for Wasim from Gray Nicholls, his sponsor. Wasim had arrived on tour hopelessly ill-equipped. He only had one pair of bowling boots, and the reason his knee had been bruised by Hadlee was that the pads that he was wearing were a cheap pair given to him by Javed.

Wasim had no real expectations of playing in the third Test. 'I hadn't played that well, and I was told that they were going to pick Mohsin Kamal for the Dunedin game. Then, the day before, Mohsin got injured, and the selectors informed me I would be playing. That night I was told that they had changed their mind, and it was only the morning of the match that I discovered I was definitely in the side.'

It was a match that Pakistan should have won, but dropped catches in the closing stages cost them dear. Pakistan batted first and made 274, with Qasim Omar and Javed taking the honours. New Zealand replied with 220, 5 of the wickets, including the Crowe brothers, falling to Wasim. In their second innings Pakistan totalled 223, leaving New Zealand 278 to win. At one stage New Zealand were 220–8, with

Wasim again taking 5 wickets, and the last pair at the crease, after Lance Cairns had retired hurt when he was hit by a bouncer from Wasim.

'I'd hit a few batsmen in club cricket before, but this was different. Cairns wasn't wearing a helmet, and I hit him on the back of the head. He collapsed beside the stumps, and had to be stretchered off the field. I was really upset, and it put me off my bowling for a couple of overs. But I got very angry shortly afterwards when I received an official warning for over-use of the short-pitched ball. The umpires had allowed Richard Hadlee and Brendon Bracewell to bowl 3 bouncers an over without saying a word.'

Coney and Chatfield made the runs, and New Zealand scraped home by 2 wickets. However, Wasim's reputation was sealed. In the post-match interview on New Zealand TV, Wasim further endeared himself to the Pakistani nation with his unassuming modesty. The new *wunderkind* of cricket could only manage a few words of broken English, had to rely on Mudassar for help with the translation, and yet at barely eighteen and a half he had swept himself into the record books as the youngest player to take 10 wickets in a Test match.

Immediately after the tour to New Zealand, Pakistan left for Australia for the 'World Championship of Cricket'. Imran had been playing for New South Wales in the Sheffield Shield whilst he fully recovered from injury, and had passed himself fit to rejoin the national side. Wasim was delighted to meet him for the first time. 'He immediately came up to me and, in front of all the other players, said that he had been following my progress with interest on TV, and that he was very impressed by my bowling. To be praised like that by Imran meant the world to me.'

Pakistan opened their campaign with a loss to India, in what proved to be a dress rehearsal for the final, but Wasim's performance in the next game against Australia justified the plaudits he had already received. In reply to Pakistan's total of 262 from their 50 overs, Australia were reduced to 42–5, with Wasim having taken all 5 wickets. He had yorked Kerr, beaten Wessels for pace, caused Dean Jones to play on, Allan Border to tread on his stumps, and Kim Hughes to try and pull a ball that was too close to him. It was a devastating spell from which Australia never recovered, and Pakistan went on to beat England and the West Indies, before losing the final.

By the end of the tournament Wasim was regarded by many as an integral part of the Pakistan side. Imran was even moved to say, 'Wasim is going to be the best left-arm fast bowler since Alan Davidson. He has so much control that he can put the ball exactly where he is asked, plus he has an excellent temperament and doesn't get rattled when hit. Needless to say, I am delighted that I have found a pace bowling partner.' Not a bad tribute to someone who little more than six months earlier was unknown even in Pakistan.

It was a while, though, before Wasim felt at home in the side. 'I had a lot of problems with some of the senior players on that first tour. I was treated like a servant, and once I was even threatened when I was going out for the evening. I won't mention the player involved, but he said, "Go back to bed, or I'll have you sent back to Pakistan." Nowadays there isn't nearly such a divide between the senior and junior players. It's partly because we're all roughly the same age, but it's got a lot to do with the atmosphere Imran generates. He treats the team as adults, and consequently they treat each other with respect.'

After the World Series Cup, Pakistan immediately went to Sharjah for the Rothman's Trophy, for what Wasim describes as his worst ever tour. 'I found it very difficult to bowl on the soft, heavy, sandy soil, and my calves and hamstrings used to stiffen up very quickly. I didn't play too badly myself, but the nadir was losing a game to India after bowling them out for 125. It wasn't even close; we collapsed from 35–1 to 87 all out.'

When Sri Lanka toured Pakistan later in the year, Wasim was chosen for the Test maches, but not for the one-day games. 'I couldn't understand this, as I had thought I had done OK in the one-day games I had played. It took me a long time to have confidence in the selectors, as players can go in and out of favour very quickly in Pakistan.'

Imran had returned to the Test side after an absence of nearly two years, and his inclusion gave Wasim the opportunity to bowl in tandem with him for the first time. Wasim bowled tidily throughout the series, but it was Imran and Tauseef Ahmed who took the honours, as Pakistan won the series 2–0. After a close one-day series against the West Indies, Pakistan's tour to Sri Lanka in February of the next year was a bad-tempered affair. Imran had resumed the captaincy, but Sri Lanka appeared determined to prove they were a front-line Test playing country. As Wasim points out, 'I know they wanted a winning team, but the umpiring was bad; and when I say bad I mean atrocious. Ranatunga was out at least once or twice every innings without being given by the umpire, and we were getting leg before decisions against us from balls that would even have missed a second set of stumps.'

Pakistan were cruising to victory in the first Test with Sri Lanka struggling on 45–4, needing another 80 to avoid an innings defeat, when Ranatunga just walked off the pitch pursued by the umpires, claiming that he was being 'sledged'. Javed takes up the story. 'Even though we felt we had nothing to apologize for, Imran went and apologized; the game was only delayed for half an hour, and we won easily. Winning was our goal and we weren't going to let anything get in the way of that. I was surprised that Mike Gatting didn't adopt that attitude at Faisalabad; if he had apologized immediately, regardless of what he really felt, the game would have restarted first thing the next morning.'

Amid further umpiring controversies and threats from the Pakistan team that they would withdraw from the tour, Sri Lanka levelled the series in Colombo, and a further drawn game at the same venue ensured the series finished all-square. Wasim had again bowled steadily throughout, especially in the second Test, but his end of tour comments that, 'It was incredibly hot, and I didn't enjoy the cricket because the umpiring was so dishonest,' probably summed up the feelings of most of his team mates.

Straight after this tour Pakistan went to Sharjah for the Australasia Cup, a series of games Wasim will never forget. 'I bowled really well in the semi, taking 3–10, and I took 3 more wickets in the final against India, but the tension when we needed 4 to win with just one ball left was unbelievable. Mohsin Kamal was crying because he thought we had lost, I was on the verge of tears, and everyone was praying for a miracle.' The only person who wasn't overcome by the occasion was Javed. 'My only plan was to hit the ball as hard as I could. I was very lucky that Chetan Sharma bowled a full-toss that I could slog over mid-wicket for 6.'

The Pakistan team was fêted like film-stars. Adoring supporters showered the players, especially Javed, with gifts of gold and money. Wasim returned to Pakistan with twelve gold chains and countless other trinkets, but most importantly, he returned with the belief that he was now an established Test player, and that his tenure in the side was secure.

3

Good Batting and Bad Umpiring

The West Indies tour to Pakistan in October 1986 marked a watershed for Pakistani cricket in the mid-eighties. For a number of years there had been no doubting the talent in the side, and yet the team had consistently failed to play to its potential. Many of the players had been more interested in their own performance than in the team's, and it had become almost axiomatic that in any tight finish one could expect Pakistan to lose.

Imran Khan's reappointment as captain for the previous series in Sri Lanka had signalled the change. Pakistan had always looked a more formidable side whenever Imran had been in charge, and this was again proved to be the case. Quite apart from the balance that his fast bowling and middle-order batting brought to the side, what Intikhab describes as 'Imran's obvious sincerity' communicated itself to the players. Imran's straightforward and 'unself-interested' approach fostered a new team spirit. The players believed in their captain, and in turn they began to believe in themselves and their ability to win.

The West Indies team of the mid-eighties was widely held to be virtually invincible; Richards, Marshall, Greenidge, and Haynes were in their prime, and they had never lost under Viv Richards' captaincy. Their pace-bowling attack had annihilated all that stood before it, and for the first three and a half days of the first Test at Faisalabad there was no reason to think that history would not repeat itself.

Pakistan batted first and were bundled out for 159. Qasim Omar had stood on his wicket after being hit on the head by a Tony Gray bouncer, Salim Malik's wrist had been broken by Courtney Walsh, and only a fighting 61 from Imran had saved Pakistan from complete humiliation. The West Indies were restricted to 248, thanks to a career best 6–91 from Wasim, but Pakistan were in deep trouble at 224–7 in their second innings when Wasim came into bat.

'I went for my shots right from the start, because I didn't know how to play any other way. After a couple of early fours through the covers I began to get more confident, and I realized that I could stay in and make runs. By the end, I was hitting Marshall and Gray for 6 over mid-wicket, and I went on to score my first ever Test half-century.'

Thanks to Wasim, along with some stubborn and brave resistance from Tauseef and Salim Malik who was batting with one arm in plaster, Pakistan were able to set the West Indies a last innings total of 239. On a crumbling pitch the Caribbean team was swept aside for 53 by Imran and Abdul Qadir, for whom Wasim is unstinting in his praise. 'On his day, he is a magician. He has so many variations of spin and pace, and I've never seen anyone turn the ball further than him.'

Pakistan's victory was confirmation that they could now compete on equal terms with the best in the world, and win.

The significance of this was not lost on the media. Christopher Martin-Jenkins wrote, 'It is clear that Pakistan are capable of not just repeating the fantasy of Faisalabad, but also of achieving much more consistent success over a long period.'

The West Indies exacted swift revenge in the second Test, but Pakistan held on in the third, and the rubber finished all-square. Wasim played little part in these games, bowling only nine overs in Lahore, having twisted his ankle in the field, and missing the game in Karachi altogether. However, the series was an important turning-point for Wasim, too. It was wonderful to take so many wickets in the first Test, especially those of Greenidge and Richards, but the highlight was my batting. I know it was a bit of a slog at times, but I discovered that I could make runs at Test level. After this, people began to think of me as an all-rounder.'

Two short visits to Sharjah and Australia, for the Perth Challenge, followed, before the five Test tour of India in early 1987. The first four games were all drawn, in matches where the bat dominated. Shoaib and Imran made centuries for Pakistan in the first, with Wasim chipping in with another half-century, and with Srikkanth replying with a ton for India. The same pattern was repeated in the next three games with Azharuddin collecting a couple of hundreds, and Shastri, Rameez Raja, Ijaz Faqih, and Vengsarkar, making one apiece.

'The wickets were really slow. The Indians had obviously designed them that way on purpose because their strength lay in their batting; but it seemed to us that they weren't particularly interested in winning the series, but were just anxious to avoid losing. Despite the flat wickets, Wasim had still managed to take 5 wickets in India's first innings at Calcutta, but nothing had prepared the Pakistanis for the final game.

'We couldn't believe the wicket at Bangalore. The ball turned square from the first day. I'm convinced that the Indians had no idea the wicket would play like that either. We were skittled out for 116 in the first innings, and the whole team was really down. I said to Imran, "That's it, we've lost." He turned to me, and replied, "We'll bowl them out cheaply too. We'll win this game." He was so confident.'

Imran's predictions were spot-on. Tauseef Ahmed and Iqbal Qasim span out India for only 145. Pakistan put up sterner resistance in their second innings scoring 249, leaving India to make 220 if they were to win the match and the series. 'I took a couple of early wickets, and after that the spinners worked their way through the batting. They were 9 down for 185, but then Roger Binny started throwing the bat, and I thought they would scrape home. Finally, he nicked Tauseef to the keeper; it was definitely out, but we were very relieved that the umpire gave it with the match in such a delicate position.'

Pakistan had won by 16 runs, and had realized a dream of winning in India. 'That match was one of the tensest I have ever played. Beating India is always important, but to do so in India for the first time is very special. The tour was extremely demanding; we were well treated by the Indian players and officials, but the crowds were often very hostile. At Ahmedabad and Nagpur, three of our fielders on the boundary resorted to wearing helmets, because they were being pelted with stones. It's incredibly tiring being put under that kind of pressure, but you can't complain because exactly the same thing happens to the Indians when they tour Pakistan.'

'The series of one-day games were also one of the best in which I've played. We won 5–1, and the Indians only won their one game thanks to Abdul Qadir. We needed one run off the last ball to win, having lost fewer wickets, and he decided to go for a second run. He was run out and we lost. It was incredible. He did the same thing at Edgbaston in the fourth Test against England the next summer. We were struggling to hold on for a draw, and I said to him before he went out to bat, "Whatever you do, don't get run out," and needless to say he was run out. He's run me out on two other occasions as well; he's just a bad runner, I suppose.'

The Sharjah Cup in April underlined the importance to the Pakistanis of winning against India. To win the tournament, Pakistan had to not only beat India in the final game, but do so in style to lift their run-rate above England's. Wasim is characteristically blunt about it. 'We didn't make much effort to score quickly, because we wanted to be sure of the match first. Beating India, especially in Sharjah, is more important than a cup.'

Much has been written on the Pakistan tour to England in the summer of 1987, particularly in the light of the events in the return series in Pakistan later that year. Like many cricketers, Wasim asserts that on-field niggles and incidents are forgotten once the game is over. While it is true that such episodes are probably accorded a greater significance by officials and the media, it is also quite likely that these affairs remain in the subconscious of the players, and have a commensurate knock-on effect.

Quite apart from any long-term feelings of discord generated between the two sides, there had been two incidents in recent years that had put the Pakistanis on their guard. There was David Constant's appalling decision at Headingley on the 1982 tour, when he gave Sikander Bakht out caught off Vic Marks – a decision which Imran believes cost Pakistan the match and the series. The second incident took place in a meaningless game in the Perth Challenge in Australia. England and Pakistan had both qualified for the final but had to play out a league match regardless. Rameez Raja was batting when he hit a no ball to Bill Athey who caught it. Rameez had not heard the call, and started to walk back to the pavilion, whereupon Athey promptly ran him out. Pakistan did not make an issue of it, but as Wasim says, 'It was a really unprofessional thing to do. Mike Gatting was captaining the side at the time, and he could have recalled Rameez, but chose not to, and in so doing he, albeit unwittingly, defined his approach to the Pakistanis. He was a captain who was not above sharp practice, and therefore not to be trusted.'

In Haseeb Ahsan, Pakistan had a tour manager who was prepared to be outspoken, something that came as a shock to the TCCB who were used to dealing with managers who considered it enough of a privilege to be invited to tour England, and had been happy to go along with anything the English officials might suggest. Pakistan had requested in the pre-tour meeting with the TCCB that David Constant should not stand in the Tests. Under the circumstances, this was not unreasonable, and indeed when England had made similar overtures to national boards when they toured overseas, their wishes had usually been granted. Whether it was to demonstrate their faith in David Constant, or to deliberately snub the Pakistanis, or a combination of the two, will remain a mystery, but umpire Constant was appointed for two Tests. At the very least this was high-handed; the Pakistanis took it as a sign that they were treated as an inferior touring team, with all the implied racist overtones, and Haseeb Ahsan was not averse to making his feelings known.

The resentment spilled over into other areas, as Wasim

explains. 'We were generally put up in poor hotels. The rooms were tiny, there was no room service, and the only furniture was a couple of beds and a chair. Whenever I've travelled with Lancashire we've had better accommodation. Likewise, at the grounds, the food was rationed. When teams come to Pakistan there's a large buffet, and you can take whatever you want. In England, they would only give you exact portions. If you were still hungry, you had to bring in food from outside.'

For all that, Wasim was aware that this tour was very important for him. 'I knew that I would be playing county cricket for Lancashire the following year, and I wanted to create a good impression. Imran had also told me that if a player does well in England, then he is recognized all over the world.'

After a closely fought one-day series for the Texaco Trophy, in which England edged home thanks to some late order defiance from DeFreitas, Foster, and Thomas in the deciding game, the first two Tests were a great disappointment to everyone concerned. So much time was lost to bad weather that both games never progressed further that the first innings. At Old Trafford England made 447, Tim Robinson top scoring with 166, and with Wasim bowling impressively taking 4 wickets at little more than 2 runs per over in a marathon spell. In reply, Pakistan struggled to 140–5 before proceedings were called to a halt. It was even worse at Lord's, as England reached 368 on the only two days when play was possible.

The third Test at Headingley only stretched to a fraction over three days, but this time the weather was not at fault, as Pakistan marched to a comprehensive innings victory. The Headingley pitch was never easy, and England could have had a justifiable moan about an injury to Botham and a poor umpiring decision against Chris Broad, but there was no escaping that Pakistan's bowling, batting and fielding were consistently a class above England's.

In ideal conditions for swing bowling, England were bowled out shortly after tea on the first day for 136, with Imran, Wasim, and Mohsin Kamal, picking up 3 wickets each. Pakistan built up a first innings lead of over 200, largely due to Salim Malik who held the middle-order together with 99, and to Ijaz Ahmed and Wasim who scored valuable runs against a tiring bowling attack. Wasim's innings, 'it was just a big slog,' comprised a remarkable 43 off only 42 deliveries, and included four sixes, two off Edmonds, one off Foster, and a straight hit back over Dilley's head.

England never recovered from the early loss of Broad and Robinson. Despite some token resistance from Botham and Capel, with the former surviving a controversial claim for a catch by Salim Yousuf, of which Wasim said, 'It was really bad. Sometimes the keeper is not sure whether he's gathered the ball on the half-volley, but this wasn't even close,' England were dismissed for 199. Pakistan ran out the worthy winners; Imran took 10 wickets in a Test for the fifth time, Wasim took 5, as the touring side went one up in the series with two games to play.

It was exactly this kind of position from which previous Pakistan sides had gone on to lose, but the present team, under Imran, had learnt how to cope with the pressure, as England were to discover at Edgbaston. Both teams had piled up large first innings totals, with Mudassar and Gatting both making centuries, and at lunch on the last day Pakistan had only lost 1 second innings wicket. In an inspired spell during the afternoon, Foster and Botham took the remaining 9 wickets, to leave England a target of 124 in 18 overs.

'We thought we had thrown away the match; Broad and Gower gave them a great start, and they should have won. Imran and I bowled unchanged throughout that innings, in one of the safest and steadiest spells we have bowled together. We were surprised that England didn't promote Botham in the order, and by the time he came in the ball had begun to swing, and my yorker was working well. In the end, we shut them out.'

England were left 15 runs short, with 3 wickets remaining. Any hopes that they might have had of salvaging the series at the Oval were scuppered when Pakistan amassed over 700 in their first innings, leaving Gatting and Botham to fight a rearguard action to avoid a second defeat. Wasim never finished the match. 'I got a really bad pain in my stomach on the Saturday night, and when I woke up the next morning my whole face was yellow. The doctor diagnosed it as appendicitis, and I was taken to hospital immediately.'

The discomfort of the operating theatre was tempered by the knowledge that he had yet again come through a demanding series with his reputation enhanced. Wasim's talent and temperament had been severely tested, and he had not been found wanting. Imran had announced that he was to retire after the forthcoming World Cup in India and Pakistan, and Wasim was already being seen as the natural and worthy successor to the mantle of Pakistan's top all-rounder.

Pakistan's first series victory in England was greeted rapturously by Pakistanis everywhere. After drawing a home rubber against the West Indies, and beating the Indians in their own country, defeating the old colonial rulers in their own back yard was the crowning glory to a successful year. While the victory may have had a special meaning for Pakistani communities that had for a long time felt as if they were treated as second-class citizens, its impact was also felt elsewhere in the cricket world.·

Pakistan were now regarded as one of the firm favourites for the World Cup to be held in Pakistan, a view that was also held by Wasim, and the rest of the team. 'We were so confident we would win; it also seemed inevitable somehow that Imran would retire on a winning note.' This level of confidence and expectation permeated the whole of Pakistan, and by the time the tournament began, the country was in the grip of World Cup mania. Whenever Pakistan were playing, the nation ground to a halt; people would miss work; students would miss school, and teachers would turn up with radios and earplugs to catch the score between lessons. People would wait outside the players' hotel just to feel part of the team, and the players themselves could not go on to the streets without attracting a mob of followers.

'The tournament had started so well; we had won our first five preliminary games and had easily qualified for the semi-final in Lahore. We were due to play Australia, and we were sure we would win. Everyone was; the Australians hadn't even made any provision for televising the final. In the end, I think we were too confident, imagining that we only had to turn up to win. On the day everything went wrong. Salim Yousuf was hit in the mouth, and so Javed had to take over the gloves. He got so tired wicket-keeping, that he couldn't take quick singles when he was batting. Imran was given out to a bad decision, and Dean Jones was given the benefit of the doubt over a run out. I also think that Imran miscounted the overs; normally, it was left to him and me to bowl at the end of the innings, but for some reason it was left to Salim Jaffer. The poor guy got hit for 18 off the last over, which was exactly our losing margin. I made a quick 20, but it was clear to me well before the end that we were going to lose.'

The disappointment of the players was felt in equal measure by the country. 'It was as if the nation was in mourning. The streets were quiet, and people were crying. Some got angry, and I think that Mansoor Akhtar had stones thrown at him in Karachi, but most people were too stunned to do anything. I felt I had let the country down, and I was so upset that I couldn't go out for a few days. The only thing that relieved the depression in Pakistan was that India lost their semi-final too.'

England were due to play a three match Test series immediately after the World Cup. The tour will be remembered in England for a long time as one of the most bad-tempered and controversial of all time. For Wasim and many other Pakistanis it was something of a non-event.

'Losing the World Cup had a profound affect on the national psyche; people were so disappointed that they lost interest in cricket completely for a while. This, combined with Imran's retirement, meant that only a few hundred spectators could be bothered to come and watch each day of the Tests.'

'There was bad feeling between the players and the management of both sides; both Javed and Gatting are very aggressive captains, and that didn't help either. The umpiring in the first Test at Lahore was bad, and I'm sure that the umpires had been put under some kind of pressure, but it wasn't as bad as Gatting claimed. Everybody involved in the game knew that England had been on the wrong end of about four decisions, but making a public statement about the umpiring only made matters worse.'

'I missed the game at Faisalabad with a groin injury. I saw it on TV, and I'm still not certain about what really happened.

The video evidence clearly suggests that Gatting hadn't warned Salim Malik that he was moving the fielder at backward square-leg, and that Shakoor Rana was right to interrupt play, but I asked Mike about it a couple of years ago, and he insists that he told Salim what he was doing. What I am certain of is that there would have been fewer umpiring errors and delays in these two games if the public had been at all interested in them. These Tests reinforced my own belief that cricket should have a panel of international umpires, as in other sports, and that from it independent umpires should be selected for each series.'

Wasim returned for the final game at Karachi. He was still only semi-fit, but that mattered little, as the wicket was as slow and dusty as the previous two, and spin bowling once again dominated the proceedings. The series offered little to Wasim, and he wasn't sorry when it ended; he had batted well in his only 2 innings, but his immediate concern was his groin injury. He had broken down again at Karachi, and would need an operation before the tour to the West Indies in early 1988.

'I wasn't fit when the tour started. Imran had come out of retirement for the tour, and he said that he wanted me to come with the team to the West Indies and just train during the five one-day games, so that I would be ready for the Tests. It was so hot and humid out there, but I would spend hours each day running and getting fit.'

Pakistan's bowling was taken apart in the one-day games and they lost all five. They went into the first Test in Georgetown, Guyana as underdogs. 'I still wasn't fit for this game as I had pulled a thigh muscle, but Imran said, "You must play," so I did.' Wasim only took 1 wicket but Imran made an inspirational return to Test cricket with an 11 wicket haul, and

Javed notched up a century, as Pakistan battled to an unexpected 9-wicket triumph.

Wasim was still not fully fit for the second Test in Trinidad, a match that produced yet another tight finish. 'Imran and Abdul Qadir had bowled the West Indies out for 174 in the first innings, and then Marshall and Benjamin dismissed us for 194. Viv Richards and Jeff Dujon both made centuries in the second, leaving us to make over 350 to win the match. We were in with a shout at tea, needing 120 with wickets left, and with Javed and Ijaz both going well. But we started to lose wickets, and when Salim Yousuf was out to the first ball of the last over we were in trouble. Viv hit Abdul, our last batsman, on the pads first ball, and I was sure he would be given out whether he was or not. To my amazement, he wasn't and Abdul played the last four deliveries safely, and we hung on for a draw.'

The final Test in Bridgetown, Barbados, was played on what Wasim describes as, 'one of the best wickets I've ever seen; it was green and hard but the bounce was even.' For the first time on the tour, Wasim was match-fit as Pakistan sought to become the first touring team to win a series in the West Indies for fifteen years. There was little between the teams after the first innings. Pakistan scored 309, thanks to early order contributions from Shoaib Mohammad and Rameez Raja, and some late defiance from Wasim and Salim Yousuf. Eventually, Yousuf had to retire hurt with a broken nose after attempting to hook Malcolm Marshall, but Wasim was full of admiration for the wicket-keeper. He isn't the tidiest keeper, but he's one of the bravest batsmen I've ever seen.'

The West Indies responded with 306, with Imran and Wasim each taking 3 wickets, and when Pakistan totalled 262 in their second innings, Viv Richards' team required 268 to win. 'We thought we were going to win, when we had taken 8 wickets with over 60 runs still wanted. I was bowling very well. I had bowled Viv with a late inswinger, trapped Marshall LBW on the back foot, and had Curtly Ambrose caught, but Dujon and Benjamin made the runs. Some of the umpiring was disgraceful, and we felt that it was pre-planned that the West Indies should win as they hadn't lost in the Caribbean for so long. I had Benjamin trapped plumb leg before, and Dujon gloved Abdul straight to silly point, but neither decision was given. I got very tired and disheartened as I had been bowling a long time, and I lost some pace and they just scraped home.'

It was a disappointing end to a tour that had started so badly, but had promised so much. 'It was one of the most demanding tours I've ever been on. Not only was the cricket extremely hard-fought, but the living and travelling conditions were tough too. Whenever we flew from island to island we would always be travelling late at night or early in the morning, and would often have to make several stops en route. They did this to us because it was cheaper, but it was incredibly tiring.

'At the grounds we were treated badly as well. The West Indians were often given mineral water, and we would be lucky to get cold water from the tap. Lunch would always be cold by the time we got it, and the players would be given vouchers for it. Once, one of our players lost his lunch ticket and they refused to give him any food. I know these sort of things can happen, but it makes me very angry that so many countries, especially the West Indies, come to Pakistan and complain about the facilities, when those in their own country are just as bad. We never went out much in the evenings; we used to stay in small villas where we would cater for ourselves. Ijaz and I were lucky that Shoaib Mohammad's wife had joined the tour, and she would cook for us from time to time. I really enjoyed that part of the trip.'

'I never really got to know many of the West Indians then. Now, since I've played county cricket, I've got to know a few like Patto, (Patrick Patterson), and Courtney Walsh, but then they seemed very superior and aloof. Viv's always been quite nice to me, but I did have a run-in with him in the Barbados Test. I had bowled him a bouncer, and followed it up with a fast inswinger, which hit him full on the knee, right in front of the stumps. I appealed, and he was given not out, and I said, "That's cheating." Viv started swearing at me, and I said, "Look Viv, I respect you as a cricketer, don't do this to me." He carried on swearing, so I started swearing back, and he then said, "I'll see you outside the ground after the game," and I replied "OK". We never did fight it out afterwards!'

Wasim missed the dismal tour of Australia to Pakistan in September, with a recurrence of the by now familiar groin injury preventing him from playing more than one one-day international. However, he returned for the Asia Cup in Bangladesh, and travelled to Australia for the Benson & Hedges World Cup series in December. 'That was a pointless tour, and the BCCP only accepted it because they were offered a lot of money. They really shouldn't make the players go on tours like it. We were only there to make up the numbers in a triangular one-day tournament, while Australia and the West Indies were playing a Test series as well. We only had one three-day game, and sometimes had a ten-day break between one-day games. We had no match practice, and consequently we played very badly and lost easily.'

Pakistan were due to play a three Test series in New Zealand early in 1989, but yet again Wasim's groin injury forced him out of a series, and the next match that he would play for his country would be in Sharjah in the company of the unknown Waqar Younis.

By late 1989, many of the great all-rounders of the early and mid-eighties were in the twilight of their careers; Ian Botham's back had given way, and he was reduced to a medium-pacer; Kapil Dev was likewise no longer the bowling threat he once was, and Imran, too, had lost his pace; Richard Hadlee was still taking wickets, but was soon to retire. Various pretenders had stepped forward to press their claims as the next all-round talent, but only Wasim had consistently done enough to suggest that he had the ability to succeed the greats. In three years, Wasim had progressed from a young fast bowler, unsure of his place in the side, to a player who was being hailed, injuries permitting, as the man who would be the world's best all-rounder in the nineties.

4

The Burewala Bombshell

When Waqar Younis made his debut for Pakistan in the
Sharjah Champion's Trophy in October 1989, the cricket
world responded with a universal, 'Waqar who?' So little was
known about Waqar, and so dramatic was his impact, that
almost immediately a legend was created. He was, so the story
went, an unknown who was plucked from obscurity by Imran
Khan, who just happened to be watching him bowl on TV. It
was a good fairy story, but like many of its kind, it was also
some way short of the truth.

The reality was more mundane. Waqar had been recognized as a great prospect for a few years in Pakistan. He had
impressed while playing divisional cricket for Multan, and
departmental cricket for United Bank, and had been chosen to
represent the national Under-19 side against India. However,
what nobody had anticipated was his improvement between
the end of the '88/9 season and the beginning of the '89/90. In
a few months, Waqar seemed to progress from a wayward
youngster with promise, to one of the fastest bowlers in the
country. It was the suddenness of his development, and not

that he was unknown, that caught so many people unawares, and made his selection for Sharjah so unexpected.

Waqar was born in the Vihari district of the Punjab on 16 November 1971, and therein lies another story. Anyone who saw Waqar demolishing the New Zealanders in 1990, or terrorizing every batsman on the English county circuit in 1991, must have been astonished that they were watching a teenager in action. John Deary, the Surrey physio, is openly sceptical about Waqar's age. 'I've never seen someone that physically developed who wasn't at least twenty-three or -four.' Even to the uninformed, Waqar looks much older than his age, and many of his colleagues at Surrey and in the Pakistan side are equally doubtful.

Various theories have been put forward for the apparent discrepancy between his age and appearance. Gehan Mendis, Wasim's Lancashire team mate and a Sri Lankan by birth, suggests that, 'in many Asian countries it is quite common in the rural areas not to register a child's birth until many years after it has been born, and many parents forget their child's birthday.' Wasim has another explanation. 'When you matric-ulate at the tenth grade, many schools allow you to re-register your birth, if you have an opportunity of playing first-class cricket. It's a way of getting into the Under-19s. You obviously stand a better chance of being chosen, if you have a few extra years to develop.' Many such 'over-age' cricketers have represented the Pakistan Under-19s and visiting Under-19 sides have frequently commented on the swarthiness and size of their opponents. Regrettably, the mystery remains unsolved; Waqar, the only person who could settle the matter, isn't saying anything, but his engaging smile and wall of silence indicate that he, too, has his misgivings.

Vihari is situated in the most fertile area of Pakistan, and like many of its inhabitants, Waqar's father was a cotton farmer. Waqar was the eldest of five children, and as is usual in Islamic culture, the hopes and expectations for the future of the family were invested in the eldest son. The family was not wealthy, but no expense was spared to see that Waqar was given the best schooling. It was good for his education, but it had its price, as Waqar explains. 'My father got a job in Sharjah as general foreman for a Chinese construction company when I was three and a half. Instead of going with my parents I was left at Azir school in Lahore, an English medium boarding school. The only contact I had with my family was with my uncle who lived in the city. For the first few months, I was very lonely and upset. I wouldn't talk to anyone, and I cried the whole time.'

Many children would have been crushed by the experience, but Waqar learnt to use it to his advantage. He grew up, and became self-reliant at a very early age; he quickly realized that he would have to work hard for any success and was determined to do so. Numerous people have marvelled at Waqar's maturity, at his ability to keep cool in tight situations. What is even more surprising is that he actually enjoys these moments. It has been a hard-won personal struggle to get to the top, and bowling at the death for Pakistan is the culmination of everything he has worked for.

When Waqar was seven years old, he left Lahore, to be reunited with his family in Sharjah. They lived in a part of the town called 'A Thousand Villas', and Waqar studied for four years at Sharjah College. 'I wasn't a very good student, and neither was I very interested in cricket. That changed in 1981 when the first international benefit match between the Gavaskar XI and the Miandad XI was played in Sharjah. I went to the game, and I saw Imran bowl for the first time. From then on cricket was in my blood.'

Shortly after this, Waqar's father was posted to the neighbouring emirate of Abu Dhabi, and Waqar moved school yet again. There were few opportunities for a youngster to play cricket in the United Arab Emirates, and the family were not only educationally ambitious for Waqar, but they also wanted to give him every encouragement to play the game. Consequently, after a short stay at college in Abu Dhabi, Waqar was sent back to Pakistan to study at Sadiq public school in Bahawalpur.

'Sadiq was one of the finest schools in Asia and very expensive as well. My father wanted me to have the best, even though it meant that he got into financial difficulties over the tuition fees. It was here that I started to play cricket seriously; even though there were no good coaches, there were very excellent net facilities, and the school team did extremely well.' Waqar's natural athleticism and ability soon saw him become the leading fast bowler for the first XI, and he also represented the school at throwing the javelin and the high jump. To this day he still holds the school record for throwing a cricket ball.

After matriculating from Sadiq in the tenth grade, Waqar moved back to Burewala, from which is derived his sobriquet 'The Burewala Bombshell', and enrolled in the Government College in Vihari. 'The college side was not very good, and I was made captain in my first year. I was also playing for the Burewala Whites cricket club, who were a first grade side in the Multan Division.' Waqar's talent soon came to the attention of Sufi Sadiq.

'He wasn't a coach so much as a keen follower of the game. In Pakistan it is quite common for an outsider to take you under their wing and give you a *Danda* – a big push. I didn't have to give him anything, and he wasn't even rich. He ran a cycle repair shop, in fact. He was very well connected with the divisional selectors though, and he would drive me to all my games and encourage me to play.'

Waqar was chosen for the Multan Division Under-19 side during the 1986/7 season. 'I was bowling very fast, but I was highly erratic. All the selectors said to me that I had a good action, but that I had no control of line and length, but I didn't really care. At that stage, I just wanted to bowl as quickly as I could.'

The next year Waqar was picked to represent the senior Multan division side. In the group league matches of the Patron's Trophy Championship which were not given first-class status, he took 9 wickets against Quetta, and followed this up with 10 more in the three remaining games, to take Multan to the top of their group. As a result, Multan qualified for the first-class round of the Patron's Trophy as well as the season's Quaid-e-Azam Trophy.

Waqar's first taste of first-class cricket did not end in glory. He only took 4 wickets in five matches at the expensive average of 60. The highlight of his season was his batting, when he made 46 not out in a last wicket stand against Pakistan National Shipping Corporation at Sahiwal, but he had impressed sufficiently while bowling against United Bank to be added to their payroll for the '88/9 season. 'Ehtesham-ud-Din, the ex-Pakistani Test cricketer, approached me after the game and asked me to sign a contract. I was desperate to play first-class cricket, and I signed immediately. The money wasn't very good, only 2,500 rupees a month (about 55 pounds), but playing for Multan I was only getting a daily allowance and it was difficult to make ends meet. I was supposed to be still studying at Vihari College, but whenever I had a game I would just skip classes.'

The start of the '88/9 season was a difficult period. Multan were playing most of their matches on underprepared pitches, and Waqar was used primarily to take the shine off the new ball, so that the spinners could get to work. He didn't have any realistic expectations of playing for United Bank, either. 'Sikander Bakht, Sajid Bashir, and Saleem Jaffer were the senior fast bowlers, and I didn't think I'd ever get a game. We were due to play our first Wills Trophy match against National Bank at Bahawalpur on the slowest wicket in Pakistan. On the morning of the game Sikander and Saleem Jaffer took one look at the wicket, and decided to withdraw with injuries. It's the sort of thing that happens quite frequently in Pakistan, and it meant that I was given a chance. I bowled very well, taking 1–25 in my 10 overs, and was chosen for other games.'

By now Waqar was beginning to come to people's notice, Javed Miandad's included. 'My younger brother had played against him, and had reported back to me that Waqar was genuinely quick and had hit one of our batsmen, and that I should take a look at him. Also, Waqar's uncle, a civil judge, is an old friend of mine, and he too was trying to persuade me to sign him for Habib Bank for the next year. Although he was doing well in domestic cricket, nobody was thinking of him as a Test cricketer, and I never got round to seeing him before he was picked for Pakistan.'

It was also at this time that Wasim first came across Waqar. 'I needed some bowling practice, so I joined United Bank for a net session. I saw this guy sprinting in, and bowling very quick on a green wicket; I didn't immediately realize he was Waqar, as I didn't know him by sight. I had heard of his reputation for being erratic, but on this day he was bowling really well, and I was impressed.'

In the first game of the Quaid-e-Azam Trophy in January 1989, Waqar took 3-65 against Muslim Commercial Bank at Hyderabad, and a few days later routed PNSC in Lahore for 126, taking a career best 6-33 in the process. This match assured Waqar of selection for the Under-19 Test against India at Gujranwala. Javed Burki had just taken over as Chairman of the selectors. 'Haroon Rashid, the manager of the United Bank team, introduced Waqar to us. We could see he had the rhythm, but he had very poor control. Nevertheless, we still decided to give him a game. He didn't actually do very well; he got movement, but he pitched his outswinger outside the off stump, and his inswinger outside the leg.'

Javel Burki's summary of his performance is endorsed by Waqar himself. 'It was the most important game I had ever played, the first time I had been on TV, and I bowled very badly. I took a couple of wickets, but I got carried away with trying to bowl too fast and aggressively. I wasted the new ball by being inaccurate and bowling too many bouncers. Looking back, I must have been mad. I was very upset to be dropped for the next two Tests, but I didn't honestly expect to be given another chance.'

Another 5-wicket bag for United Bank, this time against Pakistan International Airways in Karachi, guaranteed Waqar a recall for the final Under-19 Test. This time he bowled much more steadily, taking 4 wickets in the first innings and 1 in the second. Although Pakistan lost the match, Waqar had justified the faith placed in him, and he finished the season topping the bowling averages in the Quaid-e-Azam Trophy with 23 wickets.

It had been a fine first year for Waqar with United Bank, but even so, he still wasn't regarded as a possible choice for the full Test side. His development over the summer months took everyone by surprise, as Javed Burki recalls. 'We had always known that he had the talent, though I suspect we didn't realize quite how much, but we were waiting to see if he could control what he was doing. Again, it was Haroon Rashid who alerted us to the improvement. He phoned me in Karachi to say that there was a big difference between this season's Waqar Younis and last season's. Previously, he wasn't physically fully developed; his neck was very thin, and his head was not very steady on his shoulders as he ran into bowl. In five months he had filled out a great deal, and it was showing in his bowling.'

Early in October 1989 the two one-day champions of Pakistan and India, United Bank and Delhi, played for the inaugural Super Wills Cup in Lahore, and this was the first time that Imran saw Waqar bowl. 'Because I don't play domestic cricket, whenever I return to Pakistan I make a point of asking various top players for their opinions of the form of those I know, and especially about the up-and-coming youngsters. Some of them had mentioned Waqar, so I was on the lookout for him. Immediately when I saw him bowl, I decided to ask him to the training camp for Sharjah.'

Waqar was amazed. 'I bowled very quickly in that game; I didn't take any wickets, but I had the batsmen jumping around. Imran watched my first 3 overs at home on TV, and then came straight to the ground to see the rest of my spell. After the game, he told me to join the camp.' Waqar still did not expect to make the final squad, but Imran's mind was made up the first time he saw Waqar bowl in training. 'It was obvious that Waqar had a rare talent; just by watching him run up to bowl you could see he was a natural athlete. All I needed to know was whether he had the temperament to go with it. I decided there and then that I would play him in Sharjah. There was some resistance from the selectors who felt he was not ready, but I insisted.'

Settling into a national side is a difficult transitional period for any cricketer, and for an inexperienced teenager especially so. For Waqar the process was eased by the team spirit in the Pakistan side of the late eighties, and he experienced none of the hostility and resentment that Wasim had encountered on his first tour. 'For a start, there were other young players who had only been in the side a little while, like Aaqib Javed and Mushtaq Ahmed, with whom I got on very well. Also, all the seniors were very helpful, Ijaz, Wasim, and Rameez, in particular; they worked very hard with me in the nets, and did their best to make me feel welcome.'

Wasim remembers, 'He was just like me on my first tour; quiet, very shy, and well-behaved. He spent most of his spare time with his family in Sharjah, or with Aaqib and Mushtaq. The three of them were very close, but they were good company. Even before we became friends I used to enjoy going to their room for a chat and a laugh.'

In an astute piece of team management, Waqar was made to share a room with the seventy year-old Dr Aslam, the team doctor. 'He was like a grandfather to me. When I was feeling nervous, or negative about my cricket, he would make time to talk to me. He would make sure I got early nights, and he always praised me when I bowled well.'

Waqar was chosen for Pakistan's first game against the West Indies, and made an immediate impression. Although he failed to take a wicket, he had Haynes and Simmons ducking and swaying from lifting deliveries, in a spell of fast bowling the like of which is rarely witnessed on the lifeless Sharjah pitches. Indeed, Dickie Bird, who was umpiring, said that it was amongst the fastest he had ever seen. Waqar's dream debut in front of a crowd that included every pupil from Sharjah College where he had studied as a boy came to an end after 4 overs. In the debilitating heat, Waqar got cramp, pulled a muscle, and had to leave the field.

Javed Burki was not altogether surprised. 'We knew that his bowling action took a lot out of him, and that he wasn't as yet fit enough or strong enough to sustain a long spell, but we thought that he would last 4 overs. We reckoned without the heat; in his first match, he only lasted that one four over spell. After that, myself, Imran, and the manager, decided that we had to nurse him, and we never bowled him for more than 2 or 3 overs at a time. Imran would talk to him constantly from mid-on, sometimes after every ball even, to find out how he was feeling, and to advise him on what to bowl. Of course, now that he's much stronger, you can bowl him for 5 or 6 overs on the trot.'

Although Waqar failed to complete his spell, Pakistan still won the game, thanks in large measure to 5 wickets from Wasim, including his first Sharjah hat-trick when he clean bowled Dujon, Marshall, and Ambrose with successive deliveries. Waqar missed the next game against India through injury, but was passed fit for the second match against the West Indies.

While it had already been apparent to Imran and many others in Pakistan that Waqar was a genuine fast bowling find, he was still unknown outside Pakistan. This game was to change that. In his 9 overs, Waqar took 3–28 including the wickets of both Haynes and Simmons, the openers, and discomforted everyone who faced him. Qamar Ahmed, the Pakistani cricket reporter who spends much of his time in

London, was covering the tournament for *The Times* and the BBC World Service. 'I was amazed by Waqar's fluency and pace. I'd never even heard of him before, and yet here he was, a mere teenager, frightening the life out of the West Indian batting. I wrote in my report that Waqar was the fastest bowler on either side, quicker even than Ambrose and Bishop. This story was picked up by the Australian press as well, and when I returned home everyone wanted to know all about him.'

For Pakistan it was a matter of cometh the hour, cometh the man. As Imran's pace had begun to decline, Wasim was having to spearhead the attack virtually single-handed, and so Waqar's arrival was a god-send to the team. He had not by any means matured overnight into a world-class cricketer; he still lacked control, and would clearly need careful handling in the future if his talent was not to be wasted. However, he had shown that he had the pace and the temperament to become a regular member of the team for many years to come, and that with Waqar in the side to complement Wasim, the Pakistani fast-bowling attack had the potential to become among the most feared in the world.

5

The Politics of Sport and Neutral Umpires

The Pakistan side travelled to India in 1989 as one of the pre-tournament favourites for the Nehru Cup, a six nation one-day competition. The old guard was well represented by Imran, Javed, Wasim, Salim Malik, Rameez Raja, and Abdul Qadir, but there were so many players who were scarcely out of their teens, namely Waqar, Aaqib, Mushtaq, and Shahid Saeed, that the side was nicknamed 'Imran's Kindergarten Team' by the Indian press.

Waqar was under no illusions about what lay ahead. 'I knew that I was going to be under a great deal of pressure. Not only was I a newcomer to the Pakistan side, but a tour of India, followed by a return Test series against the Indians at home creates its own special stress.' No matter that the Nehru Cup was a relatively unimportant competition, organized ostensibly to celebrate the centenary of the Indian statesman's birth, but in reality to promote Rajiv Gandhi's election campaign; beating India at any time assumes a significance that few outsiders can comprehend.

Many touring sides have had a gripe about the difficulties of touring the sub-continent. There is the heat, the travelling, the indifferent umpiring, and the unfamiliar food. While the food isn't a problem in each other's country, Pakistan and India have to contend with the added hazard of the spectators. True, England have had to play the odd Test match in Pakistan that has been halted because of rioting, but the constant barrage of noise and abuse that a Pakistan v India fixture can provoke is matchless.

To comprehend the acrimony between India and Pakistan, one has to look back to the partition of the two countries by the British in August 1947. Pakistan was formed out of the predominately Muslim eastern and western areas of old colonial India, while the chiefly Hindu central region became the new state of India.

The results of this partition were catastrophic. Immediately, the borders became a matter of dispute. The northern province of Kashmir, which was primarily Muslim, after some indecision had eventually opted to become part of India. This led to fierce fighting between the two new countries, and resulted in Pakistan regaining control of the western section of the province. Even now the matter is unresolved, and the 'Kashmir Question' is always at the centre of political wranglings.

Elsewhere, particularly in the Punjab, partition induced the mass migration of millions; Sikhs and Hindus fled to India, while Muslims sought sanctuary in Pakistan. This migration took place to the accompaniment of massacres and riots. Raj Chengappa, Associate Editor of *India Today*, comments: 'Quite simply, there was a bloodbath. Hindu attacked Muslim, Muslim attacked Hindu, and the ferocity of these assaults was breathtaking. Whole villages were wiped out. Fathers were even known to kill their own children to prevent them being tortured to death by the opposing faction.' To this day, particularly among the uneducated, even though many may have friends of the other religion, Muslims and Hindus remain deeply suspicious of each other's culture. Even the Indian cricket captain, Mohammad Azharuddin, a Muslim, is not immune to the hatred of some of his countrymen. In early 1991, a mob of Hindu extremists stoned his Hyderabad home, damaged his car, set fire to a scooter, and Azharuddin and his family had to be escorted out of the area by armed police.

Not unexpectedly, cricket is often seen as a legitimate forum for political action. Pitches are dug up in protest, and both Pakistan's projected tours to India in 1991 were cancelled because the players' safety could not be guaranteed. The spectators frequently attach a significance to victory that goes well beyond the cricket, and the pressure on the players is immense. Imran himself observes that, 'It's not like in England where there is a much saner attitude to failure. In Pakistan, it's one extreme or the other. You are either treated like a god if you win, or abused if you lose, and especially so if you are playing India. The players know the score, and once they've experienced the abuse they never want to feel it again. It's a kind of pressure English cricketers never face. In India and Pakistan you're really arguing with hell.'

The tension among the spectators is not translated into friction between the players. In fact, the resumption of cricketing relations in the late seventies has led to an increased understanding and mutual respect. Many of the Pakistani players are on friendly terms with the Indian side, for as Wasim remarks, 'Culturally we actually have a great deal in common; we share a common history. We were part of the same country and used to speak the same language.' These sentiments are reciprocated by the Indians. Azharuddin points out that, 'As far as the players are concerned there are no bad feelings at all; it's only the crowds that make so much of the games. To me, the Pakistanis are normal human beings. I don't socialize too much with them during a tour only because I need to concentrate on the cricket.'

Nevertheless, despite Waqar's assertion that 'he gets no greater sense of satisfaction than when he wins with the crowd against him', there is no doubt that the players are acutely aware of the pressure they face. 'Some of the grounds, especially near the border are very unwelcoming,' says Wasim. 'At times when the crowds are threatening, we are all very concerned for our personal safety.'

The pressure is not alleviated by the type of schedule that Pakistan were forced to endure for the Nehru Cup, about which Wasim is understandably scathing. 'It was unbelievably stupid. We arrived in India after the tournament had started because of the Sharjah Champion's Trophy, and had to play seven games in about ten days in different venues around the country. It was non-stop play, travel, and sleep. Everyone was just knackered. Sometimes, it seems as if our cricket board will agree to anything providing the money is right. The English had much more sense and insisted on at least two days between each game.'

Pakistan were comfortably beaten in their opening match against England in Cuttack. The pitch was poor, but the main contributing factor to the defeat was the tiredness of the Pakistanis. 'We had just flown in from Sharjah, and the next morning we had to get up at 5.30 to travel to the ground,' said Waqar. 'The journey took about an hour and a half by bus along a dusty, dirt track, and we were exhausted by the time we arrived. I bowled reasonably well, but I fielded atrociously. It was the first time that I had played in India, and I had never experienced so many spectators swearing at me. I was so nervous that I let two or three balls go straight through my legs for boundaries.'

The following day Pakistan easily defeated Australia in Bombay. Solid batting from Shoaib and Javed, combined with a late swashbuckling innings from Wasim saw Pakistan through to 205, and the Australians were bundled out for a mere 139. Waqar again bowled well, but was still not entirely happy with his form. 'I was very conscious that Aaqib was the senior bowler to me, and that Imran was giving me the opportunity ahead of him. I was trying so hard to perform well, that I became very anxious, and my legs would seize up with cramp as I was still not that strong.'

More problems surrounded the next gate against the West Indies in Jullundur. This part of the Punjab was the scene of fierce clashes between Hindus and Muslims, and the Pakistan side was widely attacked by the local Muslim community for not withdrawing from the tournament because of the troubles. Waqar remembers it well. 'We had to be helicoptered into an army camp, and then taken to the ground with an armed escort. The hotel was swarming with police, and we weren't even allowed out to go shopping. It was a very difficult game, as the crowd swore at us and pelted us with stones constantly.'

Unsurprisingly, Pakistan lost the game and were in danger of being eliminated from the competition. They won their next game against Sri Lanka in Lucknow, albeit somewhat fortuitously as Wasim concedes. 'We had scored 219, and Sri Lanka looked to be cruising to victory needing 8 to win with 4 wickets in hand, and almost 2 overs in which to get the runs. I suddenly bowled Ratnayake and Labrooy in successive deliveries, de Silva was run out, Mahanama was bowled by Abdul, and we had scraped home by 6 runs.'

Immediately after the game, Pakistan flew to Calcutta where they checked into the Taj Bengal Hotel at 10.15 at night. At 7.45 the next morning, they were at the cricket ground to take on India in front of a partisan crowd of 50,000, where to the disappointment of the assembled throng, they romped home to a convincing victory to qualify for the semi-finals.

After an evening to recover, Pakistan travelled westwards to Nagpur to meet England, where they were greeted by unseasonal rains that soaked the outfield and threatened the match. England would have been more than happy to have had the match abandoned, as they would have qualified for the final on superior run rate, but to Pakistan's relief, and no doubt to the organizers' as well, who had their eyes firmly set on an India v Pakistan showdown in Calcutta, the umpires decreed some four hours after the scheduled start that a 30 overs game was possible.

Pakistan won the toss and put England in on a wicket that was still decidedly damp, but the move looked to have backfired as England notched up 194 in their allotted overs. Graham Gooch and Wayne Larkins gave England a good start, Robin Smith made a characteristically pugnacious half-century including a 6 off Waqar, and Capel and Pringle put together a useful partnership later on. The wet outfield made bowling and fielding a tricky proposition, and only Wasim and Qadir were able to restrict the batsmen to 5 an over; Waqar took the important wickets of Gooch and Alec Stewart, his future Surrey team-mate, but his 6 overs cost an expensive 40 runs.

In reply, Pakistan started very badly losing Javed, Ijaz, and Imran cheaply, and falling well behind the run rate in the process. With 10 overs left, the asking rate had risen to nearly 10 per over. Wasim takes up the story. 'Salim Malik and Rameez Raja produced one of the best one-day partnerships I have ever seen. Salim, especially, was superb. He hit 66 off about 40 balls, and by the end the match wasn't even close, as we won with an over and a half to spare.'

In the other semi-final there was disappointment for the Indians, who tamely surrendered to the West Indies in Bombay. There was frustration ahead for Waqar, too. 'My back had stiffened up after the semi, and it was no better on the morning of the final. I was very depressed, but there was nothing for it other than to tell Imran that I wasn't fit, and that he should pick someone else.'

Despite India's non-appearance, over 70,000 spectators were packed into the famous Eden Garden's stadium in Calcutta, the vast majority willing the West Indies to win. The bookies had made the Caribbean side the odds-on favourites, and this prognosis looked accurate as they piled up 273 in their 50 overs, with the main contribution coming from Desmond Haynes with an unbeaten century. Aaqib bowled very tightly as Waqar's replacement, but none of the other bowlers were as reliable, and it was only a late burst of 3 wickets from Imran that prevented the West Indies from making in excess of 300.

Ijaz, Salim Malik, and Imran ensured that Pakistan kept up with the required rate of scoring, and with 10 overs left only 42 runs were needed when the young off-spinner Akram Raza joined the skipper at the wicket. Curiously, the run-rate slowed and when Raza was run out off the third ball of the last over, Pakistan still wanted 4 to win as Wasim came out to bat. 'I think that Viv Richards must have messed up the bowling, as all the quickies had finished their spells and Viv himself was bowling the last over. Imran was facing, and took a single from the fourth ball. I had a chat with him in the middle, and we agreed that the most important thing was to make sure that I got a single so that Imran who had got his eye in could try and make 2 off the last ball. However, I had already decided that if the ball was there to be hit, I would have a go at it. Viv bowled a length ball, it dropped exactly in the right place for my swing, and I drove it for 6 over long-on. It wasn't a slog, just timing.'

The celebrations continued long into the night, as Pakistan's 35,000 mile odyssey around India ended in triumph, and after their success in Sharjah, they were justifiably regarded as the uncrowned one-day champions of the world. Imran remarked that, 'the tournament was more of a test of endurance than of skills and talent,' but it was an impressive performance nonetheless. All the senior team members had played to their potential, and Imran had again showed himself to be a shrewd leader and tactician; he had consistently had the imagination to use two leg spinners and an off spinner, and he had helped to bring the best out of his young fast bowlers. The side was given a hero's welcome when they returned to Pakistan, as thousands turned up at Lahore airport to garland them. But there was little time for self-congratulation; within a fortnight they were due to meet India in Karachi for the first of four Tests.

The series was extremely hard fought throughout, but will be remembered for a long time as one of the most harmonious ever played between the two countries, mainly because of the presence of John Hampshire and John Holder as independent umpires. Wasim is unequivocal about it. 'Neutral umpires made all the difference. Of course, players disagreed with decisions from time to time, but very little dissent was shown because we had confidence in the umpiring. From that point of view, it was one of the happiest series ever.' John Holder, too, was left in no doubt. 'Imran told me how grateful he was to myself and John, and a couple of the Indian players remarked that if we hadn't been there, they would have lost the series.'

Waqar made his Test début in Karachi on 15 November 1989, the day before his eighteenth birthday, though this was rather overshadowed by the début of the Indian batsman Sachin Tendulkar, who at sixteen years old became the third youngest person ever to play Test cricket. Waqar only passed himself fit on the morning of the game. 'I'd been very worried about my back since the Nehru Cup; I'd been to a number of doctors who told me that I either had a slipped disc or a hairline fracture of the backbone. I didn't know what to do, so I called Imran. He told me that the doctors were mucking me about, that their diagnosis was bullshit, and that what I needed to do was to rest completely for ten days, before starting training again. It was only after a last net session that I was confident that I was totally fit. When Imran told me I was in the team I was so excited that I phoned my mother immediately.'

India won the toss and elected to field first on a wicket, which, while by no means green, had a lot of grass on it, and promised to be the quickest of the series. Despite the fact that the match was against their arch-rivals, the Pakistani public had become so conditioned to one-day cricket, that Test cricket held little interest any more, and the Karachi stadium was less than half full as the Pakistan innings began. Nevertheless, emotions ran sufficiently strong for a Pakistani supporter to climb the twelve-foot perimeter fence to attack Kapil Dev as he walked back to his bowling mark. Many of the Indian players were involved in the ensuing mêlée, and Srikkanth, too, was attacked and had his shirt ripped.

Apart from this incident, the match progressed relatively

smoothly, with Pakistan accumulating 409 with little trouble. Shoaib and Javed contributed solid half-centuries, while the highlight was a not out century from Imran. India were in immediate trouble at the start of their innings, collapsing to 41-4 as Wasim and Waqar ripped through the upper order with 2 wickets apiece. The delivery with which Waqar dismissed Sanjay Manjrekar was described by John Holder as the ball of the match. 'It must have been about 90mph, and it just took off; Manjrekar could only glove it to the keeper who caught it well above his head.' Wasim and Waqar each took another couple of wickets, but Ravi Shastri, Kapil Dev, and Kiran More defended well to make sure that India avoided the follow-on.

It had been a wonderful performance from Waqar on his début, but it was ruined by a reoccurrence of his back injury. 'I was bowled for too long, and I could feel it go again; this time I was utterly disheartened, and was convinced I would never play again.' It was quite understandable that Waqar should have overstrained himself on his début, but it was a sign that Imran had still not completely learnt how to handle the youngster, as Javed Burki explains. 'It's so tempting to overbowl someone who looks as though he can take a wicket any time through sheer pace, but Waqar was still not very strong. He should never have been given 6 overs on the trot in the humidity of Karachi, and it was not surprising that he broke down.'

Pakistan declared their second innings on 305-5 at tea on the fourth day, leaving India four sessions to survive to draw the match. With Waqar unable to bowl more than 2 overs, and with the help of a number of dropped catches, India hung on with ease. Wasim, in particular, was on the wrong end of most of the dropped catches. 'It was just unbelievable, and it went on throughout the series. I think we put down about 24 catches in the four games, at least 13 of them off my bowling. The slips fielded like schoolchildren; Javed, Malik, Ijaz, and Shoaib all started dropping dolly catches. In the end, none of them had any confidence, and they didn't even want to field there because they expected to drop anything that came their way.'

Waqar missed the next two Tests, which was a disappointment for Wasim as well. 'Wicky made a big difference to me; bowling in partnership with another strike bowler makes life much easier. For a start, it meant that I could be used as a strike bowler myself, rather than as a stock bowler, and so I could conserve my strength by bowling fewer overs. Also, it meant that the batsmen never had a chance to relax. I felt that without him, batsmen would concentrate on blocking out an over from me, in the knowledge that the pressure would ease at the other end.'

Pakistan should have won the second Test at Faisalabad, but again it was a catalogue of missed chances. Srikkanth and Sidhu had made a useful start for India, when Wasim suddenly struck with 3 wickets in 4 overs, including the vital dismissal of Azharuddin, leg before first ball. It should have been 4; Manjrekar edged to Shoaib at third slip when he had only made 3, and the regulation catch was floored. Manjrekar went on to top score with 78, and in partnership with Tendulkar who notched up his maiden Test half-century, saw India through to the comparative safety of 288. Pakistan replied with 423–9 with Aamer Malik completing his first Test century, and all the other batsmen making solid contributions. India battled through their second innings, with some good fortune; Wasim once beat Azharuddin four times in an over;

catches were dropped, run out chances were missed, and the draw was forced.

From the very first ball, the third Test at Lahore never looked like producing a result. The pitch was just rolled mud, without a single blade of grass, and was in John Holder's opinion 'the ideal wicket for a timeless Test'. India suffered a couple of early alarms when Srikkanth was clean bowled by Wasim for 0, the sixth time in successive Test innings that the Indian skipper had fallen to the paceman, and Sidhu was leg before to Imran, but from then on the bat dominated, as the Indian total exceeded 500 and Manjrekar compiled his first Test double-century.

In turn, Pakistan reached 699-5. Every single one of their front line batsmen made at least 50, and there were centuries for Aamer Malik, and Javed, while for Shoaib there was the prize of an unbeaten double hundred. Any outside chance of a result was quashed by the weather; early morning mist delayed the start each day, and bad light in the evening further curtailed the proceedings. The match degenerated into a bore draw without either side beginning their second innings. Ultimately, it was a match that was only memorable to the batsmen. For the bowlers it was one to forget, which was precisely the attitude of the paying public who stayed away in droves; there were rarely more than 1000 spectators per day in the vast Gaddafi stadium.

The two Test absences was a harrowing time for Waqar. 'I had again been told by a doctor that I had fractured one of the vertebrae in my back, and that it was unlikely I would ever bowl fast again. I felt desperate as I had paid a large amount of money to a lot of doctors, and they were all telling me that my career was as good as over. I again called Imran who said that he had once had a similar problem and that the pain that I was getting was muscular. This time he sent me to see his own specialist, Dr Qurashi, in Karachi. He gave me a few injections in my back, and told me to rest for a week. I just spent the time alone in my hotel room. Gradually, I started doing a few back exercises, and when I got no bad reaction from that I was allowed to start running. It was a slow process, but I was fit in time for the last Test at Sialkot.'

Imran's eagerness to help Waqar and have him back in the side so soon after his recovery from injury is indicative of how highly he valued him. It was a glowing testament to a youngster who had only played one Test, but also an indictment of the Pakistan attack, Wasim apart, that had lacked penetration.

The wicket at Sialkot looked as though it had been prepared with a result in mind, a possibility that Wasim readily admits. 'With Waqar back we knew we had a much stronger fast bowling attack than the Indians, and we wanted a pitch to suit us. The strip had long, lush, coarse grass and was only distinguishable from the rest of the square by the white crease markings. The consensus was that it would be a bowler's paradise, and that the game could be over inside three days. To everyone's surprise, especially Azharuddin's, the pitch was quite playable. 'It was fairly bouncy but the ball came through evenly. It was never easy, but a batsman could cope.'

Once again, Pakistan let India off the hook with dropped catches as they allowed the Indians to score 324 after putting them into bat. John Holder had looked on in amazement throughout the series as catch after catch was spilled, but the performance at Sialkot stole the honours for ineptitude. 'There were 2 misses off Wasim that were beyond belief. There was a simple lob to forward short leg that flew ten feet in the air and all the fielder had to do was wait for the ball to fall into his hands; instead he made a wild lunge for it and dropped it. The other chance came when Akram got a delivery to rise off a length and cut across Azharuddin's body; the ball took the edge and went very gently to Javed in the gulley. He missed it completely, letting the ball hit him in the chest, whereupon it fell at his feet. Javed sank to his knees, and shook his head in disbelief. John Hampshire could barely contain his laughter; it was just so amateur considering that the over before Javed had made a magnificent attempt to take a catch off a full-blooded cut.'

Despite the missed catches Wasim was the pick of the bowlers finishing with 5–101. He bowled very fast, swung the ball both ways, but was critical of his own performance. 'I think I bowled too short at times. I was getting very frustrated and upset with the fielders, and I let it get to me.' Waqar was used much more intelligently by Imran than he had been in the first Test, but only picked up a couple of wickets. 'Even though I was fully fit, I couldn't get the injury out of my mind. I kept thinking that my back might go again at any time; it made me very hesitant as I ran in, and I only bowled at about 85 per cent of my usual pace. I should really have taken a few more wickets on such a green track.'

In their first innings Pakistan totalled 250, as the Indian bowlers capitalized on the conditions, and it required dogged batting from Rameez, Salim Malik, and Wasim to ensure that they got that many. There was a window of opportunity for Pakistan in the Indian second innings when Imran and Wasim had the visitors on the ropes at 38–4, but the old spectre of missed chances returned to haunt them, and Sidhu and Tendulkar made certain of a fourth successive draw.

So, Pakistan retained their unbeaten home record against India, but it was an indifferent result against a side that had been hailed as one of the poorest ever to leave India. In retrospect, this might have been a harsh judgement on a team that showed itself to have good fighting qualities, but a 3–0 series win had, quite literally, been within the grasp of the Pakistan side. In the end, the dropped catches had been the deciding factor.

Javed Burki had his own ideas about the missed catches. 'Waqar and Wasim were just too speedy for our slip fielders. Over the previous few years, as far as fast bowling was concerned, it had been Imran who had been taking most of the wickets. He got most of his dismissals with the ball that moved into the bat, and so for a long time we had slips who were not required to take catches at pace. Wasim had become markedly quicker, and although he and Waqar had the ability to move the ball both ways, they both frequently found the edge with the away swinger. Our fielders just weren't prepared for the speed at which the chances came, and put them down.'

Imran maintained that, 'the only good thing to have come out of the series was the appointment and performances of the neutral country umpires.' As a general comment on the rubber this had a degree of truth, but it overlooked a great deal. While Imran may not have learnt anything new about the team's capabilities, he had seen actively demonstrated what he had previously only intuitively guessed at; that Wasim and Waqar were the ideal new-ball partnership. Wasim had shown that he was perfectly at home as the senior bowler, and was by a long way Pakistan's most effective and economical bowler with 18 wickets at an average of just over 30, but it was only when he was bowling in tandem with Waqar that Pakistan really threatened to dismiss India quickly and cheaply.

6

Wasim On Top Down Under

'I love playing cricket in Australia. They have the best wickets, grounds, and crowds, and off the field people are really helpful and friendly. Everything is so relaxed. In England, especially at Lord's, if you want to practise at the ground you have to ask ten people's permission first; in Australia you can just turn up, and they'll let you play.'

Three previous visits had left Wasim with a favourable impression of the country, but the Pakistan tour to Australia in early 1990 was his most important to date. 'I'd been in the Pakistan side for five years, and I'd only ever played one-day games against the Aussies. Test matches are where it really counts, and I'd never had a chance to prove myself against them at that level.'

For Waqar the three Test series was a learning experience. 'It was my first major overseas tour. I'd been to India and Sharjah, but in many ways they are both fairly similar to Pakistan. Australia was the first western country I had ever visited, and I found it a bit overwhelming at first.' The attractions of city life were initially irresistible for the teenager, as Wasim recalls. 'Waqar was a very naughty boy at the beginning of the tour. He had started off sharing a room with Aaqib, but they had behaved so badly together that they were separated, and Waqar was again made to share with Dr Aslam. Imran even had to place a curfew on them, which was most unusual.'

Even this was no deterrent to Waqar, as he himself admits. 'I'd been out late at the disco with Aaqib and Mushtaq, and it was well past the 11 o'clock curfew. It was no problem for the other two, as they were now sharing together, but I had to get past Dr Aslam. I turned my watch back from 1 o'clock to 11, and knocked on the door. Dr Aslam got up to open it, and asked me what the time was. I said, "I'm not sure, I'd better have a look. Ah! It's eleven exactly." He replied, "So it is," and I went to bed, thinking that I'd got away with it. I didn't realize that he had looked at his watch before opening the door; he told Imran, and at the team meeting the next day I was given a severe telling off, even though the rest of the side was killing themselves with laughter.'

It wasn't just off the field that Waqar had trouble adjusting to conditions. 'I'd been used to bowling just short of a length on the slow, flat wickets of Pakistan, and I found it very hard to change to a fuller length on the hard, bouncy pitches. The length that I was bowling made me very easy to hit, and it was almost impossible for me to take any wickets, because, if the batsman missed, the ball would invariably go over the top of the stumps.'

Inexperienced though he was, Waqar was still considered to be one of the front-line bowlers. In line with Imran's long held belief of giving promising youngsters an extended run in the first team to get used to the rigours and relentlessness of the five-day game, Waqar's continuing education would be an ordeal by fire in the Tests. Statistically, the Tests were to yield poor dividends for him, but this is a clear case of the figures concealing as much as they reveal, for he was a far better bowler by the end of the tour than he was at the start.

Waqar is typically demure about his improvement. 'I had two good senior bowlers in Imran and Wasim who could teach me. I spent hours watching them swing the ball, and then tried to do the same thing myself. They both made it very easy for me to pick it up quickly.' As far as Wasim is concerned there is much more to it than that. 'He had such a positive attitude towards his bowling, and was greedy for wickets. I've never seen anyone improve as quickly; in a short space of time, he had grasped what it had taken me three years to learn when I was his age.'

The series was seen by the Australians as an opportunity to decide who was the second best Test playing country after the West Indies, and Pakistan were up against it from the start. Rameez Raja and Salim Malik, both key batsmen, were injured, and for the first two weeks of the tour Pakistan lost every side game they played. Confidence was not high as the team gathered in Melbourne on the eve of the first Test. It was already clear that the batsmen had not adjusted to the bouncier wickets, and that much of the bowling would depend on Wasim.

Australia were put into bat on what Wasim described as one of the fastest wickets he'd ever played, and were all out for 223 on the second morning, having at one stage been 90-0. It was a fine bowling performance by the Pakistanis, and by Wasim in particular, who returned his best Test figures of 6-62 including his 100th Test wicket, that of Terry Alderman caught by Aamer Malik; but it could have been so much better. As in the last series against India, Pakistan's close catching was again woeful, and continued that way throughout the tour, with Wasim being the main sufferer. 'In that first innings, I had Mark Taylor dropped early on by Javed at slip, and we put down at least three other chances. It was just as bad in the second innings, and in the next test at Adelaide. It's absolutely vital to take your catches at Test level, and when you don't you can feel the confidence of the side slipping away. It affects everyone, not just the fielder who's missed the catch; players begin to hope that the catches won't come to them, and don't want to field where they might be exposed. It's just not the sort of thing that should happen at Test level, though sometimes it does have its funny side. Once Waqar dropped a straightforward catch on the boundary off my bowling. I said to him, "What's going on?" and he replied, "I held out my hands, but the ball just went straight through where my finger is missing!"'

Pakistan began their second innings disastrously, and were soon reduced to 71–8. Carl Rackemann, Merv Hughes, and Terry Alderman, all bowled very tidily, and the Australian fielders held their catches, but the main cause of Pakistan's downfall was their inability to come to terms with the bounce of the wicket, as batsman after batsman steered balls that were well outside the off stump straight into the waiting slip area. It was a fighting 9th wicket stand between Tauseef Ahmed, the off-spinner, and Waqar that took the total into three figures, and offered Pakistan a glimmer of hope for the second innings, as Wasim recollects. 'They both stayed in for an hour and a half, and showed us that you could bat on that wicket. Imran said to me that after watching the pair of them, he now knew what to do. If it bounced, duck it; if it was wide, leave it; and if it was on the wicket, block it.'

Waqar's contribution was 18. 'It was the most difficult

innings I've ever played; not only was the wicket very bouncy, but it had huge cracks in it, about an inch and a half wide, on a good length. I worked out what to do from Tauseef; I saw how he played, and thought that if he could manage, so could I.'

The Australian second innings began with a 116 run advantage, and the home side swiftly capitalized on the situation, in the face of some indifferent Pakistani bowling, increasing their lead to 376 with 3 wickets standing by the end of the third day. Indeed it was only 4 wickets in the last hour from Wasim that prevented the Australians from reaching an even more commanding position. Earlier, Mark Taylor had moved comfortably to his 5th century in his last ten Tests, a milestone that was greeted with profound indifference by the Pakistani team who were convinced that he had edged Wasim to the keeper on 93.

The next day Australia batted on for a further 52 runs, enabling Wasim to take his second 5-wicket haul of the match in the process. Border declared at 312–8, setting the Pakistanis an improbable 429 to win, or more realistically, asking them to survive for over a day and a half on a difficult pitch to draw the game. The Pakistanis started their second innings as if they had every intention of losing within four days. Aamer Malik, Shoaib Mohammad, and Mansoor Akhtar were easily removed by Alderman and Hughes, and it required a stubborn partnership between Ijaz and Javed to steady proceedings, but when Javed was dismissed shortly before the close, Pakistan once again had their backs to the wall.

Australia duly completed their victory on the final day, but a marvellously aggressive century from Ijaz, and stern rearguard actions from Imran and Salim Yousuf, ensured that they only did so with 22 minutes to spare. In retrospect, the incompetence of their close catchers had undoubtedly played a major part in their defeat, but the Pakistanis were convinced that some eccentric LBW decisions in Terry Alderman's favour on that last day had cost them the game.

Imran declined to comment on the umpiring after the game, but he has since made his feelings known. 'The decisions against Yousuf, Waqar, and myself were atrocious. The ones against Salim Yousuf and myself were also given at crucial stages of the game; both times we had built substantial partnerships of 80 or so, and there was a real possibility that we might even win the game. If it had happened to an Australian team in Pakistan there would have been a major incident, and the Australians would probably have threatened to abandon the tour. As it is, the Australians know that they can get away with this sort of thing with the Pakistan team. For a start, our Board and officials have this attitude that we are a third world country, and that we mustn't upset our hosts. Also, the Australians are not afraid of our media; if an English team was treated badly, the English press would give the Aussies a roasting, and that is a big incentive for them to behave. As it is, they really don't give a damn what the Pakistan media says about them.'

Three days later, the two sides met at the Adelaide Oval for the second Test, a game that was to produce Wasim's finest all-round performance so far. Pakistan chose to bat on an ideal batting strip, but were disappointingly dismissed on the first day for 257. Several batsmen played themselves in, only to get out once they had done so, and the final total would have been even lower but for an aggressive knock of 52 from Wasim. During this innings Wasim had a head-to-head confrontation with Merv Hughes, the Australian paceman. 'I was going for a quick run and Hughes just stood in the middle of the wicket so I bumped into him. He started swearing at me, and so I retaliated by pointing my bat at him, and shouting, "What's your problem?" He thinks he can get away with this sort of thing because he imagines he's a great bowler; he isn't, he's simply average. If he had to bowl on dead pitches as in Pakistan he would get smashed all over the place. But all the Australian team are like this, even Allan Border; they shout and swear at you constantly, and they don't even say hello to you off the pitch. They think that this kind of attitude makes them tougher, and scares the opposition. It doesn't, it's just rude.'

Australia totalled 341 in their first innings, a score that left both teams dissatisfied. Wasim once more was left to rue his luck as chances went begging, and the miss by Aamer Malik when Dean Jones had made 19 was particularly expensive, for the Victorian batsman went on to his eighth Test hundred. For their part the Australians felt that they had rather missed out on a decisive lead as their last 5 wickets tumbled for 13 runs. Wasim took another 5 wicket bag, and Waqar showed that he was coming to terms with the conditions by chipping in with a couple, bowling Border off his body, and having Ian Healy caught hooking.

Whether the Australians should have scored more runs or not seemed something of an irrelevance as the Pakistani batting disintegrated to 22–4, with Hughes doing the damage. Pakistan were fortunate not to be 22–5 shortly after, but David Boon failed to hold a half chance from Imran at short leg, and Javed and his captain rode out the storm to stumps.

Javed was out early the next morning, and as Wasim walked out to bat, Pakistan were effectively 6–5, and in imminent danger of going 2 down in the series. 'I thought we were going to lose the game,' said Wasim. 'Imran had a word with me in the middle when I came in. He said that he was going to concentrate on defence, but that I should go ahead and play my usual attacking game. So that's what I did. I started off fairly quietly, but once I got going I hit the ball to all parts of the ground. It was my best innings ever.' Wasim went on to score 123, his maiden Test century incorporating one six and eighteen fours, and it couldn't have come at a better time. In partnership with Imran, who likewise hit a highest Test score of 136, Wasim saw Pakistan through to safety. It would be wrong to characterize his innings as a slog, though; some of his cover driving was peerless, and drew fulsome praise from his skipper. 'He was so fluent; he made me feel like some laborious blocker.'

Pakistan declared their innings early on the last morning, and almost achieved a surprise victory as Australia ended the game on 233–6, chasing a total of 304. Dean Jones completed his second century of the game to be the saviour for Australia, but was again put down early in his innings. Two more chances went astray later on, and Pakistan were left to ponder on what might have been.

Less than two full days' play were possible in the final Test, as Cyclone Nancy swept through New South Wales, rendering the Sydney Cricket Ground unplayable after torrential rain. There was time, though, for the by now predictable early order collapse of the Pakistan batting, and the equally predictable century from Mark Taylor, before the game petered out into a draw.

So Pakistan lost the series 1–0, but there was consolation for Wasim as he was named 'Man of the Series'. He had found the informality of Australia much to his liking, and it had shown in his cricket. He had thrived on wickets with pace and bounce, revelled in the responsibility of being Pakistan's senior bowler, and turned in performances that were comparable with those of the great all-rounders of any generation. The only dark cloud on Wasim's horizon was the recurrence of his groin injury.

'I could feel it go again in the first innings at Adelaide, and it steadily got worse. By the time we played the Benson & Hedges one-day tournament at the end of the tour, I was in agony every time I stepped on the field. I wanted to keep playing for the sake of the team and the captain, and so I was given massive pain-killing injections in my groin before the start of each game; even then I was often nearly crying with pain.'

Pakistan rounded off the tour by losing the Benson & Hedges finals, despite two fine innings of 86 and 34 from Wasim, for whom hospital now beckoned. Intikhab had got in touch with a number of orthopaedic surgeons, chiropractors, and physios, and had eventually been recommended to a doctor called Neil Halpin who had had great success in treating injuries of Rugby League players. 'He convinced me that Wasim needed an operation to cut the muscle away from the bone in the groin area. Wasim was naturally very frightened about the operation, but I spent a long time reassuring him, and preparing him for it.'

Wasim was operated on in Sydney in March 1990 and was playing again within a month. Although far from match fit, Wasim was such an essential part of the Pakistan team, that he was included in the squad for the Australasia Cup in Sharjah. This six nation tournament between Pakistan, India, Australia, New Zealand, Sri Lanka, and Bangladesh brought Waqar the rewards for all his hard work in Australia. He devastated India, Sri Lanka, and New Zealand with spells of 4-42, 6-26, and 5-20 to take Pakistan into the final against Australia.

In that game, Waqar struck with a further couple of wickets, but the match belonged to Wasim. He was still getting a great deal of pain in his groin, but he managed 49 not out in Pakistan's innings of 266-7. When Australia batted he personally delivered the *coup de grâce* to wrap up the innings, by claiming his second Sharjah hat-trick, clean bowling Hughes, Rackemann, and Alderman, to give Pakistan an emphatic victory.

By now such deeds were becoming almost expected of Wasim, by the crowds, the team, and perhaps even by himself, as he continued to enjoy a remarkable run of success. However, the Australasia Cup also marked Waqar's coming of age as an international bowler. He had now combined his lethal pace with consistency and accuracy; never again would he be regarded as merely a 'promising youngster'. So great was his improvement that when Wasim was asked whom he would pick to play for his life he replied, 'Richard Hadlee, but in a couple of years look out for Waqar Younis.' It was to prove to be a very shrewd assessment of Waqar's potential.

7

Ball Tampering and Pitch Doctoring

There is little doubt that by the end of 1990 Wasim and Waqar were the most effective pair of quick bowlers in the world; for sheer consistency of wicket taking they even bettered the West Indian quartet of Marshall, Ambrose, Walsh, and Bishop. Wasim had missed much of the English season recovering from injury, but even half fit, his prodigious swing and unexpected pace still made him too much for most batsmen. Waqar was now a known quantity; throughout the English summer he had terrorized the county circuit with his speed and his toe-crushing inswinging yorker. However, even though batsmen had learnt what to expect, it didn't mean they were any better prepared to handle him.

The New Zealand tour was billed as a mismatch from the start. Imran Khan had publicly declared his unavailability for Pakistan, claiming that the New Zealand team was little more than a second string eleven. Wasim agreed with this assessment. 'Where was Andrew Jones, John Wright, Jeff Crowe, and John Bracewell? With Richard Hadlee having retired, Martin Crowe was the only world-class player in their side.

Mark Greatbatch was highly rated after a couple of centuries against England but he turned out to be fairly ordinary. He couldn't play the bouncer at all. He just closed his eyes; next ball we'd bowl a yorker and he'd always get out. To me, the New Zealanders were no better than an average county side. How can you send a 'B' team to play one of the best sides in the world? It's just ridiculous.'

Faced with such indifferent opposition whose bowling posed little threat, Pakistan stacked the odds even further in their favour by preparing 3 Test wickets that were unaccustomedly green, hard, and bouncy, in the expectation that Wasim and Waqar would rampage through the Kiwis batting; neither of them was to disappoint. Wasim was unrepentant. 'Every country, except England, makes pitches to play to the home-team's strength. I don't know why, but England always prepares slow wickets, even if they're playing Sri Lanka. I'd heard so much about green English wickets, and how the ball did this and that, before I toured in 1987. I couldn't believe it when I tried to bowl a bouncer in my first Test at Old Trafford. The pitch was so slow the keeper virtually had to stand up to take the ball on the full.'

Javed Miandad, captaining the side again in Imran's absence, had little hesitation in putting the New Zealanders into bat on winning the toss in the first Test at Karachi. Immediately, Wasim and Waqar found bounce and movement to which the batsmen had few answers. Only a stand of 116 between Greatbatch and Ken Rutherford lifted the New Zealand score out of double figures, as they tottered to an all out total of 196. Wasim and Waqar each took 4 wickets, and bowled with such confidence that they frequently had no fielders behind the wicket at the bowler's end.

Shoaib compiled a painstaking not out 203, and Pakistan

were able to declare their first innings 237 runs in front, with 4 wickets still standing. The lead was more than enough, and New Zealand tumbled to an innings defeat. Wasim again took 4 wickets, Waqar took 3, and Aaqib Javed weighed in with a couple on his Test début.

The second Test at Lahore was almost a replay of the first. Pakistan cruised to a 9-wicket victory that could easily have been converted into another innings win had all the catches been held. New Zealand were again routed by the Pakistani pacemen, Shoaib again scored a century for the home team, and only an unbeaten hundred from Martin Crowe, who was dropped early on behind the wicket off Wasim, took the match into the fourth innings.

Waqar returned his finest Test figures of 7–86 in the New Zealand second innings. 'I didn't vary my bowling that much in any of the Tests, but they didn't seem to know how to play me. I'd bowl three successive outswingers and then slip in the inswinger which they'd miss. Most of my wickets were leg before or bowled.'

There were further problems for Wasim as he continued to suffer from his groin injury. 'It went again in the second Test, and I could only bowl a few overs in the second innings. I flew back to London for treatment. They did a lot of tests, and told me that because one of my four adductor muscles had been cut away from the pelvis bone that my left leg was 50 per cent weaker than the right and that it would need to be strengthened, since it couldn't cope with the stresses of bowling fast. I was put on a scientific weight-training course to build up my left leg, and since then I haven't had too many problems with it.'

Wasim missed the third Test at Faisalabad which was a much closer affair. The wicket in the old mill town was far from its usual flat self, and Pakistan collapsed to an all out total of 102 in the first innings, as the New Zealand medium-pacer Chris Pringle took 7 wickets. When New Zealand batted Waqar improved on his Test figures of Lahore with 7–76 to restrict their lead to 115, but Pakistan rallied well in their second innings, with the aid of a third successive century from Shoaib, to set a target of 243. Yet again, the pace of Waqar was too much as he collected another 5 wickets, and Pakistan squeezed home by 65 runs to complete a 3–0 series victory.

The latter part of the series was shrouded in allegations by the New Zealanders that the Pakistani quick bowlers had tampered with the ball. So heated were these claims that Wasim and Waqar were even accused of taking knives and bottle-tops on to the pitch to rough up one side of the ball to make it swing further. They both vehemently denied this. 'It's bullshit. How can you make the ball swing with a bottletop? It was simply that the New Zealanders couldn't play the moving ball. On Pakistani wickets, the ball gets rough automatically on the mud and the sand; all it needs is for the ball to be snicked for 4 early on over the rough outfield into the concrete of the stadium, or into some tin advertising hoardings, and it looks 30 overs old. Nobody could possibly need to do anything else to it.'

However, the accusations persisted, and even Mudassar Nazar, the Pakistan national 'B' team coach joined in the debate. 'The outlawed practice of roughing up one side of the ball to enhance swing must be eradicated in Pakistan. It's got to stop; it will be hard to enforce, but we will be firm.' Prising the truth is never an easy matter; bowlers the world over have always tried to gain an edge by fiddling with the ball and polishing it. There is inevitably a very fine line between what is illegal and what is acceptable. A ball will get tears in the leather in the normal course of a game; it's only natural that a bowler will seek to smooth down the scratches on one side, and exaggerate them on the other, even to the extent of making them larger with their finger nails. It is this practice to which batting sides object; but the reality is that the smoothing of rough edges is every bit as much an act of ball doctoring, and yet no one ever complains about that.

Gehan Mendis has some interesting observations. 'Everyone's always trying something to get an advantage, and the cricket grapevine's very small. If someone hears that Imran has been doing this and that to a cricket ball, you can count on most other bowlers on having a go at the same thing. But it works the other way, too, because umpires hear about these things and are on the look-out for them. If the only way Waqar and Wasim could swing the ball was with the help of a bottle-top, then they wouldn't have taken many wickets in the English county championship, as they would have been pulled up by the officials. Waqar took 113 wickets, and Wasim got 56 before he was injured, so you can draw your own conclusions. The point is that many bowlers try all sorts of methods to make the ball swing, but don't get the same results. I personally believe that Imran taught Wasim and Waqar how to shine the ball. I remember from my days with him at Sussex that he spent a long time perfecting the art of ball polishing. The reason that the Pakistanis get the ball to swing so much more than anyone else, may in the end simply boil down to a racial characteristic. Perhaps their sweat has different properties to other people's, that makes it ideal for shining the ball.'

Nothing should detract from Waqar's performance in the three Tests. He had taken 29 wickets at an average of just over 10, a haul only bettered for Pakistan in three games by Abdul Qadir, who took one more in the infamous series against

England in 1987, a statistic about which he modestly remarked 'I am sure that I wouldn't have taken nearly so many if Wasim had been fit throughout'. It had been Waqar's pace as much as his late swing that had confounded the New Zealanders; time and again batsmen were out because they just didn't have enough time to play the ball. Waqar remembers the crucial dismissal of Martin Crowe in the second innings at Faisalabad. 'It was probably the fastest ball I've ever bowled, and I don't think he ever caught sight of it from the moment it left my hand. He played in desperation at it, as if he was looking for the ball; it took his glove and went through to the keeper on the rise.' For his part, Martin Crowe was left in no doubt about Waqar's ability by the end of the series. 'Waqar is the best that I have faced – ever.'

Pakistan followed up their series victory with a further 3–0 whitewash in the one-day internationals, and when the West Indies tour began shortly after, they defeated them too by a similar margin in the one-day games. Waqar was again the destroyer with 3 returns of 5 wickets in the six matches, showing he was equally at home in either form of cricket.

The Tests against the Caribbean side were keenly anticipated by the Pakistani public who had found little to enthuse about the New Zealand tour. The absence of Imran, and the general perception that the New Zealanders had sent a second-rate team full of players the spectators had never heard of, had contributed to spectacularly low crowds at all three games. The West Indians were a different matter; to begin with, Imran had returned to captain the side, but more importantly, as Wasim points out, there was a great deal of prestige at stake. 'We had drawn our last two series against them, and we felt that if we beat them this time we could claim to be the best team in the world.'

The importance of the games to the Pakistanis was reflected both in choice of umpires and pitches. The New Zealanders had been offered neutral umpires at the beginning of their tour, but crass remarks by Martin Crowe ensured that the offer was withdrawn. For the West Indians there was never any suggestion of independent umpires. To Wasim it was all quite simple. 'The last time they came here we gave them neutral umpires, but when we asked for a similar arrangement in the West Indies, they refused. If they were never going to do what we want, why should we bother to do anything for them?' It goes without saying that the West Indian umpiring in the final Test in Barbados in 1986 was not far from his mind when he said this.

Likewise, the West Indians could expect no favours from the pitches, which would bear no resemblance to those used less than a month earlier against the New Zealanders on exactly the same three grounds. Gone would be the green, bouncy surfaces, and in their place would be slow, low underprepared tracks which would take the sting out of the West Indian quickies, whose preferred method of attack was the short-pitched ball, but at the same time still giving Wasim and Waqar, along with the Pakistan spin attack, some assistance.

The Pakistan press was quite certain what was required. Kamran Sekha wrote in the *Pakistan Cricketer*, 'We must forget the idea of being sporting by not doctoring the wickets. One will not see Qadir-type pitches in the West Indies, so why should we prepare Marshall-type wickets in Pakistan? The best bet would be to prepare wickets of the type we did in 1979–80 when Lillee was murdered and of the kind when the 1982–3 Aussies were whitewashed 3–0. Let the West Indians complain, nobody likes Pakistan anyway. We have the world's best players of spin bowling while the West Indians have possibly the world's weakest players of spin bowling. We also have the world's best spinners, so for God's sake let's plan properly otherwise we will commit a hat-trick of suicides against the West Indies.'

The series was contested in a generally good-natured manner, a feature that Wasim attributes to the players' familiarity with one another. 'I knew Des Haynes from the county game, and quite a few of the others knew each other too. You don't spend much time socializing with opponents on tour, but it's nice to be able to have the odd chat. I don't think I really talked to any of the New Zealanders except Martin Crowe because I don't know them. There was never any of the unpleasantness that you get with the Aussies, but there was a certain distance between the teams.'

Despite the good feeling, the series took place to murmurings of discontent about ball doctoring. The West Indians had been forewarned to be on their guard, and were not slow to condemn. According to Imran, 'Haynes was keeping an eye on our ball as if it was a hand grenade that could explode at any time. When we won the first Test, Gibbs and Haynes were going to release a statement until they were shown the ball that they had bowled with. There was no difference as the rough pitch had equally effected the two balls.' Of course this proved nothing, as the West Indians may well have been tampering with the ball. For his part, Mudassar Nazar was convinced that the West Indians were 'worse than us' when it came to roughing up the ball, and indicated that one West Indian had told him that they had resorted to the practice in the last two Tests in the Caribbean against England the year before. In the end, the murmurings remained murmurings; perhaps both sides realized that if there was anything untoward going on, then both sides were at it, and no one was gaining an appreciable advantage.

The first Test was due to take place at the National Stadium in Karachi, a ground that had never been Waqar's favourite since he had injured his back in his first Test match. 'I don't know why, but I always have this lingering worry whenever I play there that my back is going to go again. I always take extra special care whenever I'm warming up, but I still find it hard to let myself bowl at my fastest.' Even so, the West Indians, Desmond Haynes apart, had little answer to Waqar and Wasim as they were all out in their first innings for 261, having chosen to take first use of the wicket.

It was a happy come-back to Test cricket for Wasim who had pronounced himself fit, on his return from England having completed his treatment on his groin. 'I still didn't have my rhythm back properly, and I wasn't bowling with my usual pace, but Waqar and myself got a lot of swing. The wicket was very slow, slower even than Sharjah wickets, so we could bowl a full length, and for some reason the ball often moves a lot in the air in Karachi; maybe it's something to do with the sea breezes. Des Haynes played brilliantly for his century, but Waqar got 5 wickets and I took 3 as none of the other batsmen could play us with any confidence at all.'

It took good batting from Shoaib, Salim Malik, and Imran to give Pakistan the first innings lead. Apart from these three, none of the other batsmen made it into double figures, though Waqar showed good obdurate qualities in a last wicket stand of 27 with his skipper. The West Indians looked to be making good progress after clearing the arrears of 84 for the loss of just 1 wicket, but their last 9 wickets fell for under a hundred to set Pakistan a winning target of 98. Again it was Waqar and Wasim who were the principle wicket takers with 4 and 3 wickets respectively. Their late inswing was so effective that of their 7 second innings wickets only 1 required the assistance of a fielder. Shoaib and Salim Malik took their time making the runs on the last day, but they duly did so by tea-time to complete a comfortable 8-wicket victory for the home side, in front of an ecstatic crowd of 6000 who had been allowed in for nothing to see the denouement.

History repeated itself as the West Indies fought back to win the second Test, exactly as they had four years earlier. Indeed, the resemblance was uncanny; once again the match was all over inside three days. There was nothing wrong with the wicket at Faisalabad, though, according to Waqar, 'It was an average kind of wicket, slightly bouncier than Karachi, but nothing very difficult. When we first looked at it we thought it was an ideal batting track, and that we would have no problems winning or drawing the game.'

For Wasim the problem was easy to pinpoint. 'Maybe we were a little too relaxed after the first game, but our batsmen played terribly. Only Salim Malik who scored 70 in each innings played with any authority, but all the other batsmen just lost confidence. I'd never seen Javed ask to go lower in the order before, but in our second innings he asked to go in after Malik; maybe he wasn't fully fit, but I don't think that was all there was to it.'

Pakistan were all out for 170 on the first day, but Waqar with another 5 wickets, and Wasim with 3 kept them in the game by dismissing the West Indians in their first innings for 190. Indeed at one stage in the Pakistan second innings, they were in with a real chance of victory. 'We had made about 145–4, and were going along quite comfortably,' said Waqar. 'We then lost our last 6 wickets for 10 runs. Malcolm Marshall produced a tremendous spell of 4 wickets in as many overs, and effectively won them the match.' There was time in this spell, though, for Wasim to enter the record books again, albeit in an undistinguished fashion; he became the fifteenth player to be run out in both innings of a Test match.

A total of 129 never looked likely to give the West Indians too many problems, and so it turned out. Wasim took 3 wickets to apply some pressure, but there was no joy for Waqar, and Akram Raza, the young left-arm off-spinner, could make no headway on a wicket that had begun to take some turn, and the West Indians cruised to a 7 wicket victory.

The deciding game was played at the Gaddafi Stadium in Lahore, and was the closest of the three. Pakistan eventually hung on for a draw, but if so much time had not been lost to early morning dew and bad light in the evening, it is probable that the West Indians would have forced victory. The pitch turned out to be a surprise to the Pakistanis. 'We wanted another slow, low wicket that would take a bit of spin,' said Wasim. 'We weren't looking for a draw to square the series; we wanted to go out and win it. The pitch turned out to be very underprepared; it wasn't a great wicket for a Test match, as it took a lot of spin from the start. Unfortunately, our batsmen were still out of touch, and our spinners bowled pretty badly, I'm sorry to say.'

The West Indians batted first and were in difficulties at 37–3 before a 4th wicket partnership between Brian Lara, on his Test début, and Carl Hooper stemmed the tide. 'Lara was out for 0, caught behind off my bowling,' remembers Wasim. 'Unfortunately, I was called for no-balling. Hooper's innings was the best I have ever seen him play. His timing was superb.' Hooper went on to score 134, his second Test century, as the West Indians finished their innings on 294, with Wasim taking 4 wickets.

Pakistan's first innings was a disaster as they capitulated to Ambrose and Bishop. Wasim was the only player to bat with distinction, as he compiled a solid 38 out of a total of 122. The West Indian second innings was limited to 173 as Wasim collected a further 5 wickets. The end of the innings was a strange mixture of success and disappointment for Wasim. 'I had Dujon caught behind by Moin, and the next ball I bowled Ambrose with an outswinger from around the wicket. Bishop came in to face the hat-trick ball; he got a leading edge to a straight ball, and it lobbed to Imran at mid-on, who just stood there and dropped it. Everyone was expecting a bowled or leg before, and I don't think the skipper was concentrating. Bishop took a single, and in the next two balls I bowled Malcolm Marshall and had Courtney Walsh leg before. I had taken 4 wickets in 5 balls, but I had missed out on the hat-trick.'

Pakistan were set 346 to win, and the draw was always their priority. The cracks in the pitch were growing progressively wider, but although the wicket gave some help to the bowlers, the West Indians didn't have the spin bowling to exploit their position. Defiant innings from Shoaib, Rameez, Masood Anwar, Imran, and Wasim saw Pakistan through to safety.

So, yet again, a West Indies and Pakistan series had been inconclusive, and judgement would have to be witheld on who was the stronger team. For Pakistan there were worries in the batting and the spin bowling departments, and the debt they owed to Wasim and Waqar was evidenced in the bowling averages for the series. Wasim had taken 21 wickets, and Waqar 16; the next most successful bowler was Imran with 4.

Waqar and Wasim had taken their wickets with high quality fast swing bowling, and in so doing had challenged most people's thinking about quick bowling. For some years, everyone had grown so used to West Indian fast bowling quartets banging the ball in short, that many had come to assume that this was the key to fast bowling success. Obviously, this meant that the West Indians were always likely to be more effective on a hard track. The two Pakistanis had shown that full-length bowling at the stumps could be equally unplayable, and for them the rewards promised to be infinite, as they were at home on any type of surface.

By the end of the series, Waqar had rocketed to the number 2 position in the Deloitte world ratings, and it was only a matter of time before the number 1 slot would be rightfully his. Wasim was number 6, and the best all-rounder in world cricket. If Pakistan could get their batsmen to equal the performances of these two, the unofficial title of world's best team would be a racing certainty.

8

The Nigel Plews Affair and Wasim at Lancashire

'I came to realize that what Patrick Patterson had told me when I was a newcomer at Lancashire was correct; the county uses you. When you're playing well everybody says, "Oh Waz you're terrific," but when you get injured some of them don't talk to you properly. I know that the overseas player is better paid than most county pros, and that this causes some resentment, but we're definitely better cricketers too; that's why we're signed. Players sometimes seem to forget that you're human.'

Wasim has had to face his fair share of difficulties in his four years of playing for Lancashire, but his experiences are by no means uncommon. The role of the overseas player in English county cricket has long been the centre of controversy. He is employed to win trophies for the club, to swell the ranks of the membership, and is seen as a vital part of the team, yet at the same time there is a strong lobby that thinks that the overseas player retards the development and opportunities of the domestic player. Imran was amazed by this ambivalence when he was playing for Sussex. 'I went to a meeting of the Cricket

Association in 1978 where 60 per cent of the members, many of whom I knew well, voted that there should be no overseas players in the English game. I was really shocked to discover how many people despised the contribution of the overseas player.'

Wasim's disillusionment with county cricket was precipitated by his treatment by Lancashire over what has become known as the 'Nigel Plews' affair. 'We were playing against Warwickshire at Old Trafford. The pitch was terribly slow, the ball was old and soft, and we were struggling to bowl out Warwicks. Dermot Reeve was batting; I bounced him and he pulled me for 4. I put a man back on the boundary, bounced him again, and he ducked. Roy Palmer who was umpiring at my end told me to spread them out. I said nothing, bowled a couple of length balls and then two more bouncers. Again Roy Palmer told me to spread them out. I said, "Why do I always have a battle with you?" He just told me to carry on bowling. I bowled another bouncer, and he gave me a warning.

'Neil Fairbrother was captaining the side, and he changed the end I was bowling from to take me away from Roy Palmer. I then bowled a couple of bouncers at Paul Smith, one of which he hit for 4, the other which broke his finger, whereupon Nigel Plews gave me my second warning. Half an hour later, Tim Munton came in at number 9, and started to play very comfortably, because the wicket was so slow he knew that he could safely play forward to anything that was pitched up. I then bowled him a bouncer that didn't even get above chest height, and immediately Nigel Plews said to me, "Spread them out." I said, "It's the first bouncer I've bowled at him. What do you expect me to do? Bowl a full length that can be blocked or hit for 4?" He just told me to carry on bowling.

'I bowled another bouncer at Munton, and Nigel Plews gave

me a third warning, so I couldn't bowl again. I took my sweater from Nigel Plews, and as I was walking away from him I said "Shit umpiring". It's the sort of thing that I often say to myself when things have gone wrong, or I've bowled badly, and I didn't even think the umpire had heard. He certainly never said anything to me at the time.'

However, Nigel Plews did hear Wasim's comments and the incident was reported. The other Lancashire players were in no doubt that Wasim had stepped out of line, but what followed angered everyone at the club, as Graeme Fowler relates. 'It was clear that Wasim had gone too far, in the way that fast bowlers sometimes do when they are trying their best and getting no results. Waz would have been much better off swearing in Urdu, but seeing as he swore in English, Nigel Plews, who is one of the best umpires on the circuit, was bound to report the matter. Likewise, the club had to discipline Waz, but the way it was carried out was disgraceful and upset all the players.'

Wasim takes up the story. 'I'd left the ground without saying a word to anyone, and when I arrived the next day everyone fell silent and stared at me when I entered the dressing-room. I had a look at the papers and they were full of stories of how "Wasim had been such a bad boy swearing at the umpire", and I realized that somehow the press had got hold of the story.'

'The Chairman, Bob Bennett, came up to me and said, "Look Wasim, now that this has happened we have to have a meeting, so please come down and see the Committee." I went down to the Manager's room, and there were five of them, Bob Bennett, Alan Ormrod, David Hughes, the Treasurer, and the Secretary sitting round the table. They passed me a sheet of paper with an account of the incident written on it, and Bob Bennett asked me what I thought about it. I said, "As far as I'm concerned nothing happened. I was trying my best for Lancashire, and I didn't swear at the umpire. I just said 'shit umpiring' under my breath."

'Bob Bennett replied that they were going to have to discipline me, but I would have the right to appeal against any punishment to the Disciplinary Committee of Lancashire. I said that I wasn't interested in appealing, and that they could do what they liked. I then walked out, and was recalled half an hour later to be told what they had decided. Bob Bennett said, "We're going to fine you a thousand pounds." I looked at him and replied, "A thousand pounds is a f— of a lot of money, but I'll pay it anyway."

'When I told the players in the dressing-room everyone was really sympathetic because they knew what had happened on the ground, and they all offered to help me pay the fine.'

It wasn't just the amount of the fine that upset the players, but the publicity that went with it, as the story appeared in countless newspapers and even made it on to News at Ten.

Although Wasim has paid the fine, with generous contributions from his team mates, he has still not received a reply to the letter he wrote to the Committee expressing his disappointment over the proceedings, and questioning the accuracy of its reporting to the media. The incident left a bad atmosphere in the dressing-room, as Gehan Mendis points out. 'As a player, I hate to think that it had a bearing on our performances for the rest of the season, but I'm sure it did. I personally believe that it is still not resolved. Many of the players are still uncertain whether he'll come back and try for us in 1993. He works so hard physically, even to the extent of creating injuries by working so hard, and then often bowls for us with those injuries. He goes through all that pain, and what for? At the end of the day he still feels left out.'

However, it would be misleading to say that Wasim's experiences at Lancashire had been totally dispiriting. 'I really appreciated the support that the other players, Neil Fairbrother especially, gave me over the whole affair. In general, though, Lancashire is one of the best counties. They have great facilities, and the money is definitely a lot better than at most others. Also, the cricket is one of the best organized I've ever played, better even than most international tours. The county arranges everything; you only have to say to the manager, "I need this," and it happens.'

Wasim first played in England in the summer of 1986. 'Imran had told Mohsin Kamal and myself that we should get ourselves used to English wickets in preparation for the tour the following year. Imran got in touch with a friend of his in Birmingham, Masood Chusti, who had good contacts in England, to try and arrange something for us both. I ended up playing for Burnopfield in the Durham League, and Mohsin was, I think, signed to Gateshead.

'We really both went for the experience, as neither club was offering much money. Burnopfield gave me only £50 per week, and my three-month stay ended up personally costing me more than £2,000. We used to play twice on the weekends, and sometimes mid-week. I did quite well taking 60 odd wickets and scoring 5 – 600 runs, but I found the whole summer fairly depressing. I was very lonely, and Mohsin and I froze to death in our tiny flat in Durham. I'm not even sure that I learnt that much; we always seemed to be playing on poor pitches at small, wet grounds with no facilities, and we even had to keep playing in the rain. Without being rude, most of the cricket was of a fairly average standard, and many of the players were unfit and old. Maybe the only experience that I did get was of the weather. I certainly learnt to wear a T-shirt under my cricket shirt!'

Lancashire had had their eye on Wasim for a couple of years, before they eventually signed him. 'I first saw him in Australia in 1985, when he beat players like Kim Hughes and Kepler Wessels for pace, and bounced out Allan Border in a one-day international,' said David Hughes. 'However, our interest really started in Australia in early 1987, when I took over as Captain of Lancashire, and Alan Ormrod took over as Manager. We were hoping to sign Botham and Dilley who were on the all-conquering Ashes tour, but we were also looking for another overseas player to complement Patrick Patterson. Pakistan were out there for the Perth Challenge, and that's when we made our first approach to Wasim.'

Negotiations continued in Sharjah in April of that year, when England were invited to play in the Sharjah Cup, as Neil Fairbrother remembers. 'It was all very hush-hush. Lawrie Brown and I had to sneak out of the hotel where we were staying to meet Wasim, without telling the rest of the England party what we were doing.' Ironically, Wasim had never realized what kind of approach Lancashire was making. 'When Lawrie told me that Lancashire wanted to sign me, I was certain that he was talking about the League, as it had never crossed my mind that I might be wanted as an overseas player by a county; I just didn't think I was good enough. I was thrilled when I discovered that the county wanted me, and accepted immediately.'

Clearly, Lancashire wanted to leave nothing to chance; Bob Bennett and Alan Ormrod were on hand at the Pakistani hotel the very first night the team arrived in England for their five

Test tour of 1987 to finalize the deal with Wasim. 'I wasn't at all experienced at that sort of thing. It was a big help to have Imran there. He had known Alan Ormrod from his Worcestershire days, and he assured me that Lancashire were making me a good offer. Haseeb Ahsan, the tour manager, was also very kind to me, and negotiated a lot of the details on my behalf. I finally signed a six-year contract to begin in 1988.'

Wasim arrived late for his first season at Lancashire because of the Pakistan v West Indies Test series in the Caribbean. 'Alan Ormrod was at the airport to pick me up, and took me straight to Nottingham where we were due to start a three-day game the next day. He took me to the hotel, and introduced me to the players; I knew some of them well enough to say hello to, but that was about it. I felt very lonely. When I woke up the next day David Hughes told me that I had to wear a proper Lancashire blazer and tie to go to the ground.'

This was Wasim's first taste of the formality of Lancashire, and he finds it every bit as difficult today as he did then. 'I know you have to look smart, but why can't you dress in smart casual clothes? It's not necessary, and many other counties don't have this rule. At Lancashire, for a three-day game, you must wear a blazer and tie on the first day. For the second day, it's a sweater and tie, and for the final day, you can dress casually providing you don't wear jeans. It's all so prim and proper. I hate having to wear a tie in the morning if I've been playing for several days on the trot, and I'm tired after travelling to the next game the night before. It's so pointless; you have to get up, shower, put on the tie and blazer, only to take it off again the moment you arrive at the game.'

Wasim took 3 wickets in the Notts first innings on his début. 'I was terribly nervous. I knew that everyone was watching to see how I would perform; I felt under a great deal of pressure as people expect the overseas players to do well. I got my first wicket in my second over, when I clean bowled Newell, and that calmed me down a bit. I took a couple of wickets in the second innings, too, and all things considered I was quite pleased with the way my first game had gone.'

Graeme Fowler remembers Wasim's first appearance at Old Trafford. 'The local TV station turned up at the ground to film the new overseas signing in the nets. Wasim was totally unprepared for this as he was wearing jeans and trainers. Nevertheless, he bowled off four paces to me and he could hardly get the ball anywhere near the wicket because he was swinging it so much. I thought it was pretty strange that even off four paces he couldn't put the ball in the right place. However, I soon realized he was just going through the motions for the cameras, and that he wasn't concentrating on what he was doing. When we actually started training properly, he bowled superbly, and I couldn't believe how much he swung the ball.'

Wasim began his county career at Old Trafford in fine style with his maiden first-class century in the match against Somerset. He came in when Lancashire were in some difficulties at 127–5, and by the time the innings closed at 329–9 Wasim was still unbeaten on 116. 'It was a tremendous feeling; not just because I had proved myself to the club, but because I had proved something to myself as I had never scored a hundred before.' He followed this up with a good bowling performance against Northants, taking 7 wickets in their first innings, but the crowning glory of his first season was the game against Surrey at Southport.

Surrey batted first and were cruising along quite happily at 213 for 2, when Wasim struck with 5–15 in 10 overs. This devastating spell included a hat-trick, trapping Ian Greig leg before, and clean bowling Keith Medlycott and Mark Feltham. Surrey were dismissed for 253, and Lancashire stumbled to 140 all out, which might have been worse but for a half-century from Wasim. Lancashire were asked to make 272 in 70 overs in their second innings, and were again in deep trouble at 129–5 when Wasim walked out to bat. He went on to score 98 off just 78 deliveries before holing out on the boundary attempting a fifth six. 'He was unlucky,' said Graeme Fowler. 'He hit it very hard and flat, but straight to the fielder. He was furious when he came in; not at missing out on a century, but getting out when we were going well and only needed a few runs to win in the last over. It was a great innings, but Wasim is the sort of player who you remember more for particular shots, as some of his strokes are breathtaking.'

Wasim learnt a lot in his first season, as Alan Ormrod was quick to point out. 'He made a hell of an impact for his first season in the toughest domestic competition in the world. He made some very good scores, and in fact the only problem he had in adjusting to English cricket was in trying to do a bit less with the ball. That might sound daft, but time and again he found himself in conditions favouring seam bowlers, and he simply made the ball do too much to gain the rewards he deserved.' The overall experience was not entirely enjoyable for Wasim, though. 'I was very homesick at the beginning, and I got injured half-way through the season. I eventually said to the club, "I'm fed up, and I want to go back to Pakistan because I'm missing my home." They said that was fine by them, so I went straight home and missed the end of the season.'

It took Wasim a while to get used to the Lancashire dressing-room as Graeme Fowler again recalls. 'He was very quiet and polite at first, he never refused to do anything, and always joined in. The Lancashire dressing-room is renowned for its sense of humour; players from other counties love to come in just to listen. After a while, Wasim began to say a few things, but no one could work out what they meant. Eventually, it dawned on us that he was taking the piss out of us, and that he had a great sense of humour, too.

'There's no discrimination or racism in the dressing-room. Everyone gets picked on, and if it's your five minutes you have to grin and bear it. For instance, the club is always being given free samples of this and that, and on one occasion we were given some liquid ginseng. Wasim didn't know what it was, and as he started to take a swig of it, Winker (Mike Watkinson) told him that it was essence of pig juice. Waz spat it out immediately, but he took the joke in good spirit because he knew no malice was intended.

'Waz is also a great one for taking the piss out of himself. Last year we went off on a pre-season tour to Australia, and we had a stop-over in Singapore. There was no cricket there, and we all had a lot of fun together. Some of us took a rickshaw ride down to the market at Newton's Circus. Wasim decided to see this fortune-teller. The first thing she said to him was "You are a very sexy man". Of course this is the one thing Waz wanted to hear above all else, and for the rest of the trip he would always be asking whether we thought he was sexy! Needless to say, when we stopped over on our way back, Waz went straight back to see the fortune-teller again, and she said exactly the same thing.

'He's now one of the most respected blokes in the dressing-room; he's very intense at times, but he's also one of the nicest blokes you could meet. I was having a barbecue once, and Waz came round with six cans of cider. I said, "What have you brought that round for, as you don't even drink it." He replied,

"I know, but you do." Most people would have brought nothing, or just something that they themselves wanted to drink. Not Wasim; and that's the measure of the man.'

Wasim's second season was one of his happiest at the club. 'The club had helped me find a house to buy in Altrincham, and I was feeling less unsettled. I played in about twelve county championship games and took over 50 wickets. Things began to fit into place; I was concentrating on my bowling so I didn't make too many runs, but I also felt that I wasn't overbowled as Patto played in the other matches. I played the one-day games, and the highlight of the season was winning the Sunday League. It was Lancashire's first Trophy for ages, and I was very pleased to be the county's leading wicket-taker in the competition, with over 40 wickets.

'I really enjoyed that season, but I still found it strange that David Hughes was captain. I had nothing against the man personally, as he'd always tried to be kind and helpful to me. But how could you play someone as captain who bats at number 9 or 10, and seldom bowls? The players did their best to openly respect him as he was the man appointed by the Committee, but inside they didn't respect his cricketing ability any more.

'I think one of the main reasons for our success was the arrival of Phillip DeFreitas from Leicestershire. He had improved a great deal, and worked very hard at his game. You have to work hard as a cricketer. The problem with about 80 per cent of the English pros is that they just turn up for the show. They go to the ground, play, and go home. They don't practise. If you don't train in Pakistan you'll probably get kicked out of the team. Some of the pros are just lazy, but I also think they get tired of playing too much cricket. Some of them even prepare for an innings by watching a horse race on the

TV. What kind of attitude is that? It even affects our youngsters. Graham Lloyd and Nick Speak are great prospects, but they just don't practise hard.'

1990 was Lancashire's *annus mirabilis* as they won the two major domestic one-day competitions, the Benson & Hedges and the Nat West trophies. For Wasim the season was a mixture of triumph and disappointment. 'I was injured for much of the time and played very few games.' Wasim had never made it through a full season for Lancashire, and it was beginning to cause some anxiety and resentment among the players and the members. 'As an international, he plays too much cricket,' said David Hughes. 'On two occasions we were challenging for the championship in August, and he got injured. It was very annoying. I'd always tried to bowl him well within himself. I gave him short bursts, unless he thought he could get a few more wickets by staying on a bit longer, and I always used to chat to him towards the end of the spell to see how tired he felt. I suppose my overall feeling is that he would leave us in September fit enough, by and large, to play international cricket in the winter, and he would return to us in April unfit to play for Lancashire.'

Concern reached its peak when Wasim joined the Pakistan side for one-day competitions in New York and Sharjah. His contract allowed him to do so, but at the time he was effectively on the Lancashire injury list. It is quite probable that the members' reaction would have been a great deal less heated had it been an English player departing for international duty while injured, but it was not the most tactful behaviour on Wasim's part. It indicated very clearly that his fundamental loyalties lay with Imran and the Pakistan side, and understandably so, though many dyed in the wool Lancastrians found such an attitude almost incomprehensible.

Wasim was still injured when he returned from Sharjah in May 1990, and missed most of the season, though he still made some telling contributions, most noticeably in the Benson & Hedges final against Worcestershire. 'It was my first ever final at Lord's and the atmosphere was incredible. The whole week's preparation had been very special, and it felt as though the whole county was looking forward to the occasion. There was such a great attitude in the side; we were so cocky and aggressive, that we felt we were bound to win. On the day, I was so relaxed that I felt like I was flying when I ran into bowl. I just said to myself, "I know that I can perform anywhere. I don't have to feel the pressure of being the overseas player." It worked, too.'

Lancashire batted first and were slightly bogged down at 136–5 when Wasim and DeFreitas joined forces to breathe fire into the innings. Wasim hit a rapid 28 which included two sixes off Neal Radford, the second of which was one of the biggest straight hits ever seen at the ground, and Lancashire climbed to the comparative safety of 241 off their 55 overs. When Worcestershire batted, one spell of hostile fast bowling from Wasim virtually settled the game. He came on as first change after Allott and DeFreitas had taken the new ball, and with his second delivery found the outside edge of Tim Curtis's bat. Graeme Hick, who was being hailed as England's saviour-to-be found Wasim equally unplayable. Hick lasted for 17 uncomfortable balls, in the course of which he never once threatened a hint of permanence, and it was no surprise to anyone, least of all the batsman, when he too edged to the keeper. Wasim went on to take the wicket of Phil Newport later on, but it was these 2 wickets that were decisive. 'It was one of the least tense games I've ever played in,' said David

Hughes. 'I knew we were going to win by the time the Worcestershire innings was just 15 overs old.'

Although Mike Watkinson was adjudicated Man of the Match, Mike Selvey, writing in the *Guardian*, was in no doubt as to whom the game belonged. 'Wasim epitomizes the rise of the red rose ... The two moments of genius came from Wasim Akram, the one player to transcend the occasion and play cricket at a level removed from anyone else. Wasim is the business, no two ways about it ... Three years ago Imran Khan was saying he would be the finest all-rounder in the world; now he is just that.'

The champagne flowed again in September as Lancashire completed a notable double by lifting the Nat West trophy. 'It was another easy win,' said Wasim. 'We set out to enjoy ourselves whether we won or lost. Daffy bowled one of his best spells on a seaming wicket that suited him down to the ground. When he dismissed the first five batsmen cheaply, the match was never in doubt. After the game we went out to dinner and on to Stringfellows, just as we had after the Worcestershire match; it was a good evening!'

The regulations for the registration of overseas players were changed for the 1991 season. Whereas a county had previously been allowed to have two overseas players on their staff, though only one could be played in each county fixture, the rules were now amended to limit the registration of overseas players to one per club. For Lancashire it meant that they would have to choose between Patrick Patterson and Wasim. It wasn't a pleasant decision, but neither was it particularly difficult, as David Hughes explains. 'Patrick never enjoyed one-day cricket, especially the Sunday League since he relied on his run-up for his pace. Wasim could generate his speed off a few paces, and was generally more athletic. Wasim was just as effective in the three-day games, and of course his batting was invaluable. All things considered, Wasim was the better all-rounder cricketer.'

Wasim was not kept waiting to discover his fate. 'The Manager told me right from the start that the club was going to keep me, though he asked me not to tell anyone else.' According to Geham Mendis, Patterson also knew which person the club would choose. 'Patto told me that there was only one way the club was likely to go, and that he was already looking around for another county. I felt very sorry for him; Patto isn't a wealthy man and he relies on what he can earn from the game.'

However, while cricketing ability may have been the primary consideration in the decision, the differing attitudes of the two players may have played a part, as Graeme Fowler suggests. 'Wasim is a very bright bloke, and he worked out very quickly what he had to do in order to become one of the best cricketers in the world; he obviously learnt that from Imran. He got his head down, and quietly got on with it. I don't think Patrick ever quite worked it out. He never understood whether he was meant to be a swing bowler or a strike bowler, and what he had to do to keep playing for the first team. Also Waz is an out and out trier; he'll give 100 per cent day after day. Patrick wouldn't bowl really fast unless it was a fast wicket. Waz's attitude would be that the true test of a great quick bowler would be to bowl fast on a slow wicket; and that's what he would try and do.'

Wasim's determination to be the best also showed in his attitude towards training. At the beginning of the 1991 season Wasim was having problems; he wasn't taking wickets, and he was bowling badly with the new ball. His solution was to go to the nets with Gehan Mendis. 'On our days off we would go to the ground and Waz would ask Alan Ormrod for a new ball. He would bowl about 12 overs to me, and then take the ball back to Alan and ask for another one. Harvey (Neil Fairbrother) thought I was mad, but who am I to miss out on practice against one of the world's best bowlers?'

A short while into the season, the practice began to pay off, and Wasim raced to 50 championship wickets, and helped take Lancashire to the final of the Benson & Hedges cup, second place in the county championship, and top of the Sunday League. David Hughes remembers the game against Hampshire at Basingstoke in particular. 'We were 5 down for just over a 100 in our first innings when Wasim came in; he had to graft and build an innings, which he did, and went on to a good century. The match appeared to be dying a death on the last evening; it was 5.30, Hampshire had only lost 5 wickets, and there seemed to be no chance of a result. Mike Watkinson fiddled a wicket with his off-spinners, and then Wasim got rid of Nicholas, Connor, Aaqib, and Bakker in next to no time, and we were back in the pavilion by 5.45.'

The Benson & Hedges final was a disappointment to the team, as they lost to Worcestershire, the previous year's runners-up. Pressure had been mounting within the club for David Hughes to step down as captain, and he duly did so for the final. 'As long as the other players were pulling enough weight for eleven it was fine to have David as captain,' said Graeme Fowler. 'He had great motivational skills, but once the other ten players weren't functioning to the best of their ability, as started to happen in 1991, David's contributions as a player was exposed. Ultimately, it was this that led to his resignation. I don't know whether it all ended on a sweet or sour note, but I suspect the latter.'

Wasim was far from happy with his own contribution that

day. 'The wicket was grassy and uneven, and I just couldn't find my rhythm. I took 3 wickets, but I also got hit for 18 in an over after I got cramp in my leg.' It wasn't one of Wasim's best games, but there was a lurking suspicion that he had been mishandled by Neil Fairbrother who was standing in as captain. Curtis and Moody had fallen early on to the new ball attack of DeFreitas and Allott. Given Graeme Hick's discomfort against Wasim the previous year, Hick's arrival at the crease would have been the ideal time to introduce the Pakistani paceman. As it was, Hick was given time to play himself in before Wasim was called up, and the Worcestershire number 3 went on to play a match winning innings.

With this defeat the season began to deteriorate for Lancashire and Wasim. Ten days later came the controversial game against Warwickshire at Old Trafford, and it was with some relief that Wasim missed most of the rest of the season through injury, though for once it was not his groin that was the problem. 'He got hit by a harmless slow full toss that broke a bone in his foot in the first round of the Nat West against Dorset,' said Gehan Mendis. 'In a way I'm glad that he got it; now he knows how painful it is to be hit on the foot by a yorker.' Seventh place in the County Championship, and runners-up in three one-day competitions might have been deemed a successful year in many a county, but not at Lancashire, especially after such a promising start. David Hughes' resignation and Wasim's fine and injury unsettled the side, but there was no disguising that many key batsmen lost form, and that the club had no quality spinners to dismiss the opposition on dusty, August wickets.

Wasim's inability to complete a full season yet again did little to endear him further to the members, many of whom thought he could play if he really wanted to. This belief was strengthened when Wasim went to play in a fund-raising game for Imran in Liverpool. 'What the members didn't realize,' said Gehan Mendis, 'was that he was only making an appearance. He was in whites, and he was on the field, but that was about it. He didn't bat, he didn't bowl, and he fielded in the slips. He was only doing it for Imran as a favour, but the members don't hear that side of it. They hear what they want to hear, and they get angry.'

Even before the 'Nigel Plews Affair', Wasim had begun to feel out on a limb, and unappreciated at Lancashire. 'When the club toured Australia at the beginning of the season, all the senior players like Atherton, Fairbrother, DeFreitas, and Allott were given sponsored cars, and yet the Manager didn't have the courtesy to ask me whether I wanted one. I've played over a hundred one-day internationals and over forty Test matches for Pakistan, and yet I get worse treatment than the England players, some of whom haven't even been at the club as long as me.

'I also found it hard to make friends. Gehan Mendis and I became very friendly, and we learnt a lot about each other's culture, but otherwise I found it difficult. I used to invite people to come and have a meal with me, but nobody invited me back apart from Graeme Fowler and Paul Allott. I know that the other players are from a different culture, but I found them much less welcoming than what I was used to. They were friendly enough at the ground; whether or not they went out with one another after matches I don't know. They certainly didn't with me.'

To an extent this highlights the problem of the overseas player, who is brought up in one culture and is then overnight thrown into the deep end of another. 'We spend nearly six months of the year in each other's pockets,' said Gehan

Mendis, 'and the only thing that some of us have in common is that we play for the same team. If everything's going well, then we get along all right. Sometimes people get a bit edgy when we're doing badly; under those circumstances it can be unbearable to be cooped up in a dingy dressing-room while it's raining. I find I need to get away from the game and the other players. Wasim is a genuine friend, though, and I like going out with him in the evening.

'Some of the players don't know Waz as anything other than a great cricketer, but you can't get on with everyone. Wasim does have his infuriating habits; whenever Waqar or one of the other Pakistanis comes to the ground he always speaks Urdu, which makes the other players feel excluded and annoys them a great deal, but Wasim seems to be oblivious to their feelings. I suppose it's just a clash of cultures; if Wasim didn't speak Urdu his Pakistani friends might think he had become anglicized, and that he had turned his back on his own culture.'

Nevertheless, certainly within the confines of the dressing-room, Wasim is well-liked and respected. 'It's difficult for someone who comes from overseas to relate to the county.' said David Hughes. 'I will give my all for the club because I'm a born-and-bred Lancastrian. Wasim is great in that even though he isn't, he will still give his all. I couldn't have asked for any more than that.'

Graeme Fowler offers a similar viewpoint. 'He motivates people by his example and his enthusiasm, though I think he sometimes fails to realize that we don't all have his natural talent. I often feel that we are a better team when he's playing. He's turned in some great performances for the club, though I think we've yet to see him at his best with the bat. Partly this is due to him concentrating on his bowling, and to him feeling he often doesn't have the time to build an innings coming in at number 6 or 7. But it's also due to the fact that he can't see properly! I wear contact lenses to bat, and my eyes are twice as good as his, and yet sometimes he goes out to bat without them. At Worcester he even took his lenses out in mid-innings! I know it takes time to get used to them, but he's got to persevere. If you can't see properly, you've got to be struggling.'

Unquestionably, the 1991 season left deep scars on Wasim, many of which are as yet unhealed. 'Lawrie Brown tried to get me to play in the Refuge Assurance Cup final, saying, "You can play, you'll be all right." I said, "I'm not fit, I've got a fracture. How could I possibly be OK?" I didn't even go the ground for that game. On the day I left to go back to Pakistan I spoke to Alan Ormrod who told me, "If you're not happy at the club, just let me know." I didn't say anything because I was feeling slightly better about it all. But it's still a problem. How do I know that I am appreciated if they treat me like that when I'm trying my guts out for them?'

One way to make Wasim feel valued has been suggested to the club by Graeme Fowler. 'I proposed that they send him a telegram in Pakistan to wish him every success in the World Cup, and that they were looking forward to having him back in 1993, the year after the Pakistan tour of England. It would only cost the club a few quid, and it would mean the world to Wasim.'

Wasim is contractually bound to return to the club. Whether he is motivated to perform at his best, and to put that extra bit of effort in when the going gets tough, to an extent depends on gestures like these. It is as much the duty of the club to make the overseas player feel at home, as it is the duty of the player to try to fit in. At the moment, communication between both parties has broken down. No player should be bigger than the club, nor be seen to be so, but while it is the right of the club to discipline a player as it sees fit, it should also take note of the fact that all the team members were angry at the way Wasim was treated. Wasim isn't a loudmouth superstar who courts controversy; he's a sensitive and insecure twenty-five-year old who needs reassurance, and Lancashire cannot afford to lose the services of a man of his talent.

9

Surrey Get A Match Winner

It's hard to think of another overseas player who has created a greater impact in county cricket during his first two seasons than Waqar Younis. Jimmy Cook and Graeme Hick made a remarkable number of runs for Somerset and Worcester, but in terms of match-winning potential even they have to concede second best to Waqar. In less than half a season in 1990 he took over 50 championship wickets, many of them on an Oval pitch that had given up 1850 runs for the loss of just 19 wickets in the fixture against Lancashire in May, and with the new smaller seamed ball at that. The following year, it was Waqar who almost single-handedly took Surrey to the Nat West final, and kept them in contention for the county championship up until the closing weeks of the season.

What makes Waqar's success all the more astonishing is that prior to his arrival at Surrey he was virtually unknown in England, and had already been rejected by another county. Imran takes up the story: 'I approached Sussex, because I knew they were struggling. Even back in 1988, my last season with the club, I knew that Sussex did not have a strong enough team to sustain themselves in county cricket, and I told them so. They didn't do anything much about it, and the season was a disaster. The next year was pretty much the same, and so I immediately thought of them in 1990. I spoke to everyone at the club; Paul Parker, the captain, Norman Gifford, the coach, and John Barclay, the ex-captain who was on the committee. I said, "I have this strike bowler who's exceptional; you must sign him while you have the chance, because next year he'll be snapped up by someone else. Take him for nothing this year, but just make him play; you can judge his capabilities for yourself, and decide whether to re-sign him for 1991." In those days you were still allowed to have two overseas players on the staff, so it would have been quite possible.

'They came back to me, and just said no. They had offered Tony Dodemaide a contract for the year after, and they wanted to stick with him. I tried to explain that Waqar was an out and out strike bowler who would win matches. Dodemaide was a perfectly good cricketer but he was a medium-pacer like hundreds of others in county cricket. Sussex didn't seem to understand this.'

It is highly unlikely that Sussex could have been under any misconceptions about the strength of their bowling, so why were they unwilling to take Waqar, even on trial? The answer again exemplifies the ambivalence in which the overseas player is held. They were probably wary of being used as a finishing school for one of Imran's Pakistani colts. Of course, Imran had a vested interest in Waqar being signed to the Sussex staff; the organization and the quality of the cricket and the pitches at domestic level are of a standard matched only in Australia, and Waqar would certainly have benefited from the experience. So conditioned were they by the notion of the overseas player 'taking something from the game', that

Sussex failed to appreciate that the arrangement could, and should, be mutually benficial.

Surrey, though, were more interested. Imran had met up in Sharjah with Ian Greig, his old Sussex team mate who was now captain of Surrey, where Pakistan were playing for the Australasia Cup, and where the Surrey side had come for some pre-season warm-up games. Greig had confided in Imran that the club was worried about the fitness of Tony Gray, their West Indian fast bowler, and that they were concerned about his enthusiasm for county cricket. In turn, Imran alerted Greig to Waqar's potential, though no firm commitment was immediately forthcoming from Surrey.

Pakistan then went on tour to America, where they played two unofficial games against Australia in New York and California. 'Imran was still trying to get me signed to an English club,' said Waqar. 'He told me that even if they didn't pay me any money I should go for the experience. The week after the American tour ended Imran phoned to ask me to join him in London. When I arrived he told me to go straight to the Oval for a trial in the nets.'

Ian Greig was still sceptical about Waqar's potential, but he had sufficient faith in Imran's assessment to see for himself. He had thought it unlikely that Waqar would be good enough to replace Tony Gray in the first team, but that he would be a welcome additon to the second eleven. Indeed, Greig had already pencilled Waqar in for the second team match against Somerset at Yeovil. 'You've got to give Greig a lot of credit,' said Imran. 'He realized how good Waqar was straight away, and the club phoned me and the BCCP to ensure that he could be registered in time for the Benson & Hedges quarter-final game against Lancashire at Old Trafford the next day.'

Alec Stewart was the guinea pig in the nets that day. 'I had played against Waqar in a couple of Nehru Cup games, but he hadn't made too big an impression; it was my first major tour and I tended to stick with the England players. I had made runs in one game, and been bowled second ball by Waqar in the other, but to be honest I remembered him more for a couple of misfields. He bowled at me for about half an hour; by the end of that session, I think we all realized he was a bit special.'

Waqar was very nervous for that first game. 'I didn't know any of the Surrey players, and I was totally surprised by the size of the crowd,' he said. 'I'd never played in front of so many people in Pakistan, not even in a one-day game; Old Trafford was absolutely packed. In all honesty, I didn't bowl at my best, giving away 55 runs off my 11 overs.' He did, however, take a couple of wickets, those of Graeme Fowler and ironically enough, Wasim. It might have been more, too, as Gehan Mendis's first scoring shot was a decidedly streaky edge between slip and gulley off Waqar.

Surrey lost the game, but despite Waqar's indifferent performance he was asked to sign for the rest of the season immediately on the team's return to the Oval. 'They only offered me £7,000, but I was delighted. I would probably have signed for almost nothing, just to have the chance of playing county cricket.'

Waqar's inclusion in the side gave some much needed fire-power to a bowling attack that had looked distinctly anodyne on the flat Oval wickets. He made his county championship début in early June against Derbyshire at the Oval, a match in which John Holder was umpiring. 'I was very surprised to see him again, and I was also amazed at his improvement since I'd last seem him in India. He seemed to adjust to the cold and miserable conditions quite easily, and he was very quick indeed.' Waqar took 4–77 from 30 overs in Derbyshire's only innings, but the match petered out into a rain affected draw.

Understandably, Waqar found it diffcult to fit into the social set-up of the club at first. 'I didn't speak very good English, and I found it very hard to understand all the other players. The skipper spoke with a South African accent, Tony Murphy with a northern accent, Monte Lynch and Tony Gray with Caribbean accents, and the rest of the team with various London accents.'

'I spent the first five weeks staying with friends in East Ham who came from my home town in Pakistan. They were very kind to me, but I knew that I couldn't stay with them for long. It was awkward because I knew that Surrey didn't want to pay for accommodation as they were already paying for a flat for Tony Gray, but I didn't have enough money to find somewhere for myself. Eventually, I explained the situation to the club and they found a little one-bedroomed flat in the East End for me, and I felt a lot more settled after that. I also had a great deal of trouble getting used to the food, and suffered from bad stomach upsets.'

Many of the Surrey players went out of their way to include Waqar in social activities, but even so things went wrong at times. After returning with the team from an away game, Waqar was left at the Oval while the other players drove home. It was late at night, and Waqar had no car, the trains had stopped running, and he didn't have enough money for a taxi. In desperation, he phoned Imran who told him to take a cab to his house, and he would pay the fare. Imran was furious with the club, and told them so. The skipper and the players were reprimanded, and there was no repeat performance, but it does show how easily an overseas player can be made to feel an outsider. There was no malice on the part of the Surrey players, just thoughtlessness, but it is sensitivity to these details that can make all the difference to the overseas player fitting into the club and turning in the level of performances for which he was originally hired.

Initially, the Surrey members were somewhat suspicious of the young Pakistani. He didn't have the tall, muscular build of the traditional fast bowler, and his spells tended to be unpredictable. There would be more than the usual number of high full tosses and wides mixed in with the unplayable delivery. However, as Waqar proved himself a match-winner, he rapidly earned the respect of both the members and the players.

'I didn't expect to play that much to start with,' said Waqar. 'Tony Gray was still the first-choice overseas player, and I thought that Surrey would be looking to give him the chances. However, whenever Tony played he seemed to get injured, and I gradually became the first choice. I know there were a lot of rumours about Tony not wanting to play county cricket, but I'm not sure how true they really were. I know that after I arrived, he got pretty desperate about missing games through injury. He was always very friendly to me, and I felt terribly sorry for him.'

Waqar was the driving force behind two wins on the trot at the Oval in early July. He routed Northants in a game shortened by rain, with 6–36 off just over 18 overs, and followed this up with 11 wickets against Warwickshire, including a career best 7–73 in the first innings. By the end of that week, Waqar topped the national bowling averages with 27 wickets at an average of 15.85, and was now beginning to win the admiration of the English cricket press. David Foot wrote in the *Guardian*: 'Younis is no more than medium build and possesses a good natural action. He is young enough to tear in like a sprinter; he keeps the ball up to the bat and has a lethal yorker up his sleeve. Above all, he bowls straight.'

It was Waqar's competitiveness, as much as the results he achieved that won the hearts of the players. 'He was every bit as aggressive in the nets as he was in the middle,' said Graham Thorpe, the Surrey England 'A' team International. 'In fact, he bowled me with the first ball I ever faced against him in the nets. Without taking too much away from the other players, he helped give the side a killer instinct. No matter how many runs your batsmen are making, it still comes down to the fact that by and large it is the bowlers who win games and championships; and with Waqar in the side we began to believe we could win.'

Surrey were never able to maintain a strong challenge for the county championship, and finished the season in ninth place, though Waqar continued to gain the plaudits of all those who saw him. Fine efforts against Leicestershire, Hampshire, and Middlesex, helped him to finish the season with 57 wickets from his fourteen matches, by far the most successful return of any of the Surrey bowlers.

For Ian Greig, the Surrey captain, Waqar's arrival was most timely. Greig had been appointed skipper in 1987, after he was released by Sussex, specifically to clean up the Surrey dressing-room that had become renowned for its backbiting and backstabbing. This he had done, but there had been a price to pay, as he was left with a relatively young and inexperienced side after the release of several of the senior pros. 1990 was the penultimate year of his five-year term, and he was ambitious to end on a winning note. The batting had begun to take shape with the quintet of Darren Bicknell, Alec Stewart, Graham Thorpe, David Ward, and Monte Lynch all capable of putting together a long innings, but before Waqar, the only pace bowler of any consistency was Darren Bicknell's brother, Martin. Martin Bicknell was beginning to be seen as an England prospect, a view that was born out with his selection for the Australia tour of 1990/1, but there were genuine fears that lack of support would lead to his being overbowled.

Not only did Waqar furnish that support, he also gave a much needed fillip to the other bowlers, as Ian Greig explains. 'Waqar provided someone for Martin Bicknell, Tony Murphy, and Mark Feltham to live off. With Wicky bowling from one end, batsmen were much more likely to take chances at the other.' In turn, the other Surrey bowlers had nothing but admiration for Waqar's pace and accuracy. Without a hint of envy, Mark Feltham moaned that, 'Even if I was twice as fit and twice as strong I could never bowl that fast. He has such a whippy arm action, that I sometimes wonder if he's double jointed.'

Waqar's success did not only come by bowling a much fuller length than other quick bowlers, and thereby not suffering so much from the dry wickets of 1990 which had reduced others' potency considerably, but also from his ability to swing the ball so late. Dermot Reeve, the Warwickshire bowler, was able to achieve a prodigious swing, but the swing started early in the ball's flight, which made it comparatively simple for the batsman to pick up the trajectory. What made Waqar so effective was that the ball would appear to be travelling in a straight line, and then deviate at the last moment; this, combined with his extreme pace, made him lethal. Geoff Arnold, the Surrey coach, is known to be a rigorous judge of a bowler, but even he said of Waqar, 'He is very sharp indeed, but he is special because he swings the ball at will. Very few modern bowlers swing it consistently with the balls we now use, and nobody in the world swings it so late, and at such speed, except Wasim Akram.'

At the end of the season, Surrey were forced to choose between Tony Gray and Waqar, a decision that Waqar had made straightforward, and after a few hiccups in the negotiations, Waqar signed a new five-year contract. Waqar had more than justified the claims that Imran had made about him to Ian Greig, and Greig had reaped the reward for having had the open-mindedness to listen. The club benefited on a financial level too; 57 wickets for £7,000 represented the bargain of the season, and Waqar's presence at the club augured well for membership subscriptions and attendances in 1991. Undoubtedly, too, Waqar's success prompted Hampshire to sign Aaqib Javed, another Imran protégé, while their regular overseas player Malcolm Marshall was touring with the West Indies. Aaqib didn't disappoint, either, finishing the 1991 season as the county's leading wicket taker with 53 victims.

For many players, the second season in county cricket is the most difficult as their novelty value wears off. The first season can be a honeymoon period; the bowlers have not learnt exactly where the weaknesses in a new batsman's technique lie, and a batsman is not quite sure what to expect from an unknown bowler. Batsmen knew exactly what to expect from Waqar in 1991, but if anything, batsmen found Waqar even more unplayable than the previous season, and he went on to have an extremely successful year.

Waqar returned to Surrey for pre-season training at the beginning of April. 'I had phoned the club before I arrived to make sure everything was ready for me, and they told me everything was fine. When I got to London, it turned out that the flat they had rented for me in Streatham didn't even have a phone. After a week I told them that I wanted something better. I found a two-bedroomed flat in Bow that had good security, and had access to a swimming-pool and gym, where I could get some peace and quiet. It was more expensive than the club would have liked, but they rented it for me because they wanted to keep me happy.'

Surrey were to have gone on a pre-season tour to India, but this was cancelled when it became apparent that no opposition of sufficient ability could be guaranteed, and instead a short trip to Lanzarote was hastily arranged at the last minute. 'It was physically very tough, but I enjoyed it,' said Waqar. 'Most importantly, it was a time when I got to know most of the other players. I got to know all about them, and they got to know all about me, and we came to understand one another's problems.'

In the very first game of the season Waqar showed that he had lost none of his enthusiasm. A 4-wicket blitz in the Sunday League fixture against Somerset almost won a rain-affected game for Surrey, but even then he was not satisfied. As he returned to the dressing-room, he buried his head in his hands, cursing himself for bowling what he considered to be the wrong ball at the wrong time. His knack for taking wickets didn't desert him all season. In his first county championship game he took 11 wickets against Lancashire, and repeated the performance in the very next game against Hampshire at Bournemouth.

Thereafter, scarcely a game went by without a significant contribution from Waqar, and by the season's end he had taken 113 wickets in 18 games, with no fewer than 13 five wicket bags, at an average of under 15 runs per wicket, to head the national bowling averages. Of his 113 wickets, over 60 per cent were bowled or LBW, an astonishing record of accuracy and unplayability; most fast bowlers would be thrilled to achieve a percentage of 30 per cent. However, what made Waqar even more impressive was his sheer consistency, as Alec Stewart points out: 'He's the only bowler I've ever played with or against who you feel could take a wicket at any ball, regardless of the state of the wicket or the state of the game. A batsman could be on 0 or 150; it doesn't make any difference.' John Holder confirms this: 'I was standing in the game between Surrey and Leicester. James Whitaker had been batting very solidly for 46, when Waqar bowled him a bouncer just before lunch. The next ball, he delivered the most perfect yorker, and I could tell it was going to cartwheel the stumps from the moment it left his hand.'

Inevitably, Waqar's success did cause some problems, albeit of the kind that most teams would be thrilled to have. 'I think we did get a bit complacent at times,' said Graham Thorpe. 'We tried to guard against it, but it did creep in. When you've got Waqar in the side, even if there doesn't seem to be much happening, you think that all you've got to do is to give Waqar the ball and he'll take 3 or 4 wickets and we'll be back in charge of the game. If our back-up bowlers had taken more wickets, we might well have won the championship. I'm not saying that they didn't do their best but we probably subconsciously took the pressure off some of the other players and put it on to Waqar.'

Certainly Waqar felt this pressure from the captain. 'Ian Greig was very heavy-handed with me at times, a bit like a school teacher. No one can take wickets in every game, but when I didn't he looked at me as though I was doing it deliberately. If I didn't take 5 wickets it was as if they were not getting their money's worth. Sometimes I'd bowl flat out in the nets, and the ball would fly through. Greig would see me get a lot of bounce, and say, "I wish you'd try that hard in the middle." He didn't seem to realize that the wickets in the nets were quick and green, while most of the pitches we played on were flat and low. I never argued with him because he was the captain. If he said something I disagreed with, I just kept quiet.'

In a bizarre parallel with David Hughes' experience at Lancashire, Greig, amidst unconfirmed rumours of a dressing-room vote of no confidence, announced his retirement from the captaincy at the end of the season, though he continued to act as skipper for the rest of the year. His personal dissatisfaction with his batting and bowling form was matched by the rest of the team. 'I think it was a good decision,' said Waqar. 'He scored under 400 runs and only took 10 wickets, so it was hard to say he was worth his place in the side. I don't know whether Alec Stewart will be a better captain, but he's more my own age, and I find it easier to talk to him about the game. Apart from anything else, he's a current England Test player, so I feel he knows what's what.'

Nevertheless, under Greig's captaincy, Surrey reached the Nat West final. While the county championship is arguably a truer measure of a player's ability, it is the one-day competitions that attract the crowds. The Nat West games provided the perfect setting for Waqar to showcase his talents to a wider audience, for without his contributions Surrey would almost definitely have lost both their quarter-final and semi-final games.

Surrey's Nat West campaign got under way with a win against Oxfordshire. 'It rained so hard for two days that we were never able to properly finish the game,' said Waqar. 'It came down to a shoot-out between the bowlers in the indoor nets. Each team had to nominate five players to bowl two balls at a set of undefended stumps, and whoever scored the most hits won. Oxford won the toss, bowled first, and scored two hits. We were confident after that, especially as none of our bowlers had missed in practice. I went first, and missed with my first ball, and I could sense that people were thinking, "What's going wrong?" I hit with the second, but then Monte Lynch, James Boiling, and Martin Bicknell, all missed with both their deliveries. We were sweating a bit then, and we were sure we were out of the competition. Tony Murphy was the last to bowl; he just picked up the ball, walked back to his mark, and, without hesitating for a second, ran in and bowled. He hit, and then he did the same thing again, and we were through. There was a lot of screaming and shouting after that game.'

After a straightforward victory against Kent in the second round, Surrey were due to meet Essex, one of the most experienced one-day sides in the game, in the quarter-final. Surrey batted first and made 253, with David Ward scoring an aggressive 62, and Waqar providing some welcome tail-end heroics with a sparkling 26 in a matter of minutes, that included two huge sixes. Surrey's total was at best only par for the course on a perfect batting wicket against a team with the likes of Graham Gooch, John Stephenson, Salim Malik, and Nasser Hussain in its ranks, and at tea, with Essex on 83–0, the home side were in trouble.

However, wickets began to tumble. Gooch fell immediately, as he touched a Waqar outswinger, and Alec Stewart took a smart catch low down, James Boiling caught Prichard in the gulley, and John Stephenson went to a catch by Monte Lynch that verged on the unbelievable. Stephenson had driven Bicknell low and hard into the covers, and Lynch standing close in, caught a ball that had never risen more than a few inches from the ground. It was a sublime piece of fielding, but there was also much that was ridiculous, as Darren Bicknell, Jonathan Robinson, and Ian Greig all put down chances that at the time appeared crucial. In the end, the pressure was too much for Essex and they were all out for 222; Salim Malik was run out by a good boundary throw from Martin Bicknell, and inevitably Waqar weighed in with 3 more wickets, those of Garnham and Seymour in successive balls, and of Derek Pringle, the last man out, to take the Man of the Match award.

If the Essex game was tight, the semi-final against Northamptonshire was a nail-biter. Surrey won the toss and batted first on a pitch that offered movement to the seam bowlers, and shortly before lunch were in desperate straits at 91–6, which became 124–7 shortly after, as Graham Thorpe the last of the recognized batsmen holed out to point. Thereafter, the innings was shored up by Martin Bicknell with a best ever score for Surrey of 66 not out and by James Boiling with 22, to take the total to 208–9 by the close, and thereby giving the Londoners a ghost of a chance.

The Northamptonshire innings was progressing nicely at 68–0 when both openers Larkins and Fordham were out in successive overs, and the match then became a cliff-hanger. Waqar was too fast for Bailey and Capel, Lamb was sensationally caught in the gulley by Boiling, and Waqar came back in yet another hostile spell to bowl Baptiste and Williams with late inswing. By 7.30 in the evening, Northampton had reached 188–8 with 6 overs left, and in light that was rapidly deteriorating Greig recalled Waqar for his last 2 overs. The threat of Waqar was enough for the umpires to offer the light, and Allan Lamb had no hesitation in instructing the 2 not out batsmen, Curran and Walker, to accept.

In retrospect, this was clearly an error, but even at the time

Waqar thought that Lamb had made a mistake. 'Curran was playing very well, I was tired, and it was not easy to sight the ball in the field. The next day, I felt much fresher and had Curran caught low down at slip off my very first ball. Even if he had got the edge the evening before, I am sure he would have got away with it, as it would have needed a miracle to catch the ball at that pace in the dark.' Waqar was unable to take the last wicket, but with Curran out, the run rate steadily mounted, and Walker was run out in the last over attempting a suicidal single. Surrey were through to the final, and again Waqar was Man of the Match, though in many ways Martin Bicknell's runs and his 3 wickets were equally telling.

In the weeks that led up to the final, Surrey continued to play with confidence and determination, and Waqar was as relaxed as he had been at any time during the season. In between taking 12 wickets in a county championship game against Hampshire, their Nat West opponents, a few days before the final, he found time to do some clothes modelling, and to fool around in the dressing-room wearing a Saddam Hussein mask.

Surrey were firmly established as favourites for the final, and the deciding factor in this assessment was Waqar. No one seemed to be in any doubt that he could virtually win the game on his own. It was a big burden to place on a young player, but Waqar appeared oblivious to it. According to Jonathan Barnett, Waqar's agent, Waqar's big worry before the final was whether he would be able to find someone to sponsor him for a batting helmet. 'I know it sounds absurd, but it's true. I managed to get Alfred Reader to give him a helmet; I told them that in all probability they could have it back unused after the game!'

Traditionally, the Lord's wicket helps the side bowling first in the Nat West final, as the September dew takes time to evaporate, and Surrey were disappointed to lose the toss and be put into the bat. The expected lateral movement never materialized, but the pitch was never as benign as most commentators imagined. Jonathan Robinson, the Surrey opener, explains, 'It was a very two-paced wicket; in one over a bouncer from Aaqib flew over my head, and I could duck easily, but in the next, a similar ball hardly got up at all, and hit me on the head.' After Robinson retired hurt, the Surrey batsmen regarded the pitch with deep suspicion and dawdled to 97–1 off well over 30 overs by lunch. Stewart, Thorpe, and Ward then got the scoreboard ticking over and 240–5 represented something of an achievement, bearing in mind what had looked likely at one stage, but was still 20 or 30 runs short of what Surrey would have felt comfortable with.

Greig had won acclaim throughout the season for his positive and imaginative captaincy, and for his intelligent use of Waqar, especially in the one-day games. He had tended to use Waqar in 4 or 5 short spells at various stages in the game, rather than adopting the customary method of giving the leading strike bowler half of his overs at the beginning of the game and half at the end. It had been singularly effective against Essex and Northamptonshire, but it was not what Waqar would ideally have liked. 'Every fast bowler takes at least an over to find his line, length, pace, and rhythm. Surrey were depending on me, and yet a few of my overs were wasted in getting me warmed up.' This was not the only piece of captaincy to which Waqar took exception. 'At the very start of the Hampshire innings I asked for a short leg. The skipper said that he'd rather have a mid-off to keep the runs down early on. I told him that nobody would be driving me at that stage, but he insisted. Off my second ball, Paul Terry lobbed a catch straight to short-leg.'

Waqar bowled fast, but was not at his best, and Hampshire moved on comfortably to 90 before their first wicket fell, when Paul Terry was thrown out by Graham Thorpe. Robin Smith and Tony Middleton put together a useful partnership of 70, and although Surrey began to come back into the game with yet another hostile spell from Waqar, a Hampshire win always appeared the likely result, and they scraped home in the last over, aided by some overthrows and a misfield.

'Everyone was very depressed,' said Waqar. 'Some of the guys were even crying; there was cases of beer and champagne in the dressing-room, but no one was drinking. Personally, I think you've got to be hard about it. There's no point crying. You have to lose sometimes; that day we lost, and that's an end to it.'

The Surrey season rather fell apart after the cup final defeat. 'We lost a game against Middlesex that we should have won,' said Waqar. 'I took 10 wickets in that game, but the batsmen couldn't get anywhere near the total of 175 that we needed to win. I got a shin injury, and I missed the final match against Lancashire. The skipper put a lot of pressure on me to play that game and if we had won we would have finished in the prize money for the county championship. I told him that I had done my best for the club all season, that I had a lot of cricket coming up, and I wasn't prepared to risk aggravating the injury.'

One unsung aspect of Waqar's efforts for the county was his batting. His runs were vital in the Nat West quarter-final, but Surrey were also involved in more than their fair share of tense run chases, the majority of which were successful. On several occasions, they relied on Waqar for success. He was there at the death in a last over victory against Hampshire at Bournemouth, but his most amazing performance was against Yorkshire at Guildford. 'I had bowled really well on the last afternoon, taking 5 wickets in 6 overs, to set up what should have been an easy win as we needed to make under 200 in about 60 overs. The batsmen cocked it up, and when I went to the wicket we needed 54 in 6 overs. As I went out, the skipper told me to block out the overs to stop them winning. I said, "What do you mean block? I've worked hard at this game, and I want to win it." I went out and started slogging, and the ball seemed to always find the middle of the bat. We needed 8 off the last over from Carrick, and I hit the first ball over long-on for 6. I was out after that, but thankfully Tony Murphy managed the rare feat for him of getting the bat on the ball and we won with a couple of balls to spare.'

31 runs off 19 balls was a marvellous feat of hitting by Waqar, but he didn't get too carried away with it. 'I used to pester the skipper the whole time to get him to put me above Mark Feltham in the batting order, but it was a just a joke really. I don't concentrate that much when I'm batting; at the moment I like to go out and have a bit of a slog.'

Waqar has fitted in remarkably well at Surrey, and it is clear that by and large he feels his efforts are appreciated. 'The first season was tough, and I used to hate away games because it meant spending a great deal of time in hotel rooms watching TV as I didn't know anyone. Now I go out to clubs with Tony Murphy, Graham Thorpe, and David Ward, and I have a good time. Mushtaq has been living with me in Bow, and I have seen quite a lot of Wasim, Aaqib, and Salim Malik as well. Some of the Surrey members have been really nice to me too, inviting me to meals in their homes.

'Geoff Arnold has been a big help to me, and I'm having a

great time at the club, but I don't know whether I'll renew my contract in four years' time. It's not that I want to play for anyone else, I just don't want to get injured by playing too much cricket. At the moment, I'm young and fit, so there's no problem. It's not difficult playing here; it doesn't get hot as it does in Pakistan or Sharjah, and there's often little pressure when you're playing in front of a few hundred people. In fact, if anything, at times it's a struggle to get motivated.'

Alec Stewart is delighted at the way Waqar has settled down. 'He gets angry when things go wrong, or when he feels that the batsmen are wasting an opportunity he's created, but that's only to be expected. I feel that he can understand far more English than he pretends to at times; when the coach is telling him off, he always seems to understand very little! The only problem we've had is with his time-keeping. He's never missed the start of a game, but if we're due to be on the field for warm-ups at 9.45 he's often not there until nearer 10.00. Before he left to go back to Pakistan for the winter we gave him an alarm clock. Let's hope he uses it!'

Without Waqar, 1992 will be a tough year for Surrey. Much of their success last season was owed to him, and it was a thankless task for Rudi Bryson, the South African pace bowler, who had been signed for the year whilst Waqar was on tour with Pakistan, to follow in his footsteps. In some ways, Waqar's absence may be a blessing in disguise for Alec Stewart, the new captain. No one was surprised that Surrey didn't repeat their success, and he will be able to ease himself into his new role without too great a burden of expectation. Around the county grounds that year there was be a collective sigh of relief from batsmen with egos and toes bruised by Waqar; around the Test match grounds it was a completely different story.

10

The Selling of Wasim & Waqar

The most enduring image of a player's agent in recent years is that of Tim Hudson, Ian Botham's erstwhile agent. Hudson deliberately set out to upset the cricketing establishment by promoting Botham as a 'Rock-and-Roll' cricketer, and encouraged him to put blond streaks in his hair and to wear brightly striped blazers. The Hudson-Botham star blazed briefly throughout the Ashes summer of '85, but faded soon after during the disastrous West Indies tour, as promised film deals never materialized, and speculation about Botham's personal life grew.

As a promotion and publicity campaign, it was singularly ill-judged, better suited to minor celebrities like Samantha Fox and Peter Stringfellow rather than to England's premier all-round cricketer. However, it did highlight the fact that for years cricketers had gone unrepresented in the commercial world, and had undersold themselves as a result. Even a footballer of moderate ability has an agent to negotiate contracts and endorsements, yet most cricketers are happy to agree a salary and terms of employment without anyone with any legal or financial nous on hand to advise them.

For the overseas player the position is doubly absurd. He is liable to be one of the finest cricketers in the world, and it is hard to think of any other sport whose top performers are expected to handle their own business dealings. Also, while it is feasible that a home-bred player might have some idea of the English contract system, the overseas player is quite literally an innocent abroad. Wasim and Waqar were twenty-one and eighteen years old respectively when they signed their first contracts with their counties. Neither had much grasp of what they were putting their name to. Wasim signed because Imran and Haseeb Ahsan said that it was good deal, and Waqar signed because Imran said it was OK.

Wasim and Waqar are not financial whizzkids, and do not want the headaches of managing their business affairs to distract them from their cricket. Wasim even delegates all his personal financial matters to a friend, Naeem Quyoum. 'I run his home in Altrincham. He gives me a cheque book with signed blank cheques, and I pay all the bills for him. I found it very difficult to explain the Poll Tax to him; under the old system he paid £1,200 and now he has to pay £298, and he just can't understand why he should pay so much less. He used to get an alarm call every morning from British Telecom but when I told him how much they were charging him for it, he asked me to ring him in the morning. Whenever he goes back to Pakistan or is on tour I try to rent out the house for him, but if it is empty I go and check that everything's OK once or twice a week.'

Entrusting personal finances to a friend is one thing, but business matters are another. Waqar's first contract with Surrey ran out at the end of his first season, in September

1990; he had made such an impact that there was likely to be a rush to secure his services for the future, and Imran wanted to make sure that Waqar was offered what he was worth. 'Personally, I had had some bad experiences with agents. I had no idea about money or business, and I wanted someone to negotiate on my behalf; I don't know whether I picked the wrong agents, but they never did anything much for me. Nonetheless, I felt that Wasim and Waqar should be represented. They were potentially the two best fast bowlers in the world, and I didn't want them to be taken for a ride because they had no experience in the commercial world. I introduced them to Jonathan Barnett who was working for the Levitt Group at the time.'

Jonathan Barnett was Managing Director of Levitt Sports and Entertainment. 'I had done a few deals with Imran on a friendly basis; no contract, just a handshake. I had straightened one or two things out for him, and had finalized the deal with the BBC for a Cricketing Legends video. He asked me to negotiate Waqar's contract for him, and he brought Wasim and Waqar in to see me. Imran acted as their spokesman throughout the meeting, and shortly afterwards I became their agent.'

Ironically, far from protecting Waqar's future with Surrey, Barnett's appointment as agent almost terminated Waqar's association with the club. 'It was getting near the end of the season, and the club had given no indication to Waqar that they wanted to retain him for 1991, even though he desperately wanted to stay,' said Barnett. 'I phoned up Surrey to let them know that I was acting for Waqar, but I got the complete brush-off. The Secretary told me that the club didn't deal with agents, and, that the the captain would speak to the player concerned if and when they had decided to keep him. I asked if they could give me any idea if they were likely to want him, and they again said no.'

Barnett then made numerous attempts to speak to Ian Greig but his calls were never returned. Eventually, he did get through, only to meet with the same stonewall response that he had received from the club Secretary, namely that the club didn't talk to agents, and that they still didn't know whether they wanted to keep Waqar. 'I warned him that it they didn't give me an answer fairly soon, I would have to see if any other clubs were interested in him,' said Barnett. 'Greig replied that I could do whatever I liked.

'I was getting worried at this point, and so I had a chat with Imran. He said that Waqar's livelihood was at stake, and that I should start sounding out other counties. At least three were very interested, and were prepared to negotiate contracts the moment Waqar was no longer on the Surrey staff. I let Surrey know what was going on, but they were completely disinterested, as they were still giving me the "We don't talk to agents" routine. I came to assume that Surrey were willing to let Waqar go, as by now the season was almost over, and negotiations with one county in particular had reached such an advanced stage that we had substantially agreed the deal.

'Quite by chance, a member of the Surrey Cricket Committee came into the Levitt offices on unrelated business. The person he'd come to see happened to say that Levitt Group had a sports company that acted for Waqar Younis. The committee man was a great admirer of Waqar and asked to be introduced to me. He told me how important Waqar was to Surrey and what a good season he had had, and I said that if that was the case it was a shame that the club was on the brink of losing him. He asked me what I was talking about; I explained the problems I was having, and said that if something wasn't agreed by the next day, Waqar would sign for another county. The committee member left my office to make a phone call, and within minutes I had Jimmy Fulford, the Surrey Chairman of Cricket, on the line asking to speak to me. He made it clear to me that the rest of the club had been out of line in refusing to deal with me, and that the club would be happy to deal with an agent if that was the price of keeping Waqar.'

The next day, Jimmy Fulford and Jonathan Barnett hammered out a five-year deal that was good both for the club and the player, in less than an afternoon. What is astonishing about the whole episode is not so much that the club appeared to be ready to risk losing the quickest bowler in county cricket over a matter of principle, but that the principle should ever have existed in the first place given the professionalism and commercialism within the game. The committee members who run the finances of the county are hard-headed businessmen well versed in the commercial practices of the nineties, and it is clearly hypocritical to expect their players to adhere to a code of ethics that more properly belongs to a bygone era.

There is little doubt that Surrey's change of heart was precipitated by their reluctance to lose a player of immense value to the club, and shows, perhaps, an unforeseen benefit to the English county professional of the presence of the overseas player. At the end of every season, each Surrey player is summoned to the committee room to hear his fate for the coming year; whether he will receive a rise in salary, or whether indeed he will even be required by the club. 'All the players are lined up like school-boys outside the headmaster's study,' was how one player described it. 'We then go in one by one to be confronted by the captain, coach, and various members of the committee, and to be told what we will be offered.'

When Waqar goes in to discuss terms, he is now accompanied by his agent, and the prospects of him agreeing to poor terms are much diminished. Having dealt with an agent once, Surrey will be much more likely to do so again, which can only be good for the other players, who, if properly represented, can ask for the most advantageous terms. Already, the influence of the agent has spread elsewhere in the dressing-room, and Alec Stewart has had various deals negotiated on his behalf. Again, far from taking money away from the English players, the overseas player might be indirectly responsible, in the long run, for putting money back into their pockets.

To their credit, Surrey have overcome their inital apprehension about agents, and every inquiry that the club receives about Waqar is now handed over to Jonathan Barnett. It is an arrangement that works well for the player, as he can maximize his earnings outside the game, and for the club who know that the player will be able to concentrate on his cricket if there is someone else to manage his affairs. It also helps to have a third party to dampen any potential friction between the club and the player.

Jonathan Barnett left the Levitt Group before Waqar's contract ever arrived, and the matter was left in the hands of a junior, who failed to realize that one of the most important clauses, entitling Waqar to receive a full annual salary from the club whilst on tour with Pakistan in England during the summer of 1992, was missing. 'This came to my notice towards the end of the 1991 season,' said Barnett, 'and I immediately brought it to the club's attention. Surrey were very honourable, and after a week or so they agreed that this clause should have been in the contract. During this time Waqar was saying to me, "I won't play in the Nat West final if they refuse to pay me." Waqar could have irreparably damaged his relationship with the club if he had done his own negotiations. As it was, I was able to pacify him, tell the club that he was perfectly happy, and still get him what he wanted. If Lancashire had been willing to use me as a buffer between them and Wasim over the umpiring incident last season, there would probably have been much less animosity.'

It's not just the counties who are upset by having to deal with agents. Shortly before the Nat West final in 1991 *The Times* approached Waqar for an interview because they wanted to run a feature about him. Not only were they angry to be refused because Waqar had signed an exclusive deal with another newspaper, but also because had Waqar been available, *The Times* would have been asked to pay. The next day, an article appeared in the paper bemoaning the fact that cricketers were becoming more like footballers every day. What the article failed to mention was that cricketers are notoriously underpaid compared to most other high-profile national sportsmen and -women, and that just because they have not made the most of their money-making opportunities in the past, is no reason for them not to do so now.

The relationship between the press and players has always been uneasy, as to an extent they are mutually dependent on one another. A player needs good press to come to the public notice, but a pressman requires the trust of the players if he wants to find out what is really going on. Wasim and Waqar are happy to appear for post-match interviews, but want to be paid for any features on their lives. This is partly for financial gain, but also, because both have been misrepresented in the media, an arranged interview is often the best way to ensure that they can be accurately quoted.

'Only one paper, the *Manchester Evening News*, bothered to ring me up to find out my version of the "Nigel Plews Affair",' said Wasim. 'I would have welcomed the chance to put the record straight. Journalists who weren't even at the ground started writing about it, and just accepted Lancashire's official interpretation of events.'

The problems are not confined to the press of this country, as Wasim and Waqar have had similar trouble at home in Pakistan. When Waqar was a newcomer to the Pakistan side, a journalist asked him for an interview in Lahore. 'I said that I had a very busy couple of days, but that I would be happy to talk to him after that. He said OK, but the next day there was this report that Waqar would rather go sightseeing than talk to journalists. There are some good journalists, like Fareshteh A. Gati, and good magazines, like *Allrounder*, but there are also a few unpleasant characters.'

Unsurprisingly, it is the English tabloids who best understand the situation, as cheque-book journalism is part and parcel of the business. There are dangers in courting the tabloids for Wasim and Waqar, since the style of reportage can be very hurtful, as Ian Botham, among many, can testify, but so far everything has run smoothly. To date, Waqar has sold articles to the *Sunday Mirror*, and modelled clothes for the *Daily Express*. He has approached both these ventures with a strange mixture of sound commercial acumen and innocence. Financial security is very important to him, more so than to Wasim, as he has seen his father struggle to afford the best lifestyle for his family and he is aware that these are lucrative opportunities, but he can also display a remarkable naïveté. 'In one article Waqar said that he didn't drink, smoke, or go out with girls,' said Jonathan Barnett. 'The Surrey players stuck up a copy in the dressing-room and gave him a lot of ribbing over it. He phoned me shortly afterwards to ask what would happen if someone saw him out with a girl; I replied that the newspaper would sue him for breach of contract. He got very scared and upset, and it was some time before he realized I was pulling his leg.'

Both Wasim and Waqar have been involved in mainstream advertising in Pakistan and have appeared in TV commercials, which is an accurate reflection of the esteem in which the Pakistanis hold their cricket heroes. Wasim has appeared in five different adverts, though he has only charged for two; the anti-smoking campaign and the appeal for Imran's Cancer Hospital in Lahore he did for nothing. Waqar has appeared in just the one; a Pepsi commercial that also featured Wasim and Imran and was shot in November 1991.

The endorsement of cricket equipment is a natural source of revenue for most players in England. In recent years, Wasim has doubled his bat contract with Duncan Fearnley. It is obviously more difficult for bowlers to attract sponsors as they don't use any equipment, though there are plans to launch a 'Waqar Boot'. The situation is much more confused in Pakistan. 'The bat companies used to sponsor us, but they never wanted a formal contract,' said Wasim. 'They used to give us cash in hand so that they could avoid paying tax. They would promise us 200,000 rupees each, (about £4,000), give us 50,000 rupees advance, and then never pay us the balance at the end of the series. Because we didn't have a contract, there was nothing we could do, so now all the players are wary of sponsors.'

Overall, Wasim has made less use of his agent in England. In part, this is because he is in mid-contract with Lancashire and so there has been less to negotiate, but in part, it also reflects a difference in attitude between himself and Waqar. Of the two players, Wasim is definitely the more laid back; he wants to make money, but he values his free time too, and tends to use his agent as a confidant as much as a businessman. Because of this, it is likely that Waqar will exploit his commercial opportunities more thoroughly. But this is to a large extent a matter of personal choice, as Imran explains. 'It's up to them what direction they take. I believe that you make your own standing in cricket and the world. It all depends on what your achievements are and the way that you conduct yourself. They both carry themselves very well. Success has come much earlier to both of them than it did to me, but they have shown they are true sportsmen and they have a natural humility.

'I think they have the potential to be successful in a number of different areas. I have just tried to ensure that they are financially rewarded for their talents, and that they are not used by the media. There was a time when a photographer would make them do all sorts of things to get the shot he wanted; the photographer would go away happy, but the player might look a complete idiot. I've always warned them about being used like that, but in the end it's their choice what they do.'

11

On Bowling and Batsmen

'Wasim is probably one of the best left-arm fast bowlers of all time; Waqar will be the best in the world, and even now bowls spells that are better than anyone else in world cricket.' At first glance Imran's appraisal of Wasim and Waqar might seem like the typical hyperbole of a partial captain; a wildly extravagant claim to make about one player who is just twenty-five years old, and another who, officially at least, is only twenty. Closer analysis reveals that Imran's assessment is no more than the truth.

From the very beginning of his career, Wasim invited comparisons with the Australian Alan Davidson, the greatest of all left-arm fast bowlers, not just because they were both all-rounders, but because they had a very similar bowling action. At first, these comparisons were premature and highly flattering to Wasim, but as his bowling and batting have improved, it is Davidson who may be the more thrilled to be mentioned in the same breath. As for Waqar, he has gone on to prove his captain's prediction of October 1991 correct; following the recent Test series against Sri Lanka, Waqar established himself firmly as the best bowler in the world today by being ranked number one in the Cooper Deloittes ratings.

As a pair, Wasim and Waqar are formidable opponents, and in Mohammad Azharuddin's opinion 'the finest opening bowlers in today's cricket.' The combination of left-arm and right-arm bowler has always made life difficult for a batsman who constantly has to get used to a different angle of attack, but coupled with this is the fact that Wasim and Waqar both bowl much further up to the batsman than most fast bowlers. Instead of the attritional style of relentless short-pitched bowling with only the occasional delivery in the batsman's half of the wicket, they both bowl a full length at the stumps; the batsman gets very few balls that he can leave alone, and the pressure of knowing that if he misses he's out, can be very draining on a batsman's concentration. At times, Wasim can overdo the bouncer, but in general, he and Waqar keep this delivery as a shock tactic.

What makes Waqar and Wasim even trickier is that they have very different styles of bowling. Waqar is six foot tall, sprints into the wicket off a long run, and has an explosive leap in his delivery stride, not unlike Imran in his prime, though not as pronounced. He has a very whippy, almost slingy action, and the ball comes towards the batsman in a low skiddy trajectory. His standard delivery is the outswinger, with the occasional inswinging yorker thrown in.

Wasim appears to do no more than amble into the wicket off a few paces, and his speed all comes from his shoulder and wrist. His action makes him very awkward for a batsman to pick, and his bouncer can be very deceptive as he gets the ball to rise steeply off a full length. He isn't as consistently quick as Waqar, perhaps only bowling one or two really fast balls an over, but he does have more variety, and can seemingly move the ball both ways at will; his most dangerous delivery is the one that darts into the right hander in the air, and then cuts away off the pitch.

The ability that both bowlers have to move the ball so late in its flight, and to seemingly bowl yorkers at will is the icing on the cake. For 90 per cent of its journey to the wicket, a ball from Waqar will travel in a straight line, before at the last moment snaking violently into or away from the batsman. It is this late movement that confounded so many on the Test and county circuit, and has led to the high proportion of his victims being either clean bowled or leg before. Those that are given out leg before often depart to the dressing-room with a limp, after being hit on the foot. As Durham's Simon Hughes said, 'You don't need a helmet facing Waqar, so much as a steel toe cap.'

The perils of Waqar's yorker are well known; Robin Smith has said that, 'If Waqar gets the ball in the right place, there is little the batsman can do about it.' Yet Wasim has a yorker that is every bit as dangerous. Graham Thorpe describes the difficulties he has encountered. 'We were playing Lancashire in a one-day game and I was trying to score quickly. I was moving around in the crease, stepping backwards and forwards, trying to put Wasim off his length, so that I could get underneath the ball to hit it. No matter where I moved, the ball always seemed to be coming under my bat. I could hardly pick up a single run off him.'

Overall, the difficulties that both bowlers present to a batsman are enormous, as Gehan Mendis so graphically summarizes. 'They bowl so fast that you have less than a twentieth of a second to decide what to do with the damn ball. You have to work out whether to come forward or go back to a ball that may swing a great deal very late, because you're lost if you try and play it from the crease. Don't tell me that batsmen ever deliberately place the ball between the fielders when facing these two, because it's impossible. When a batsman looks around between deliveries, it's not because he's bored or he's seen a friend in the field, it's because he's trying to establish the level of risk attached to going through with a particular shot if the ball is in a certain area.'

One of the most impressive features of Wasim and Waqar's bowling is the speed with which they learnt their trade. They are both so young, yet Wasim has been an experienced Test match bowler for many years, and Waqar has progressed from a raw inaccurate youngster to one of the most complete fast bowlers in the world today.

Natural talent and ability, together with a willingness to practise hard, has been fundamental to their success, but tribute must also be paid to their teachers, and in particular Imran Khan. Previous Pakistan fast bowlers have kept the secrets of their craft to themselves, but Imran has always made a point of passing on his knowledge. 'It was Imran who taught me the yorker,' said Wasim. 'We were on tour in Sri Lanka in '86, and De Mel, the number 9, slogged me all over the place in the last few overs of a one-day international. After that game, Imran told me that I had to learn the yorker; he took me to the nets and showed me how to do it. I took a long time to master it, but I worked hard, and now I have one of the best yorkers in the game, thanks to Imran.'

Imran's influence extended to Waqar before the two players had even met. 'I used to spend hours studying videos of Imran bowling,' said Waqar. 'I had always been a natural away swinger of the ball, and I was keen to learn the inswinger. I would watch Imran bowl in slow motion; his run up, the position of the ball in his hand, and his wrist action. Then I would go out and try and copy it.'

Further refinements to Waqar's bowling were suggested by Imran once the youngster was part of the Pakistani squad. 'First, I had him work on his fitness,' said Imran, 'because it was obvious from the length of his run-up and his bowling action that he was going to have to be much fitter to survive. I then suggested that he cut down on his run-up; he used to run miles, and exhaust himself. I also got him to work on his accuracy, because he was fairly wild to begin with. I told him that the only way to improve was to keep bowling at one stump. A batsman often distracts a bowler from his accuracy, and so Waqar would bowl for hours into an empty net.'

It was not just in these technical areas that Imran was able to help Waqar. Many fast bowlers wear the boots of whatever sponsor will give them the most money for doing so, regardless of the comfort and support they offer. Imran had learnt that this was a false economy, and that the wrong boots could lead to injury, either by indirectly damaging the back, or by not gripping sufficiently in loose footholds. When Waqar arrived in England to play for Surrey, Imran introduced him to his bootmaker in Northampton. Hand-crafted boots, designed specially to suit Waqar's physique cost about 200 pounds, and yet Waqar ordered two pairs. Before the start of the 1991 county season, Surrey jokingly offered to buy Waqar another two pairs if he took 80 wickets in the season; Waqar, who knows a deal when he sees one, was deadly serious about it, and much to their surprise, the club received an invoice for two pairs of boots in August.

All bowlers need a good understanding of a batsman's psyche to enable them to probe for weak spots, and here too

Imran has been invaluable. 'He taught me how to recognize when batsmen are afraid of me,' said Wasim. 'You can see it in his eyes and in the way he walks. When Ian Botham was playing weaker teams he was really cocky, and he would have this arrogant attitude that he was going to smash the bowling all around the ground. Whenever he played against the West Indies, he would be smiling at them and chatting with them; it was a sign that he was a bit scared and that he wanted to relieve the pressure. Many English players are terrified long before they go out to bat. If someone's bowling a quick spell they get scared just sitting in the dressing-room. They'll be saying, "What am I going to do? Where's my helmet and chest guard?" It's not the right attitude to have.'

If one had to single out one flaw in either player, it would be that neither is completely happy with the new ball. On Pakistani wickets this is not a serious disadvantage, as the shine comes off the ball in a couple of overs, and consequently both Wasim and Waqar are more at home with the old ball, which they can shine on one side and thereby control the movement. On English, Australian, and West Indian wickets, proficiency with the new ball is often essential. Wasim is the more experienced new ball bowler, and has delivered the odd devastating spell, but he is aware that he is by no means consistent. Indeed, for Lancashire, the new ball is often entrusted to DeFreitas and Allott, while Wasim is brought on first change. Surrey do not have the luxury of having two England bowlers to lead the attack, and the new ball is invariably given to Waqar, though his first spell is often his least effective. Imran is in no doubt that Waqar will learn to bowl with the new ball. 'It took me until about 1982 to learn,' said the Pakistan captain, 'but with him it will be much quicker because he's got the action. It's just a question of practice. When he does learn, he will be absolutely lethal.'

'To be a great fast bowler you have to have a big heart' were Harold Larwood's parting words to the young Alan Davidson, and they are as true now as they were then. You can have all the ability in the world, but if you can't reproduce it regularly in a tight situation in front of a crowd of fifty thousand, then it is almost valueless. Likewise, every bowler goes through periods when their form deserts them and wickets become elusive; there is an old saying that 'Class is permanent, but form is temporary', and temperament is one of the key hallmarks of class.

Wasim and Waqar have demonstrated that they can deliver the goods under pressure, but what is equally important to Javed Burki is that they are both tryers. 'Imran demands that his players are big-hearted; it's almost a prerequisite for selection. You know that they will give of their best all day for the team. It's not very often you get fast bowlers like this; some are real handfuls, and captains can't manage them.' One only has to remember the problems Graham Yallop had with Rodney Hogg to take Javed's point.

Waqar has, perhaps, the perfect temperament; he never appears to get rattled under pressure. It's become something of a cliché to talk about 'fiery fast bowlers', but for Waqar this is quite the wrong epithet. He may explode from time to time off the pitch, but seldom on it. Many quick bowlers respond to being hit for four by unleashing a bouncer; Waqar is more calculating than that, and keeps bowling at the stumps, seldom wasting a delivery. In some ways it's hard to assess Waqar's temperament, since it has not fully been put to the test, for he is yet to suffer a dramatic loss of form. He showed great courage in coming back from a back injury that he thought might end his career, and he wasn't particularly successful on his first tour of Australia, though he did consistently get better, and since then he hasn't been out of the wickets.

Perhaps, though, it is Waqar's mental attitude that is helping him to keep his form. 'I don't believe in getting depressed. You have to learn to treat bad times as part of the game, and try not to worry about it. I work at being relaxed; Imran has taught me some breathing exercises to help me. Before a big game I try not to think of how I will bowl, because I'll only get tired thinking about it, and if I'm not fresh I'll bowl badly. At team meetings Imran always says, "Be positive, don't panic, and don't think of losing," and that's how I try to be. I save my concentration for when I actually need it – when I'm bowling. Then I'm thinking the whole time of what delivery I'm going to bowl, and what spot on the pitch I'm aiming for; you can't get it right the whole time, but you stand a much better chance if you're not tired.'

Wasim conforms more readily to the standard mould of the fast bowler, as his emotions are much more to the fore. For him more than most, fast bowling is a matter of getting into a good rhythm. 'I'm happy if I'm running in and everything about my action feels right,' says Wasim. 'How I feel about my bowling is more important than actually taking wickets, because I know that wickets are bound to come if I feel good. In some ways I am finding that the older I get the more temperamental I am becoming. I've been injured many times, but I used to be able to come back after a two-month lay off, and my rhythm would come back immediately. Now, I'm finding it a lot harder; when I played in Sharjah in October 1991 after a long period out of the game, I was really struggling to start with. It was very frustrating, and I was getting short-tempered on the pitch. I suppose it's because everything seemed to come very easily to me at first, but now I'm having to work a lot harder. Still, I'm putting in a lot of practice, and things are beginning to fall into place again.'

Injuries have been the bane of Wasim's career, and are clearly his Achilles' heel. 'He's not a naturally fit person, and you can see how he struggles,' said Imran. 'He's had a series of fitness problems that have undoubtedly stopped him from being the best fast bowler in the world. Wasim has to decide how hard he is going to work at his fitness. He might even have to give up county cricket in the end, because there you do not get a chance to stay fit. Only if you are naturally fit will you last at county cricket, and only then up to a point. I only kept going so long by cutting down on the cricket, and concentrating on weight training. Wasim will have to do exactly the same.'

Wasim has heeded this advice, and has incorporated an intensive fitness regime into his training; he has even had a multi-gym installed in his garage in Altrincham. He has lost weight around his waist, and gained strength in his upper body and legs. However, even this may not be sufficient to save him from future injuries, as his very individual bowling action imposes severe stresses on his groin and lower abdomen. Most bowlers have their front foot pointing down the wicket, and their back foot parallel to the return crease in their delivery stride. Wasim is unusual in that his back foot is directed backwards, so that both feet are pointing in almost diametrically opposite directions. If Wasim tried to change this, he could well ruin his otherwise perfect action, and so the only solution he realistically has open to him is to build up his strength to compensate.

However, getting injured creates problems beyond the mere physical, and requires a strong mental attitude. Wasim has often carried on bowling long after he knows he should sensibly stop, not just because his team is looking to him to take wickets, but because he knows that there are plenty of keen fast bowlers waiting to take his place. In Pakistan, it is very easy to get forgotten. 'When I got injured in New Zealand the BCCP didn't even call me to ask how I was feeling, or when I was likely to be fit again. Also, the BCCP are supposed to insure us for medical treatment, but I have never received a penny from them. Luckily, PIA, my department team, helped me out, or I would have had to pay for everything myself. It's very demoralizing.'

Apart from the trouble that he had with his back early in his Test career, Waqar has remained comparatively injury free. He is still concerned about it though; he gets very anxious in the humid atmosphere of Karachi, and he always makes sure he is wearing a back support when he is warming up. Natural athlete he may be, but Waqar leaves nothing to chance, and he has worked so hard on building up his strength, that he has impressed everyone with his dedication. 'We were in America playing some fun matches,' said Imran. 'In New York I went down to the hotel gym to work out, and I found Waqar and Aaqib already there. It was their first time in the USA, and yet they were in a gym rather than having fun. I didn't know about weight training at their age, but even if I had I doubt if I would have bothered in the States. That told me a lot about how determined Waqar really is.'

Waqar's fitness training has also paid dividends in terms of an increase to his already formidable pace. 'We had a national camp in October last year before Sharjah,' reported Javed Miandad, 'and I hadn't faced Waqar for over a year. I was quite unprepared for how much faster he had become. Anyone who can swing the ball at that pace is almost unplayable at times.

I've played against many of the great fast bowlers, including Dennis Lillee, Jeff Thomson, and Michael Holding, and Waqar bears comparison with them all.'

In many ways Waqar's arrival in the side has worked to Wasim's advantage. Wasim is very easy going by nature, and success had come to him relatively effortlessly; Waqar is much hungrier to do well, and some of this has rubbed off on Wasim who has been spurred on by the competition. What is remarkable is that neither bowler shows a glimmer of *schadenfreude*. 'I would have hated it if they had been jealous of each other, as so many bowlers were when I first played,' said Imran. 'Wasim and Waqar have a tremendous relationship with one another; there is a lot of mutual respect and liking there. I think it bodes very well for Pakistani cricket.'

In fact, they both seem to positively enjoy bowling together. 'We both have had long talks about how good we feel when we are bowling together,' said Waqar. 'I feel more confident when Wasim is bowling at the other end, because I think that we are the people who are going to take the wickets. If Wasim takes a wicket, then I think that I'm going to get one as well; if he takes two, then I think I'll take two.'

Both bowlers find Test matches the most enjoyable form of cricket. 'One-day internationals are very exciting, and there's always a good crowd atmosphere,' said Wasim, 'but you are as concerned with containing the batsman as much as getting him out. In Test matches a batsman is less inclined to take risks, and you can place extremely attacking fields, and experiment with your bowling a lot more.'

For Waqar, an over is a two-pronged assault of pace and swing against the batsman, planned with almost military precision, and conducted in close co-operation with his captain. 'Imran normally stands at mid-off, and before nearly every over we will have a talk about what to do,' explains Waqar. 'He's got over twenty-years experience to Test cricket, and so he knows what will give problems to a batsman. He seems to sense when a batsman is in trouble or is getting too relaxed, and tells me what delivery to bowl when. I was bowling against Ravi Shastri recently in Sharjah, and I had given him 4 or 5 successive outswingers. Imran came up to me, and said that Shastri was expecting another, and so I should bowl an inswinger. I did, and it bowled him.'

Wasim has even more options open to him than Waqar, and could easily deliver 6 completely different types of delivery an over. However, he too persists with a certain type of ball to get the batsman accustomed to playing at a particular line and length, and only occasionally throws in a completely different delivery that is designed to take the wicket. It's an elaborate form of psychological warfare. Often the batsman wins, but the bowler only needs to win once to take a wicket. A classic example of this was in the Karachi Test of 1990 against the West Indies. Desmond Haynes was well set on 117, as Wasim bowled 5 successive deliveries that slanted across him and moved away. Wasim bowled the last ball considerably quicker, and brought it into the batsman; Haynes just raised his bat to let the ball go by, and was trapped leg before.

However, Wasim is not happy about the new ICC ruling limiting the use of the bouncer to one per over. 'They obviously wanted to get rid of mindless short-pitched bowling, but it's entirely the wrong way to go about it. It's a stupid rule. It seems like they're trying to get rid of an important weapon in the bowler's armoury.'

Imran is even more scathing about the new bouncer law. 'It has been brought in to discriminate against fast bowlers; it has been initiated by England and Australia, and supported by Sri Lanka and India. It is harmful for cricket; England and Australia have been through a phase where they were being thrashed by the West Indies. Instead of being fair about it, and trying to beat them on even terms, they are trying to handicap them. Good fast bowlers will always dominate, and there are periods in every country's history when they go through a dearth of good fast bowlers. In the past, Australia have had Lindwall, Miller, Lillee and Thomson, and England have had Tyson, Trueman, Statham, and Snow. The balance redresses itself in time.

'I don't even think the new rule is good from a batsman's point of view. Once I know that I can't receive a bouncer I'm sure I'll start pre-empting my strokes, by getting on to the front foot. In the long run that's got to be bad for my technique.'

Wasim and Waqar are both agreed that a batsman with good technique does not need protection from the cricket authorities. To their mind the bouncer is an integral part of the game, and no more needs regulating than the yorker, and if a batsman wants to be considered world-class he has got to learn to play it. 'Batsmen like Robin Smith, his brother Chris, and Jimmy Cook have become so good because they have worked hard at their game,' said Wasim. 'I rate Robin Smith as one of the best in the world because he gives so little away. He talks to himself the whole time, trying to make himself concentrate, and he is equally strong off the front foot as the back. Graham Gooch and Mark Ramprakash are very impressive in that way too. Oddly enough, though, the batsman that I always have the most trouble bowling against is Kim Barnett. He stands at the wicket like an umpire, then moves backwards and forwards as you come into bowl, and then plays a lovely shot at the end of it. Batsmen have weaknesses in all sorts of different areas, and it's wrong to legislate against one in particular. Neil Fairbrother is a great attacking batsman, but he can be very loose outside off stump, yet no one would dream of changing the rules for him.'

What will be critical for Wasim and Waqar is how much cricket they play. Nowadays for Test match players there is little distinction between where one season starts and another ends. Such are the financial demands of the game, and such is the public's enthusiasm for more and more international fixtures, especially for the one-day game, that cricket has become a year round sport. It not only puts great physical strain on the players, but mental pressure too as there is little time to relax or switch off. One only has to look at the current plight of England's Angus Fraser to see the toll that an international schedule can take.

Wasim is resigned to his fate. 'I can get as physically and mentally fit as possible, but what else can I do? I know I play too much cricket, but I can't turn down tours. I'm a professional cricketer, it's how I make my living.' Waqar is equally aware of the problems. 'I get exhausted at times. Sometimes last summer I was so tired that I just slept on the benches in the back of the dressing-room while we were batting. It's a vicious circle. The better you are, the more games you play, and the more likely you are to break down.'

Playing for Lancashire and Surrey respectively has been formative in the development of both Wasim and Waqar, but there must come a time after a number of years, when the advantages are outweighed by the possibilities of burn-out. Ideally, the BCCP would reward its key players financially during the Pakistan close season, so that they did not have to keep playing abroad just for the money. It's unlikely to happen though, because the Pakistan Board has no money, and even if it did, it doesn't have a proud history of looking after its players. Intikhab, the Pakistan manager, is increasingly concerned for Wasim and Waqar. 'Undoubtedly, one of the reasons that they have both developed so quickly is that they have had a lot of opportunities, and have never had to wait long to learn from their mistakes, but I would love to find a way to enable them to play less cricket now. Obviously, we are aware that they are our strike bowlers, and we're not going to turn them into donkeys, but we really have to be very careful with them.' On just how careful that is depends not only Wasim and Waqar's bowling careers, but also, very probably, Pakistan's immediate cricket future.

12

Behind The Public Image

Lahore, Karachi, Bombay, Sydney, Melbourne, London, Barbados, and Antigua; these place names sound like a travel plan for an international jet-setter, but are just part of the normal itinerary for a regular Test match cricketer. Travel is supposed to broaden the mind, but international cricketers abroad lead very restricted lives. The players are ferried from location to location, from hotel to hotel, and from cricket ground to cricket ground; everything is organized for them, and as far as possible they are cocooned against any outside disruptions. Little is allowed to distract from the primary purpose, which is to win at cricket. Waqar is very direct about it. 'You can easily forget what's going on in the outside world. Personally speaking, I'm not very interested in politics or things like that; cricket is my life.'

Cricketers the world over are cosseted on an international tour, and for some the transition to this lifestyle can be traumatic. Generally speaking, Wasim and Waqar have found it easier to adapt than most. Pakistani men tend to be well taken care of by the women of the family, and it is quite usual for even a modestly well-off family to have domestic help. Wasim makes no bones about the way he has been brought up. 'We had help, but even so my mother got up at 5am every day and cleaned the whole house. I suppose that as a result I am not a very tidy person; when I'm on tour my hotel room is often a bit of a mess. At home, whenever I get in from practice, my mother takes my clothes and washes them ready for the next day.'

However, while certain aspects of the lifestyle may need no adjustment, others do. Cricketers in Pakistan are accorded a completely different status to that which they are given in England. Thousands of trees are pulped in an endeavour to satisfy the public's craving for information about their heroes, and no piece of information is ever considered too insignificant to mention. It can be both a frightening and intoxicating experience for a young man to become public property, and as might be expected most Pakistani cricketers have mixed feelings about it.

'The Pakistani people love their cricketers, and would do anything for them,' said Wasim. 'You only have to ring someone up for help and you get it. In Sharjah, a jeweller friend of mine invited the whole team to his shop, and gave us each a gold chain. It can be hard when we lose, though, as we do get abused. Going out in cities like Lahore is very difficult; if I go to a restaurant I will be stared at throughout the meal, which makes it very hard to relax.'

For Waqar the problems are just the same. 'The phone will often ring continuously; I either have to take it off the hook or pretend to be someone else when I answer. A young girl from *The Khaleej Times* in Sharjah asked me if all cricketers were liars; I said that I had to lie at times otherwise I'd never get any privacy. It's just the same in England. I was playing in a benefit game against India at Uxbridge, and when I took a wicket there was a pitch invasion. I got mobbed, and one supporter ripped an expensive gold chain from my neck and stole it.'

Flamboyant, arrogant, generous, and sensitive are just some of the words that have been used to describe Wasim. As might be imagined from the range of adjectives it is quite difficult for an outsider to get a clear picture of Wasim's identity. According to Gehan Mendis, a close friend of Wasim's in England, he is 'young for his age, and very shy, but one of the nicest people you could hope to meet,' and as a general assessment this is probably fairly close to the mark.

The family is the most important social structure in Pakistani culture, and it is there one must turn to get a feel for Wasim as a person. That Wasim adores his family, and that they adore him is without question. Wasim's father has given him a plot of land worth 3 million rupees (approximately £65,000) in Model Town, an affluent area of Lahore, so that he can have his own home built. In turn, Wasim is equally generous; he recently paid for his mother and his sister, Sofia, to fly to Sharjah to watch him play and do some shopping for Sofia's wedding. At his home in Altrincham, he adopts an open-door policy; any of his family are welcome to stay at any time for as long as they like.

However, Wasim's close Pakistani friends hint that there is an undercurrent of tension within the family. Wasim is generally unwilling to talk about it, as he would consider it a betrayal, but was very upset when he returned to England after a brief spell in Pakistan following the tournament in Sharjah in October 1991. 'I hadn't done that well in the competition, and when I got home all my friends, and the media got after me saying, "What went wrong? How come

Waqar and Aaqib did so much better than you?" I was feeling very bad, and my family didn't even support me. My father, brothers, and even my mother were telling me that I had to work a lot harder. I tried to explain that I was doing my best, and that for some reason, I had found it hard to regain my rhythm. What I need is to be able to come home and relax, and switch off.'

It is quite usual for the normal equilibrium of the family to be disrupted when one member becomes a national celebrity, but it doesn't make it any easier to cope with. Every relationship changes as to some extent the whole family comes under the public spotlight. Where once Wasim was just the youngest son to his father, and the younger brother to Nadeem and Naeem, he is now also one of the best known faces in Pakistan. Of course Wasim's family are proud of his achievements, but his success brings its fair share of complications as well as benefits to those around him.

Some sections of the press in Pakistan and England portray Wasim as some sort of Imran clone who they imagine gallivanting around town night after night going to parties. Recently, the Pakistan paper *The News* produced a Sharjah supplement which perpetuated the image. In a spoof ABC of Sharjah cricket, a cartoon of Wasim appeared surrounded by adoring women, accompanied by the caption. 'W is for Wasim: whose line is perfect and will go to any length to field at silly maid-ons.'

Of course Wasim enjoys his success; he likes buying clothes, doesn't want for much materially, and as Gehan Mendis points out, 'he still gets very excited about things like being asked on TV, or appearing on the front cover of famous magazines.' However, there is a much softer, and more sensitive side to Wasim that most people seldom see. He is extremely generous to his friends. 'Most cricketers are happy to give away their complimentary tickets,' said Naeem Quyoum, a close friend, 'but wouldn't dream of dipping into their own pockets for their friends. For the last Benson & Hedges final Wasim spent around £500 on tickets for his friends, and asking them to pay would never have crossed his mind.'

Likewise, his female admirers would be astonished to realize how insecure Wasim is about his looks. 'I always find it unbelievable when I hear that some people think of me as a good-looking playboy. As a kid I always thought that I was ugly, and I still do; I don't really care what anyone else thinks. I look at my nose, and I think, God, what happened to it? My brothers are good-looking, why aren't I?'

Wasim is also a fairly lonely man. He has a great many friends whom he likes, and who like him, but there are few whom Wasim trusts sufficiently to share his most intimate thoughts and feelings. Far from spending his life in a social whirl, he appreciates a simple existence. 'In Lahore, I like to spend my evenings quietly at home with my friends. In England, I occasionally go out to dinner with Gehan, but by and large I like to go home and watch the TV and I often see two videos a night.'

Wasim's lifestyle is often misunderstood by those around him in England. Many people at Lancashire failed to realize how lonely he was in England, and when he brought over a family domestic help, it was thought that he was adopting the manner of a *grand seigneur* by employing a house-keeper. 'Everyone was saying how ostentatious Wasim was to have a cook,' said Gehan Mendis. 'In Asia there just isn't the same connotation to having help as there is in England. When I grew up in Sri Lanka I was one of three kids, and we all had our own domestic. We don't call them servants, or treat them badly, and it's not seen as something menial. Qasim had no parents, and in Asia you can starve on the streets. Wasim's parents took him in, fed him, and sent him to school, and in return Qasim did some chores like cooking and shopping. Wasim and Qasim grew up together, and in many ways are lifelong friends; Qasim came over to Lancashire to keep Wasim company every bit as much as to look after him.'

Because Wasim prefers to dress in jeans and T-shirts when in England and Australia, rather than the traditional salwar kamis, it is easy to forget how deeply embedded are his Pakistani roots. 'I love England, and I would always like to have somewhere to live there, but Pakistan is my true home,' said Wasim. 'Most of my friends are from Pakistan, and I could never imagine marrying a woman who wasn't from my country. In England, I even had an account with the Asian bank, BCCI. The first I knew that the bank was in trouble was when a jeweller's shop in St John's Wood refused to accept my BCCI American Express card, and I got very angry and embarrassed when they told me that they were going to have to cut up my card. I lost about £3,000 in the collapse.'

Any professional sportsman requires an abundance of single-minded determination to get to the top, and Wasim certainly has that. His entry to the Pakistan side was to some extent effortless, as he was plucked from a training camp to tour New Zealand after only one first-class game, but he would never have had remained in the team unless he had the mental strength to go with his talent.

Part of Wasim's single-mindedness can be attributed to the same rebellious streak he showed as a child by continuing to play sports when his parents wanted him to study. There are signs though that Wasim is beginning to mellow. Although by most standards he is, at twenty-five, still young for a Test cricketer, he is a veteran of seven years standing, and is beginning to consider a life beyond cricket. 'Sure, I still get angry and temperamental at times,' he said. 'I hate it when I'm not bowling well or I feel that I'm not being treated properly. Mind you, compared to my brothers I'm very cool. However, overall I think I'm getting calmer. I've been injured a lot, and as I get older I realize that I only have a certain amount of years left to play cricket. Nowadays, I am trying a lot harder to be kinder and more tolerant of people. If I don't respect people now, there's going to be no one around who will want to talk to me in the future. You can get away with being rude when you're famous, as people still want to know you; fame and money don't last for ever and I want to make sure that I still have my family and friends.'

Although Wasim and Waqar have similar qualities, not least of which is their ability to get on with almost anyone, Waqar's relationships with other people, especially his family, appear to be much more straightforward. His situation is eased by being the eldest son, who is traditionally looked on as the next head of the family.

'My father spent a lot of money on my education, and it paid off. Now that I'm earning good money I can pay for my brothers' and sisters' education, and I've bought a house for the whole family in the Cavalry Ground area of Lahore. I love my family very much. In our culture, because I am the eldest, my brothers and sisters have to agree with me regardless of whether I'm right or wrong, but I know that they love and respect me a great deal. I'm basically quite simple; I hate people that lie to me, and I like those who are straight with me.'

Decisiveness is an inherited trait in Waqar's family. 'My

grandfather was a headmaster of a school and a very firm man. Whenever he said he was going to do something, he would do it. My father is exactly the same.' Waqar likes to affect a light-hearted, happy-go-lucky attitude with his friends, but it masks a hard-edged resolve; of the current Pakistan side, no player is hungrier or more determined than Waqar. This determination partly stems from the fact that life has at times been a financial and emotional struggle for Waqar and his family. He was sent to boarding school as a three year old, and his family moved several times thereafter, and the upset involved may have helped Waqar fashion an iron will to succeed.

Waqar is also a man who likes to keep himself under control. 'I keep quiet if I'm with my seniors and elders. I try to show them respect by listening to what they've got to say without interrupting. I try to never lose my temper both on the pitch and off it. I can only remember one time when I got really angry. I had been selected for the training camp for the 23 probables for the Under-19 World Cup in Australia. I bowled very fast, and very well but I wasn't picked for the final squad, because the camp organizer, Saeed Razaullah, didn't like me. He said, "You'd better go home and do whatever your father does; cricket isn't your game." I was furious, and said that I would meet him again one day, and prove him wrong. I've never seen him since!'

Waqar's rise to celebrity status has been very quick, and the pace at which it has come has left him a little bemused. He has learnt to handle the media attention, but is only totally relaxed at home with his family, or amongst his friends and fellow cricketers. He has lived in England for only two years, and has consequently absorbed less of the western lifestyle than Wasim. 'I've got some good friends, and I enjoy living in London, but it's been very difficult for me to understand

English culture. I'm not trying to become part of that culture, so much as find a way to live in it.' However, Jonathan Barnett, Waqar's agent, suspects that more of the western lifestyle has rubbed off on Waqar than he imagines. 'I think he's getting a taste for the expensive things in life; before the Nat West final, Waqar, Wasim, Aaqib, and myself were all out to dinner at Langan's, and he certainly enjoyed that. Up till now, he's been happy staying in London's East End; I have a feeling that he may be asking Surrey for a flat in Chelsea when he returns to the club in '93.'

Wasim and Waqar have become good friends over the last couple of years, and there is an informality between them that is unusual for two Pakistani players of such differing seniority within the side. 'Both of them playing in England for the last two summers obviously threw them together somewhat,' said Naeem Quyoum. 'It was natural that they should gravitate to one another; cricketers from the same country seek each other out; they know all the problems and the pressures of the game, and also when they go out they can shield each other from outsiders. Even now, if you put Wasim and Waqar into a social setting the chances are they will spend the evening talking to one another.

'At first, Waqar was very guarded with Wasim but gradually he relaxed, and now even pulls his leg. For instance, they were talking about fashion and both were saying how they wouldn't be seen dead in a pair of white shoes. A few days later, Waqar found an old photo of Wasim in white shoes, and teased him mercilessly. Wasim found the situation a bit confusing; he saw the funny side, but he also said to me, "What's going on? Waqar used to be so quiet and respectful!" I don't think they would have ever become that close so quickly if they had both stayed in Pakistan.'

One thing that both share is a devotion to Imran, who has become almost a surrogate father to them. Friends will be asked for their help and opinions with any difficulties, but it is the advice of Imran that will be acted upon. 'Whenever things get tough for Wasim in his cricket or personal life he phones Imran,' said Naeem. 'Usually Imran has been through something similar, and he takes the trouble to talk through his own experiences. Once he has explained everything, he then talks Wasim through all his different options, and together they reach an answer.'

Imran has been a great help to both players in other ways, too. Popular as Wasim and Waqar are, it is still Imran who draws the banner headlines, and he deflects the attention from the other players. Some may have been jealous of this, but for Wasim and Waqar it has been something of a godsend. Had Imran retired after the '87 World Cup as he had originally intended, Wasim, and latterly Waqar, could have been burdened with the expectations of being the saviours of Pakistan cricket long before they were ready to cope with the pressure. As it is, they have been given the breathing space to mature under the shelter of Imran's reputation.

However, the real test for both players is just round the corner; as a fast bowler Imran is already a spent force, and retired after the English tour in '92. Wasim and Waqar have become the senior bowlers; if England are 150–0 half-way through the afternoon session of the first day of a Test match it is to them that the rest of the team will be looking. Off the field it will be to them that the fans look for autographs, and the press for interviews. It is a daunting prospect for both of them, but there is every indication that they are both sufficiently mature to meet the challenges ahead.

13

Sharjah 1991

Cricket in Sharjah has always been considered something of a curiosity in Britain. Indeed, most people would be hard-pressed to pinpoint where exactly Sharjah was in the Middle East. Yet over the last decade this venue has held a series of immensely popular one-day international tournaments that are recognized by the ICC.

That so little is known about Sharjah in England is largely the parochial result of the national side having only played there three times; the last time being in 1987 when they won the competition on superior run-rate because Pakistan were keener to ensure beating India than they were to win the tournament. Although it is clear the TCCB has not gone out of its way to secure return invitations, so likewise have the organizers not felt the urge to extend them. Quite simply, there is little interest in English cricket, beyond the academic, in the Emirates. The success of any tournament depends on the participation of Pakistan or India, and preferably both. Anyone else is really only there to make up the numbers.

The United Arab Emirates was proclaimed an independent

state on 2 December 1971, two days after the British withdrawal from the area. As its name suggests, it was formed out of an alliance of neighbouring emirates, of which Abu Dhabi, Dubai, and Sharjah are the largest and best known, and like the other Gulf states, it owes it economic prosperity to oil. The wealth produced by the oil price rises of 1973 led to the demand for an economic infrastructure of roads, hospitals, schools, offices, and homes, which the indigenous population was neither sufficient in numbers, or skills, to meet. Consequently, thousands of workers were recruited from all over the world, with the great majority coming from the Indian sub-continent.

To the UAE, the Indians and Pakistanis represented a plentiful supply of cheap labour whilst for the latter it was an opportunity to earn a great deal more than they could at home, and to enjoy a higher standard of living. The wide-spread recruitment of the seventies is now over, and visas and work permits are strictly controlled, but a job in the Emirates is still highly prized; the money earned in even a three-year stay can be enough to revolutionize someone's financial situation on their return home. Nowadays, nearly 65 per cent of the population is expatriate, and most of those are Pakistani or Indian. Given both countries' cricket traditions, the emergence of interest in the game in the UAE was almost inevitable.

The first international was played on 4 April 1981 when a Miandad XI defeated a Gavaskar XI on a matting wicket in what was then a rudimentary stadium in Sharjah, and with Asif Iqbal and Hanif Mohammad receiving benefit cheques of 50,000 dollars each, from the organizer Mr Abdulrahman Bukhatir. So taken was Asif by the idea of benefits for players from the sub-continent, that he suggested to Mr Bukhatir that these games should be arranged on a regular basis, and the Cricketers Benefit Fund Series (CBFS) was established. Since then, the organization and the tournaments have gone from strength to strength; over fifty players, past and present, have received benefits, the matches are now played on grass wickets, and the stadium has been improved in size and facilities, to accommodate approximately 18,000 spectators.

The tournaments may not have any greater importance in cricket terms than a Benson & Hedges World Series in Australia, but they are immensely popular with the Pakistani and Indian players. Not only are the games virtually home fixtures, but there is the prospect of being a beneficiary. In India and Pakistan there is no system, unlike in England, whereby a cricketer can look forward to being given the right to earn a tax-free sum towards the end of his career. Indeed, it is considered dishonourable for a player to go cap in hand for money, and on a par with begging. In Sharjah, if a player has been nominated to receive a benefit, all he has to do is either turn up to play, or if he has retired from the game, just turn up. Beneficiaries are now given 35,000 dollars each, and whilst the honour has been extended in recent years to a few West Indians, Richard Hadlee, and Allan Border, the overwhelming majority of recipients come from the sub-continent.

Even for those who may never be awarded a benefit, there is plenty more to play for in Sharjah than just national pride. Many players, like Waqar Younis, have family in the UAE, who they otherwise might not see that often, and for others the tournament has such a festival feel that they pay for their families to come and watch. This year, Wasim paid for both his mother and sister to fly over. But there is more than the cricket. Dubai is the duty-free capital of the world, and offers excellent value for gold and electrical goods, which may well escape the attention of Customs back home if the team has done well. Then there are the gifts. The Pakistani community are lavish with donations of money and gold to the players. When Javed Miandad hit his last ball for six off Chetan Sharma, with four needed, to beat India, he collected a Mercedes and £100,000.

Normally there are two tournaments each year, but, due to the Gulf War, the triangular series between Pakistan, India, and the West Indies for the Wills Trophy in October 1991 was the first since Pakistan defeated Sri Lanka in October 1990. The games themselves are undoubtedly accorded a higher significance by the local Asian communities than they are by the participating countries. Not that the players aren't keen to do well, but the arrival of the Pakistani team less than 36 hours before the first match, and the Indian and West Indian little earlier, suggested a certain attitude. These games were good practice in the build-up for the World Cup, and an important source of revenue for the Boards of Control. By contrast, the teams would be arriving in Australia for the World Cup some two to three weeks before the first match.

The teams were accommodated in the Grand Hotel on the shores of the Gulf. Having players and officials congregated in one place generated a tension and excitement of its own. Everyone from the press to the hangers-on and gawpers knew where to find the cricketers, and the hotel foyer quickly became a forum for gossip and rumour. Would Imran stay in Dubai, as in previous years, or would he stay with the team? Had CBFS lost a lot of money in the collapse of the Bank of Credit and Commerce International? The year before, the teams were put in what the players consider to be the superior Sharjah Continental. Whenever 'Dicky' Bird had been asked to stand, he had always stayed in the same hotel as the players, but the three neutral Sri Lankan umpires who were chosen this time were allocated to the hotel next door with the press.

The journey to the cricket stadium takes one through the centre of Sharjah to the outskirts of the town. Except for the Mosque and the souk, Sharjah is of little architectural merit. Like the other emirates, it owes its expansion to the oil boom and most of the buildings have the concrete functionalism of the seventies. There is no respite out to sea; the Gulf is littered with oil rigs wherever one looks. However, the blatant commercialism of the town has its merits. A cricket stadium with a lush green outfield on the edge of the desert is somewhat incongruous, and that it exists is a triumph both of man's ability to conquer the elements and of petrodollars. A great deal of money is needed to maintain a stadium that is so seldom used.

Squads of helpers were tending the pitch, repainting the railings that had been chipped by sand blown in from the desert, and shooing away chickens that had taken up residence beneath the stands, as the Pakistan team, except for Imran, arrived for net practice early in the afternoon. Imran would be joining them shortly, having just flown in from London where he had been organizing the fund-raising campaign for the Cancer Research Hospital in Lahore.

Wasim and Waqar were in relaxed and confident mood, having just spent two weeks at the training camp in Pakistan with the rest of the team. Wasim had recovered from the fracture of the foot that kept him out of the Lancashire side for the last six weeks of the county season, and Waqar had clearly appreciated the break from non-stop cricket. For both of them Sharjah had been a happy hunting-ground in the past, and the Pakistan side were firm favourites to win the tournament for the fifth time in succession.

Although not as bad as during the summer, it was still very hot and close. The humidity grabbed the players by the throat, stifling them; the prospect of an uninterrupted morning or afternoon in the field was distinctly unappetizing. The team were having a drinks break, when there was a commotion from the other side of the net area; Imran Khan had arrived.

Whereas before there had been a crowd of forty or fifty Pakistanis, dressed in the brown suits worn by taxi drivers or in traditional salwar kamis, to watch the practice, a throng of hundreds, chanting 'Khan sahib zindabad' – 'Victory to the Master Khan', accompanied Imran's progress to the nets. He is treated with a respect bordering on awe; unlike the other players, Imran is never asked if he will pose with a fan for a photo. The team was pleased to see him as well, and were in their own way equally deferential. Most had not seen him since the West Indies series in Pakistan in December 1990, and even Salim Malik, Wasim, Waqar, and Aaqib Javed who had spent some time with him in England, were never less than formally polite at first. There is no getting away from the fact that, in a culture that prizes charisma so highly, Imran has more than his fair share. In most countries, the idea of a captain who rejoined the side the day before a one-day international having played no competitive cricket for over ten months would be faintly ludicrous. Such is his influence and qualities of leadership in the Pakistan side that when Imran returns, it feels as though all is again well with the world.

The first game was between Pakistan and the new-look West Indies team, with Richie Richardson as skipper for the first time. The West Indies had made wholesale changes to the squad that was brought to England in the summer. There was no Haynes, Greenidge, Richards, or Marshall, and Gordon Greenidge, who was in Sharjah to receive a benefit cheque, was not averse to letting people know that both he and Viv Richards had declared themselves available for the tour. Clearly, the selectors had decided to blood some younger players, but it was a long time since the West Indies had fielded such an inexperienced side.

Due to the amount of daylight hours available, matches started at 9.00 in the morning with the side batting first completing their 50 over innings in an uninterrupted session before lunch. Shortly before the start, Imran and Richie Richardson went out into the middle for the toss, and the first controversy started to brew. Who won? The scoreboard announced that Pakistan had, while Richie later revealed that he did. It was hard to know whether the conclusion was the result of a genuine mistake, or, as the cynics would have had it, a deliberate obfuscation. Huge amounts of money are bet on these games on anything from the end result to who will take the next wicket, or even the toss, and occasions have been known when punters will try to ensure that the odds were stacked in their favour. The Pakistan team were once even approached to throw a game – a suggestion that did not go down too well.

Whoever did win the toss, there was no disputing that it was Pakistan who were batting first. The wicket was totally devoid of grass and had a glassy, reflective sheen. Early suspicions that it would give the fast bowlers little help were proved accurate, though the pitch was so slow that stroke-making was not easy either. Furthermore, the grass on the outfield seemed to have velcrose-like properties, for only shots hit with tremendous power, or exquisite timing, reached the boundary.

By lunch, with Pakistan all out for 215 having not even batted out their allotted overs, the game looked as though it had slipped away. Only Rameez Raja and Javed Miandad got going, and they were out playing loose strokes in the forties, while the rest of the team looked completely out of touch. Salim Malik was unrecognizable as the player who scored so heavily for Essex. Imran tamely lofted Patterson to cover, and Wasim ran himself out going for a non-existent second run. It wasn't even as if the West Indies had bowled well; they had visibly wilted in the heat and humidity in the latter part of the innings, and had given away 4 overs of no-balls and wides.

Pakistan got off to an ideal start in the afternoon, with Clayton Lambert given out caught behind in Wasim's first over, though even Wasim was doubtful of the decision. 'I didn't appeal at first, because the noise I heard was after the ball had passed the bat. However, Moin was sure it had come off the edge, and went up immediately.' Thereafter, wickets fell at regular intervals aided by some fine throwing, by Ijaz Ahmed in particular, and a spectacular display of wicket-keeping by Moin Khan, who had been brought in for the tour to replace Saleem Yousuf. At 158–8 Pakistan should have been assured of an unlikely victory, with Richardson and Bishop at the crease, and only Patterson to come. However, having ridden his luck early on, having twice been dismissed off no-balls, once caught behind off Aaqib and once clean bowled by Waqar, Richardson took charge with help from the tail-enders. Although Bishop was leg before to Waqar shortly before the end, Patterson stayed put long enough for Richardson to complete his unbeaten century, and win the game for the West Indies.

The Pakistanis were not overly distressed by their defeat, as it was the first time that they had played together for nearly a year. Wasim was concerned that the rhythm hadn't returned to his bowling after his three-month lay-off, and that the humidity had caused his back to stiffen up after his first 5 overs, but Waqar was quite happy with his 4 wickets, even though he had conceded more runs than usual. Besides, the really important game was against India the next day.

Whether or not, as Imran acknowledged, the tournament was 'the first stage in our preparation for the World Cup', the one game that Pakistan never want to lose under any circumstances is against India. In Sharjah this is doubly so, for it is the only venue in the world where the spectators are likely to be roughly equally divided between India and Pakistan. Although, the two communities co-exist fairly amicably in the UAE, the passions that cricket can generate between them should not be underestimated. David Munden and Ben Radford, the British cricket photographers, were travelling into Dubai by taxi, when they spotted Kiran More, the Indian wicket-keeper, and Anil Kumble, the leg-spinner, in the next car. They waved, whereupon the cab driver, who was Pakistani, announced that he 'hated Kiran More' and made a couple of attempts to drive the Indians off the road, much to the terror and embarrassment of the two snappers.

Pakistan v India is the only game that guarantees a full house. Not only that, but there will be many thousands locked outside the ground looking for some vantage point from which they can see a few square yards of the pitch or better still, the movement of the scoreboard. Inside, the atmosphere is like a Roman games, with the added bonus of a vested interest in the result. Heroes are cheered unquestioningly, opposing players are jeered mercilessly, and tears are commonplace. Wasim and Waqar have their own resident fan clubs; scores of women scream in ecstasy whenever Wasim goes near the third man boundary, and for Waqar, hundreds of his old school friends from Sharjah roar in expectation each time he runs in to bowl.

As it was, India recorded their first ever defeat over the Pakistanis at Sharjah since March 1985, with a crushing 60 run win. Pakistan had managed to limit India to 185–3 from 45 overs, without having ever bowled with any real menace or penetration. Sanjay Manjrekar was batting comfortably, if not commandingly, but it was Sachin Tendulkar, with a breezy half-century including 14 off the last over bowled by Waqar, who took the innings to the respectability of 238–4 at the close.

In Pakistan's reply, once again only Rameez and Javed looked in any sort of form with the bat; Sajid Ali looked as though he might not have the right temperament for international cricket, while Salim Malik, Imran, Ijaz, and Wasim all continued to struggle. From being in with a chance at 124–3 after 31 overs, Pakistan lost 3 wickets for 5 runs, and finally limped to an all out total of 178. The disappointment in the dressing-room was evident, though there were no great inquests. It's hard to play two games back-to-back in these conditions, but there was no disguising that neither the batting or bowling was firing on all cylinders. As Imran summarily put it, 'We're looking pretty pathetic at the moment.'

The team stayed at the ground for well over an hour and a half after the end of the game, waiting for the crowd to disperse. The traffic outside was chaotic, and the players did not want to have to run any more of a gauntlet through hostile, disappointed supporters than was strictly necessary. The price of fame is very high in terms of privacy for the Pakistani cricketers, and the fans are hard taskmasters. By and large, the players appreciate the attention, but it can get difficult, as Wasim explains, 'I know they love us, but sometimes it's a bit too much. They want to go to our rooms, hug us, take a picture, anything. Sometimes they pinch you, and make remarks about you as if you weren't even there. If you lose they treat you like dogs. Right now, I'm feeling very depressed. I've had to take the phone off the hook because I've had so many abusive calls, and some of those have been from friends who have lost money on the game. I know we haven't lost to India in Sharjah for five years, but they must have realized it would happen eventually. Cricket's only a game, and you can't win the whole time.'

The next day, India defeated the West Indies by 19 runs in a thoroughly professional performance. In both games, their batting had looked very secure, with Sidhu, Manjrekar, and Tendulkar in especially good nick, and with the new find Vinod Kambli looking a good prospect also, while their mixture of fast-mediuim and spin bowlers had been more than good enough for the slow pitch. At that moment, the Indians had by far the most balanced team on show, and were newly installed as favourites to lift the Trophy at the end of the week.

At the half-way stage in the tournament the organizers were in an invidious situation. If Pakistan lost to the West Indies in the next game, they had no chance of making the final on Friday. Not only would a final without Pakistan be a bitter anti-climax, it would also mean that the final two round-robin games were largely irrelevant.

As it happened, Pakistan did keep their tournament hopes alive in one of the most exciting one day games ever played. Pakistan won the toss and elected to bat, Imran having reasoned that on the hottest day of the tournament so far, the West Indian bowlers would be wilting in the final overs.

Pakistan made their by now accustomed indifferent start, with Sajid Ali chasing an out-swinger from Curtly Ambrose, Javed retiring with an injured back, and Malik again falling cheaply. However, Rameez with 90 and Imran with 77 restored the position. After a slow and nervous start, Imran got into his stride, hitting sixes off Walsh and Ambrose, and silencing the critics who had been carping at his return to the side. After Rameez and Imran were out in quick succession, only Wasim was able to come to terms with the pace attack, scoring a quick-fire 19 from 10 balls, and Pakistan finished on 236–6 from their 50 overs.

The West Indies quickly slipped to 57–5, and Pakistan appeared to be home and dry. Lambert, Simmons, and Lara, had all fallen cheaply in a hostile spell from Aaqib Javed, Carl Hooper went leg before to Waqar's first ball of the match, and Gus Logie was run out after a misunderstanding with Richie Richardson. From such an unpromising position, Richardson and Dujon took the West Indies to the brink of victory in a stand of 154. Pakistan did not help their cause by giving Dujon, who is always susceptible to speed, time to play himself in against the medium pace of Imran and Ijaz, nor by Imran dropping a dolly catch at mid-on from Richardson off Aaqib, but that is to take nothing away from Richardson, who was busily underlining that he was a class above his team mates.

With the West Indies on 211 and the match there for the taking, Richardson holed out at deep square-leg off Waqar for 122, a Sharjah record. 6 runs later Akram Raza ran out Jeff Dujon from backward point, and Pakistan were back in the hunt. It was left to Wasim and Waqar to bowl the remaining overs. Waqar trapped Ambrose leg before, and Wasim, in a much tighter spell than earlier on, bowled Courtney Walsh. When the last over began the West Indies required 10 to win, with their last pair Bishop and Patterson at the wicket. The first two balls from Waqar produced a single and a leg-bye, and the third was hit in a high arc over long-on for 6 by Bishop.

Waqar was astonished: 'I had been quite relaxed at the start of the over, as I didn't think they could get the runs. There was nothing wrong with the ball, it was a good length inswinger; he just played an incredible short. I've never been hit for 6 over long-on at such a crucial time before.'

Bishop was unable to lay a bat on the next two deliveries, and for the final ball Waqar bowled an outswinger which uprooted the middle stump. In the closest of finishes, Pakistan had won by a single run. One fan had collapsed and died, countless others were emotional wrecks, and the players themselves had the lifeless eyes of men drained by tension and humidity.

Back in the dressing-room, the Pakistanis celebrated their reprieve. Richie Richardson graciously congratulated Imran on his success, but there were murmurings, if not screamings, of discontent in the West Indian camp. Throughout the tournament they had been convinced that the umpires had been pressurized to ensure a Pakistan v India final, and that vital decisions had gone against them. In truth, the umpiring had seemed consistently, and impartially, incompetent in every game, and the West Indian outburst was a sign of frustration more than anything else.

On the following day, it was evident that this inexperienced West Indian side did not yet have the temperament to recover quickly from such disappointments, and lost in abject fashion to India. The West Indians collapsed to the occasional medium pace of Tendulkar, Kapil Dev took his 200th one-day international wicket, and Sidhu, Manjrekar, and Azharuddin ensured that India cruised to a 7-wicket win. This result virtually ensured that the final would be between Pakistan and India, as Pakistan would now only have to score 199, regardless of whether they won or lost, in the last round-robin game against India to qualify.

Although India had already reached the final, the team had plenty more to play for than just pride; an Indian businessman had offered them a penthouse in Hyderabad and free membership to a country club if they beat Pakistan in the last qualifier. The game itself began and ended in controversy. The start was delayed for forty-five minutes by the morning mist, as much a natural hazard to cricket in the region as the 'shamaal', the sand storms, that blow across the ground from time to time. Despite the hold-up the umpires still insisted that there would be no reduction in overs, even though it was obvious that the match would be finishing in near total darkness. It was a decision that benefitted no one. Pakistan would have preferred to have chased few runs in fewer overs to meet the required run rate to reach the final, and India would rather not have had to complete their innings in bad light.

In the event, Pakistan achieved the desired run rate with ease, posting a total of 257, the highest of the tournament so far. Aamir Sohail and Zahid Fazal, who had been flown in the night before as replacements for the injured Rameez and Javed, provided a solid start. Salim Malik at last refound his touch, and Imran again provided the end of innings acceleration with 43 from only 24 deliveries.

After lunch, Pakistan appeared to lose concentration, seemingly confident in the knowledge that they had made the final and the belief that India could not make the runs. The bowling lacked penetration; Waqar was particularly expensive. Wasim, despite a couple of wickets, was still missing his sharpness, and India were well on target for victory without having taken any undue risks. However, with 5 overs still to be bowled the light began to get very murky, and trying to maintain the scoring rate while facing bowlers of the speed of Wasim and Waqar was not just physically dangerous, but impossible too, and Prabhakar and More batted out the last over to leave India 4 runs adrift of the Pakistani total.

While there was no disputing that Pakistan had won, there was a great deal of confusion over the light. The Indian batsmen were claiming that they had appealed to the umpires to come off but had been told they must play on, while the umpires were maintaining that no such appeal had been made, but if there had, they would have called play off. Who, if anyone, would have been adjudged the winner had play been abandoned was also unclear, and the matter remained unresolved with the Indian management electing to keep a discreet and dignified silence.

The jubilation of the Pakistani supporters was boundless, but Wasim and Waqar were in surprisingly subdued mood back at the hotel. Wasim had not performed as well as he would have liked in the tournament so far. 'I am very frustrated with my form. Normally, I just slip straight back into my rhythm after being out with injury, but it's not happening now, and I don't know why. I've had the odd spell when it's begun to come together, but I've found it all a bit of a struggle.'

Waqar was likewise dissatisfied. 'I'm pleased that I've taken so many wickets, but I'm being hit for too many runs. I'm basically a strike bowler, and I much prefer five-day cricket, where you can experiment much more. I've been bowling the inswinger as my stock ball, which is usually my wicket taking delivery, but the batsmen have been working it through the on side. Imran and Javed Burki have suggested that I bowl predominantly outswingers in the final to try and contain the flow of runs.'

That evening, the official dinner to celebrate the tournament and to hand out the benefit cheques was held. Mr Bukhatir's hospitality is legendary, and his guest list read like a *Who's Who* of Arab, Pakistani, and Indian society. Actors, sportsmen, and politicians were all present, including the beautiful Simi Garewal, who is best known in Britain for being the first Indian actress to appear nude on screeen, in the film adaptation of 'Siddharta'. The ranks of the great and the good were further swollen by the presence of the ICC delegates who were in town to vote on South Africa's admittance to the World Cup. This function was a mixed blessing for Wasim. 'It's a wonderful evening, but I'm too exhausted to enjoy it. After a hard game, I'd rather relax with a few close friends than talk to a lot of people I barely know.' After dinner, the English pop singer Amazulu mimed to a backing tape, and provided the cue for guests to leave in their hundreds.

A final at Sharjah is a grand occasion, and people think nothing of jetting in from Bombay, Delhi, Lahore, and Karachi just for this one game. The car-park at the stadium is bumper to bumper with limousines and makes the MCC car-park at Lord's look like a second-hand car lot. The women are dressed in their finest clothes and jewellery. Each game is televised to India and Pakistan, and it is rumoured that wealthy patrons bribe the cameramen to make certain that their families are given coverage. The commentators for this tournament were Iftikhar Ahmed, Sunil Gavaskar, Gordon Greenidge, and, believe it or not, Henry Blofeld. 'Blowers' has become a Sharjah regular, and appears in cloth-cap and bow-tie as if he were at Canterbury rather than in the desert. In the absence of any red buses, earrings were his current passion. Many journalists had noted with interest that the photo that accompanies his column in the local paper had changed, for it was considered an uncanny resemblance to Salman Rushdie – an unfortunate coincidence in a Muslim country.

The night before the final Wasim got a bad sore throat, and it was with some hesitation that he passed himself fit. 'I hardly slept last night, and I feel ghastly. The skipper said I needn't play, but that he'd rather I did. It's an important game so I've decided to play. I only hope I can do myself, and the team, justice.' Fortunately for Wasim, Pakistan were put into bat by Azharuddin, which gave him the morning to recover in the dressing-room.

After the loss of two early wickets, Zahid Fazal with 98 and Salim Malik with 87 rebuilt the innings, and it was only cramps brought on by heat exhaustion that denied Fazal his century. Imran and Ijaz had a brief flurry at the end, and Pakistan finished on 262, an imposing score on such a slow wicket.

Ironically, despite feeling so ill, Wasim bowled his sharpest and most accurate spell of the tournament, and Waqar, too, was at his most economical, but the bowling honours in the Indian innings fell to Aaqib Javed. He took a one-day world record 7–37, including a hat-trick of LBWs. His dismissal of Shastri, Azharuddin, and Tendulkar in successive balls ripped the heart out of the Indian batting. Manjrekar and Kambli staged a brief fight-back, but when Kambli was run out and Manjrekar was superbly caught at third man by Waqar the match was effectively over. The last rites were soon concluded, and Pakistan were the victors by a margin of 77 runs.

Celebrations were muted at the hotel. Wasim went straight to bed, and Waqar spent a quiet evening with his family. The next day the team were due to fly back to Karachi, and then on to Madras for the first of five one-day games against India, and they were all exhausted. Wasim was not looking forward to the itinerary. 'I love playing in Sharjah; it's friendly, and the organizers are very generous to the players. But five games in eight days in this heat is very tiring, and to follow it immediately with a tour of India where we play five games in different cities in ten days is just too much. The Pakistani Board should not accept this sort of schedule; it's asking too much of the players, and we can't perform at our best.'

So, Pakistan kept their reputation as champions of Sharjah. While in many ways there was a perverse satisfaction in knowing they won without ever moving into top gear, there was no getting away from the fact that there was much more work to be done before the World Cup. Still, there were encouraging signs. Wasim was beginning to get into his stride; Waqar had taken wickets and had shown that he had a very cool head under extreme pressure, and Aaqib had come on immensely. Javed, Rameez, Salim Malik, and Imran were all in the runs, while Zahid Fazal looked a world-class prospect.

The Indians were left with a lingering sense of injustice. They had looked the best side for much of the tournament, yet they still lost, and they were still smarting over the bad light decision. They later appealed to the ICC to have the result nullified, and one Indian official was moved to protest that 'Sharjah was run by the Pakistanis, for the Pakistanis'. Meanwhile, the Pakistani Cricket Board went home with 90,000 dollars appearance money, and another 30,000 dollars for winning the tournament, and Imran went home having raised some more money for the Cancer Hospital after selling the car he had won for hitting the most sixes in the tournament.

14

World Cup Build-up

Pakistan's World Cup build-up began in earnest with three one-day internationals in Pakistan against the West Indies in November 1991. Following the two close encounters the previous month in Sharjah, both teams were well acquainted with each other's strengths and fallibilities, but Imran was determined to use the games to find out as much about his own team as the opposition. 'In the two Sharjah games we had batted first on each occasion,' said Wasim, 'and we knew that our bowling could put them under pressure when they were batting second. For this series, Imran said that whenever he won the toss he was going to experiment with putting the West Indies into bat first, and see how our batsmen coped with chasing the runs.'

Imran won the toss twice, but nevertheless Pakistan batted second in every game, and all suspicions of the fragility of the Pakistani batting line-up were confirmed, as they lost two matches and tied the other. Set to make 171 in 34 overs in Karachi they lost 6 wickets for 82 and slumped to a 24 run defeat, and in the final game at Faisalabad they slipped from

161–3 to 175–8 to lose by 17 runs. Indeed, Pakistan would have lost the second game in Lahore as well, but for Waqar and Mushtaq, the last wicket pair, taking 9 from the final over, bowled by Curtly Ambrose, to tie the game.

All three games were played on slow flat wickets which offered little assistance to the bowler, but for Wasim there was some relief as he began to find his form again with 5 wickets in the series. For Waqar there was no such joy, and he remained wicketless in all three games. As is often the case, this first sign of failure was seized upon by the Pakistani media and the public who had grown so accustomed to his success. 'The papers were full of "What's wrong with Waqar?"' said Wasim, 'but even though he wasn't at his absolute best, there wasn't really much wrong with him at all. However, all the speculation did get Wicky down, and he began to doubt himself. I reminded him that I suffered a similar spell in Sharjah and had come through it, and that if he kept training hard, then he would too.'

Pakistan had hoped to continue their preparations with a hastily arranged tour to South Africa which would have been an ideal opportunity to practise on fast pitches and to familiarize themselves with opponents whom they would meet in Brisbane during the World Cup. South Africa had been readmitted as a full Test playing country in the summer of 1991, but it was only at a meeting of the ICC in Sharjah in October that the previous decision not to allow South Africa to play in the World Cup was rescinded, and the whole schedule for the tournament was altered as a result. Undoubtedly, a major reason for the *volte face* by the ICC was Nelson Mandela's support for Dr Ali Bacher's campaign to allow South Africa to play in the World Cup, for as Imran said, 'If Nelson Mandela is satisfied that enough progress has been made towards the abolition of apartheid in South Africa, then Pakistan must support their admission.'

However, South Africa was not the only country that breathed a sigh of relief. The Australian and New Zealand cricket administrations had been desperate for South Africa to play in the World Cup, a desperation inspired by financial as much as by political motives, for a tournament with South Africa in it would provoke greater interest and revenue. It seems likely too, that there were side deals attached to the voting in Sharjah. Up until July, India had been vociferous opponents of South Africa, and thereafter became their staunchest supporter among the black cricket playing nations. The price for this support may well have been a series of one-day games between the two countries in India, and, in turn, for India to be the first non-white country to tour South Africa. The South African tour to India duly took place in November 1991, and the Indians made the return trip in the winter of 1992. However, it is quite possible that a commitment made to India was enough to scupper Pakistan's hopes of a South African tour in January 1992.

As it was, Pakistan had to content themselves with a three-match Test series and five one-day internationals against Sri Lanka. 'It was a ridiculous tour as far as we were concerned,' said Wasim. 'We were providing practice for the Sri Lankans but not for ourselves. We should have been playing top-class opposition on pitches similar to those we were going to come across in Australia. I don't know why the Board did this to us. The World Cup comes round every four years, and so they have ample time to arrange the appropriate itinerary; I hope they think about this for 1996.'

The first Test was played at Sialkot, and a combination of mist, slow batting by Rameez, Shoaib, and Zahid Fazal on the third day, and second innings defiance by Jayasuriya and Tillekaratne for Sri Lanka, conspired to deny Pakistan victory. In the Sri Lankan first innings, Waqar took his sixth 5-wicket haul in only his twelfth Test, but in many ways it was Wasim who stole the honours even though he took just the one wicket in the whole match. 'I could feel my rhythm coming back,' said Wasim. 'In the first innings I took 0–47 from 32 overs, but in the second I was bowling really quickly. I was getting the ball to lift very sharply from a good length, and I hit De Silva on the head a couple of times.' It was calculated aggression on Wasim's part; the new rule limiting the bouncer to one per over had come into force, but he was proving that the really dangerous delivery was the one aimed at the batsman's throat rather than above his head.

Gujranwala was the venue for the second Test, the first ever Test match to be played at the ground. Unfortunately for the players and spectators, little more than two and a half hours play was possible in the entire match, and the two teams moved on to Faisalabad for the decider. Pakistan narrowly scraped home by 3 wickets in the third Test, but they so nearly inflicted on themselves a first home Test series defeat in eleven years and presented Sri Lanka with their first ever overseas Test victory. As usual it was the batting that let them down. Sri Lanka were restricted to 240 in their first innings with Waqar taking 4 wickets, and Wasim 2. Pakistan's batsmen lost their way after reaching 102–0, and were all out for 221, but the bowlers again retrieved the initiative by dismissing the Sri Lankans in their second innings for 165, as Wasim took 3 wickets and Waqar 5, to elevate himself to the number 1 position in the Deloitte world ratings for Test match bowlers. Jayasuriya won universal acclaim for his stroke-play in that innings and throughout the series, but Wasim was far from impressed. 'Our catching was no better in this series than it had been in any other in recent years, and we frequently gave Jayasuriya a couple of chances. Also, you could tell that the reason he was playing so freely was because he was scared of our bowling. It was desperation stuff, rather than a controlled assault.'

Pakistan were set 185 for victory, and were in some trouble at 60–4 with the cream of their batting back in the pavilion, as Wasim walked out to join Zahid Fazal. 'It was one of the most difficult innings I've ever played,' said Wasim. 'The bounce was so uneven; one ball would skid through, and the next would bounce chest high off the same length. I knew that I had to stay there with Zahid, and I don't think I've ever concentrated as hard. I was in for about four or five hours for my 50, and we had just about seen Pakistan through to victory when we both got out. I played a stupid shot; I tried to hook a short ball outside the off stump and succeeded in top edging to mid-on.' Wasim's efforts won him the Man of the Match award, as Moin Khan and Waqar, not without their own alarms and excursions, nudged Pakistan to victory.

As far as Waqar was concerned, the five one-day internationals that followed the Test series were equally pointless as preparation for Australia. 'There was no sense of urgency as we won so easily; we took the first three games, lost the fourth when we relaxed too much, and then won the final game. The pitches were again slow, dead surfaces. Wasim and myself would get hit all over the place in the first 10 overs, and then as the ball got older and started to shine we would regain control.' There was some consolation for the Pakistanis as their batsmen regained some form, as the twenty-one-year-old Inzamam-Ul-Haq and Salim Malik scored centuries, and there was a 100 too for Javed Miandad, whom Wasim thought was beginning to time the ball better than he had for four or five years.

Just how inadequate the games against Sri Lanka were as preparation was revealed after Pakistan flew into Australia in early February, some three weeks before the World Cup. The team failed to win any of its side games, and as ever it was the batting that was suspect. Every player found it hard to get accustomed to the bounce and pace of Australian wickets, and again the temperament of some of the finest stroke makers in the world was suspect under pressure.

What was even more worrying than any flaws in the batting was a back injury to Waqar. He had picked up the injury at a training camp in Lahore five or six days before the team left for Australia. The problem was never thoroughly checked out at the time, and he was told to rest up, and that he would be fine in time for the World Cup. The back injury never did clear up and Waqar did not bowl a single ball in Australia. The problem was finally diagnosed as two stress fractures to the lower vertebrae shortly before the competition began; Waqar was sent home for two months complete rest in the hope that he would then have sufficient time to recover before the tour of England in the summer of 1992.

Waqar knew the writing was on the wall a week before the final diagnosis was made. 'I know it's serious and that I'm out of the World Cup,' he said. The rest of the team sensed that the injury was serious as well. 'You could tell that something was very wrong,' said Wasim. 'I've never seen Waqar so depressed; he was so quiet, not at all his usual lively self. The whole team kept the injury a secret from the media because we didn't want to make any statement in case a second opinion revealed that the injury was only a strain. Waqar was shattered when the diagnosis was confirmed. It's the worst thing that can possibly happen to a fast bowler; look at Ian Bishop. He's now virtually out of the game, and he'll never bowl fast again.'

With Waqar being a key player, there was inevitably intense conjecture in the Pakistan media about the injury. Was it an old one or a new one? Rumours began to circulate that Waqar's back had gone some time before, and that only painkilling injections and the pleadings of the selectors to turn out for just 'one more game' had prevented Waqar from getting proper treatment earlier on. 'He's had problems with his back in the past,' said Wasim, 'though whether it was a stress fracture I don't think we'll ever know, but whatever it was, it must have weakened his back somewhat, but the real damage is new. I think that the Board should have paid greater attention to the injury much earlier on though. I doubt whether he'll receive his insurance money, or even if anyone from the Board will bother to get in contact with him on his return to Pakistan. If I was him I would go to London for treatment, and I know that Geoff Arnold, the Surrey coach, would be keen for him to do so. It's important for him to be with people who will keep his morale high, as it's often as difficult to recover psychologically from injury as it is to physically get better.'

That injury could afflict one of the fittest players in the game is proof of the strain imposed on international fast bowlers who are called upon to play year-round cricket. Bowlers simply do not have the time to recover from niggling injuries, which invariably get worse, and they grow accustomed to tolerating a certain level of pain whenever they play. Curiously, in Wasim's estimation, it is not the amount of three- or five-day games that bring about the injuries but the one-day games. 'Bowling 10 overs in a limited over game may not seem much to an outsider, but it's the most tiring and debilitating form of cricket. You have to concentrate so hard every ball, and the pressure can be immense. In Test matches you at least get periods to relax, but you can't in a one-day game, and it's often when you're tense that you get injured.'

One result of Waqar's injury is that he will almost certainly have to cut down on his cricket commitments if he is to prolong his career beyond a few years. There is no question that his Test career with Pakistan would take priority, which must mean that his future with Surrey looks bleak. Imran has told him to abandon his long-term county career and to seek a contract with one of the English leagues that would pay just as well, but would involve considerably less cricket. Obviously the opposition would not be as strong, and there is a danger that Waqar could lose some of his former sharpness as a result, but if, as is inevitable, the current level of international fixtures are maintained, League cricket will become an increasingly attractive option, not just for him, but for the rest of the world's best fast bowlers too.

Wasim was one of the few Pakistani players to click into gear almost immediately, as he renewed his love affair with Australian pitches. In the three-day game against Victoria at Bendigo, which Pakistan came very close to losing, Wasim bowled with great hostility and was among the wickets in both innings. Indeed many observers considered that Wasim's performance against Simon O'Donnell was responsible for the Australian all-rounder's omission from his country's final World Cup squad. 'It wasn't premeditated,' said Wasim, 'but you always put a little extra effort in against key players. When O'Donnell came in at number 3 I told Salim Malik, our acting captain, that I was going to give him a working over. In the first innings I beat him repeatedly outside the off-stump, and had him trapped leg before which the Pakistani umpire Khizar Hayat didn't give, but then he never gives them at home either; in the second innings, I hit O'Donnell on the head and body a couple of times, before he edged me to the keeper.'

However, even for Wasim, things didn't run smoothly. Batting in a side game he was hit on the left thigh which badly strained a muscle. A fit Wasim was even more crucial to Pakistan's chances with Waqar already out of the World Cup, and the selectors decided to leave him out of the side for the final two warm-up games against Sri Lanka and South Africa, two of the least experienced teams in the World Cup. Pakistan lost both games; predictably the bowling looked anaemic, but more worrying was the way the batting panicked at the first suggestion of pressure, after a solid foundation for victory had been built early in the innings.

To compound matters, Imran had picked up a shoulder injury in training. 'I felt the muscle tear when I was bowling, but it seemed OK when I warmed up. I should have stopped immediately, because after practice my shoulder really stiffened up.' With the batsmen lacking in confidence, and their bowling attack weakened by injury, the team that had been tipped as one of the pre-tournament favourites was not in the best of shape, with the start of the World Cup only days away.

15

The World Cup: A Triumph of Faith Over Reason

'One day cricket is a game of combinations, of finding the right balance between your batting and bowling. Half the battle is over when you are happy with your combination, as the team members learn to play with one another. As a captain you learn how bowlers cope with the pressure, and at what point in the innings to bowl them. At the moment we haven't got it right; we've lost Waqar, one of our main strike bowlers, with injury, and we don't have a balanced attack. Likewise, the batting line-up we used in the recent series against Sri Lanka has become redundant here. One or two of the batsmen we thought would do well have not adjusted to the extra bounce in the wickets.'

Imran Khan had seen the writing on the wall for Pakistan even before the World Cup began, and decided that a desperate situation called for desperate measures. Only days before the final squad of fourteen was due to be announced, Saleem Jaffer, Shahid Saeed, and Akram Raza accompanied Waqar back to Pakistan, and were replaced by Wasim Haider, a young fast bowler, and Iqbal Sikander, a leg-spinner. Neither had ever played a limited over international, and would be called upon to make their debuts in the most prestigious one day tournament with little time to prepare or acclimatize. While Saleem Jaffer had not been in the best of form, many felt that his experience would be invaluable to the side in Waqar's absence, but as Wasim explained there was method in what appeared to be madness. 'We were still very worried about our batting and fielding, and we felt that Wasim Haider's extra ability in both departments would more than compensate for the extra experience that Jaffer could bring to the bowling.'

What seemed even more confusing was that, with everyone admitting that the batting was in a state of disarray, players of the calibre of Shoaib Mohammad and Saeed Anwar were never even considered. Shoaib is one of the finest batsmen in Pakistan, but has always been branded as a player incapable of adapting to the shorter game, but Saeed Anwar is a man of proven ability in one day games in Australia. When Pakistan last toured Australia in 1990 he managed to score at more than a run a ball.

The opening launch for the World Cup in Sydney on 19 February set the tone for the whole tournament; it was to be a competition arranged primarily for the benefit of the Australian Channel 9 TV network and for the sponsors, Benson & Hedges, and the players ran a poor third as far as the organization was concerned. The day began with the players being taken for a cruise around Sydney Harbour aboard HMAS Canberra. 'It was a complete shambles,' said Wasim. 'There was nothing to eat or drink, and they only allowed one or two selected press photographers on board. We just stood around while these guys took a few pictures, and that was it. There was nobody else there at all.'

In the evening there was the official World Cup launch dinner. Whether by accident or design, the seating arrangements were somewhat tactless; the predominantly white cricket playing countries on one side of the room, and the black on the other. Again, Wasim was scathing about the event. 'The dinner was very average, and they were charging Australian $150 (approximately £60) per head; they were even making the journalists pay, and consequently very few could be bothered to go. I know that none of the Asian journalists went because they felt it was immoral to spend that much on a meal, when you could feed families at home for at least a month for that amount of money. Even so there were about a 1000 people there, and the organizers must have made a fortune.'

However, the opening rites were merely the tip of the iceberg. 'When the World Cup was played in Pakistan the whole country was excited,' said Wasim. 'There were big crowds, each game was televised, and every effort was made to make sure that all the players had whatever they wanted. Here it's Australia first, and the rest nowhere. Many of the games are simply not being shown on TV; only those involving Australia and a few other selected matches are being broadcast.'

The influence of television extended to the rules for the competition and made the match scheduling a triumph of faith over reason. The World Cup was starting in the late Australian summer; this was partly because of the desire to fit in a full Test series against India and the by now traditional World Series Cup one-day internationals, but it may have also had something to do with Channel 9 having bought the TV rights to both the World Cup and the Winter Olympics from Albertville, and their wanting to ensure that one event should not detract from the other. Channel 9 were showing some four and a half hours of the Winter Olympics each night, and it was surely not coincidental that the World Cup began on the very day the Olympics ended.

Any tournament starting so late in the year should have adequate provision for rain affected matches, especially with some four matches arranged for Queensland in what is the rainy season there, but there were to be no spare days allocated for any of the preliminary matches. To make matters worse the dictates of television demanded that all games should start and finish on time, because nothing should be allowed to interfere with the programming. This meant that a match could be reduced to a meaningless reduced over slog even though there were still hours of daylight left. In three World Cups in England, only one game was ever abandoned because of the weather, but if the Australian weather was less then perfect, the 1992 competition was in danger of becoming something of a farce with teams being eliminated by the rules as much as by the opposition.

'The Australians also seem to have organized all the fixtures to suit themselves, rather than anyone else,' said Wasim. 'I don't know whether anyone from our Board checked any of their arrangements, but they should have complained. Many of our games are being played on wickets which either suit the opposition better than us, or neutralize what appears to be an advantage on paper. For instance, at Sydney where the ball traditionally turns, we're playing the Indians who are probably the best players of spin in the competition. Likewise, we're playing the South Africans at Brisbane which is exactly the kind of wicket they are used to, and of course we're up against the Aussies in Perth on the fastest track in the world where our batsmen are almost bound to struggle with the bounce. I'm sure that if Pakistan had arranged a similar schedule for the Australians, their press would have been up in arms at the injustice of it. But no one has said a word.'

This may smack of sour grapes, and cricketers are often the first to find evidence of conspiracy where none may exist, but one only had to look at the itineraries of some of the other teams to concede that Wasim may have had a point. Sri Lanka had a schedule that demanded flying across the Tasman Sea to New Zealand three times in as many weeks, Zimbabwe had a similarly arduous tour, and the West Indies were due to play three games in New Zealand on wickets that were guaranteed to reduce the effectiveness of their bowling attack, and to inhibit the strokeplay of their batsmen.

Unlike the English players who are paid to go on tour by the TCCB, the Pakistan team were being paid nothing by the BCCP for the World Cup tour of Australia and New Zealand. 'Senior players get match fees of about £500 per game from our board, and that's it,' explained Wasim. 'Otherwise we have to get by on a daily allowance from the Australian Cricket Board. We are each given Australian $80 per day (approximately £35), and out of that we have to pay for all our meals except breakfast. $80 doesn't go that far when you're staying in smart hotels, and you're also having to pay for your own laundry. On match days we are given only $60 because they say that we will be given something to eat at the ground, which shows how tight they are being with the teams. The prize money for each game goes to the players, together with any man of the match awards which we always pool, but unless we win the competition none of us are going to come home having made much money.'

Jeff Thomson, the Australian fast bowler, was once quoted as saying, 'One-day cricket is crap, and all the players know it. It's OK for a bit of a laugh, but Test match cricket is what counts.' While it is true that within a few months most of the games apart from the final would be remembered by very few people, the gathering of the media clans for the World Cup ensured that players' reputations could be made or broken by the tournament. Wasim was in no doubt of this, and had geared his preparation for the competition accordingly. 'Whatever anyone says, it is the most prestigious cricket tournament there is; it only comes round once every four years, and ever since I returned to Pakistan after the English summer, getting myself physically and mentally right for the World Cup has been my prime objective.'

Pakistan's first game was against the West Indies at Melbourne on 23 February, and the team arrived in the Victorian capital three days before the game. Although they are both similar in size, Melbourne has a completely different feel to Sydney. Where Sydney has the freneticism of a cosmopolitan metropolis, life in Melbourne takes on a more relaxed and genteel pace as trams criss-cross the city centre, and a traffic jam is a rarity. Not that the players would get much chance to experience the charms of this or any other city; for the next four or five weeks life would be a long round of airports, hotels, and cricket grounds.

The day before the match there was only a light practice in the afternoon, and many of the players took advantage of this to follow the first game of the tournament, Australia v New Zealand on TV in their hotel rooms. Salim Malik and Zahid Fazal joined Wasim and Ijaz Ahmed in their room, and amazement turned to delight as the New Zealanders pulled off the first upset of the competition. Oddly enough, the

Pakistanis' pleasure was shared by many Australians. '80 per cent of the Aussies I've met are happy their team lost,' said Wasim. 'Everyone thinks they are too big-headed and rude. The Aussie players think they are something special, but they're just normal ordinary cricketers like the rest of us.'

The umpiring in the Australia v New Zealand game caused Wasim some anxiety. 'It just wasn't consistent. If an umpire is going to call a ball wide, he must call every ball that misses the stumps by the same distance a wide throughout both innings, and it just wasn't happening here. Likewise, Khizar Hiyat gave a leg before decision that wasn't even close, and David Shepherd, who is one of the best umpires in the game, gave not out appeals that seemed absolutely plumb. Sometimes I think umpires are scared to give a decision. If it's out, it's out; otherwise it's not fair on the bowlers. That's why I'm never bothered if an umpire gives a decision in my favour when I'm fairly confident that the batsman is not out; such decisions are more than counterbalanced by batsmen being given not out when they were.'

During the same game the commentary by the Channel 9 team caused much amusement among the Pakistanis. The style of reportage has always been at best parochial with a strong home side bias, but this was beyond belief. With Australia clearly on the verge of losing the game, Bill Lawry announced when a rare Aussie boundary was struck that 'now the pressure was back on the Kiwis'. Perhaps though, Lawry was just concerned for his job; in early 1991 Rod Marsh, the former Australian wicket-keeper, was sacked by Channel 9 for daring even to suggest that one-day cricket was not that important when compared to Test cricket.

Wasim had been hoping to relax the evening before the match by watching the end of the game between England and

India in Perth, but not a ball, even in a programme of highlights, was shown on Australian TV. Throughout the afternoon live coverage had been given to the Australia and New Zealand match in Auckland on one channel, and to coverage of the women's Test match between Australia and England at the North Sydney Oval on another. However, from the newspaper reports the next day, Wasim considered that England were going to be a tough side to beat. 'Even the young players like Chris Lewis are so experienced at this sort of cricket, and they've packed their side with good all rounders. Ian Botham is a very difficult player to get away, and yesterday he got rid of the danger man, Sachin Tendulkar. I've been watching Tendulkar on TV batting against Australia in the Tests, and I think he is one of the best in the world at the moment. He's been hitting balls through the covers that the rest of the Indians were edging to slip. Azhar's right out of form now, and it's all down to the pressure of captaincy. It's the same for Richie Richardson; he hardly made a run against us in the three one-day games in Pakistan. I know that our captain is feeling the pressure too, and I suspect that Allan Border is as well.'

The Melbourne Cricket Ground, the venue for the first ever Test match in 1877, is a monument to grandeur, capable of seating over 100,000 spectators. Even before the building of the new Southern Stand when the ground resembled a concrete colosseum it was awe inspiring, and now it is even more so. The new stand stretches for over 300 metres around the southern end of the ground, reaches high into the aether, and holds more people than the entire capacity of the Sydney Cricket Ground; from the seating at the very top the players appear as if in another world. Even Wasim who is used to the large stadia of the Indian sub-continent found it breathtaking.

The 14,000 spectators who came to watch the game would have made many of the more intimate English grounds seem practically full, but were here almost lost in the tiers of empty seats.

When the two captains went out to the middle for the toss there were two surprises. There was no Imran Khan, and Javed Miandad, who had joined the tour late in order to give himself time to rest his back, was skippering the side instead. Imran had strained a muscle in his shoulder while bowling in the nets two days before, but the injury had been kept quiet in the hope that it would recover quickly. When the original tour party was announced Salim Malik was appointed vice-captain, and Wasim was amazed that he was not leading the team against the West Indies; but then so was Salim Malik. 'The first that I or any of the other players heard about it was on the morning of the game. I asked the manager, (Intikhab Alam), about it and he told me there had been a misunderstanding, and that my appointment was only for the period of the tour before the World Cup began.' Wasim was less restrained about the matter. 'There may have been a misunderstanding, but it's the manager's job to prevent it. Small things like these matter in the end, and if I were Malik I would have been mad about it. Other countries manage to get by without problems of seniority. Look at the West Indies. Malcolm Marshall and Dessie Haynes are senior to Richie Richardson yet they are happy to play under him and call him skipper.'

The West Indies won the toss and put Pakistan into bat, and the lack of confidence in the batting was soon apparent as Pakistan dawdled through their first 40 overs. Only a late acceleration of 81 in the last 10 overs enabled Pakistan to close the innings on 220–2. Although Rameez collected a century, and Javed a 50, it was by and large painful progress. Rameez crawled from 23 to 57 in singles, and only Javed provided any flair or improvisation as three times he leg glanced Malcolm Marshall from outside off stump to the boundary.

It was a frustrating time for Wasim in the pavilion. 'We had so many wickets in hand, and with batsmen like Malik, Ijaz, and myself to come, Rameez and Javed could really have taken a few more risks. The start of the innings was OK but we batted really badly in the middle, particularly against the two off-spinners Hooper and Harper who are nothing special.'

Although Javed later said that he felt that 220 should have been an adequate total to defend, it was always likely to be difficult unless Wasim and Aaqib took a couple of early wickets to expose an inexperienced West Indian middle order prone to collapse. Pakistan had gone into the game with only two front-line bowlers. After Wasim and Aaqib, there were 30 overs to find from Iqbal Sikaner and Wasim Haider who were making their international debuts, and from the occasional left-armers, Ijaz and Aamir Sohail.

Wasim was feeling the pressure. 'Waqar is the best bowler in the world at the moment, and with him in the side we felt we could defend any total. After all, not many sides could survive Waqar, Aaqib, and myself. His absence has had a marked affect on some of our players, and their heads went down when he went home. By contrast, his absence must have given the opposing batsmen a real lift. I now feel the burden is on me; if Aaqib and myself don't take wickets, who will? I also find it hard to bowl with the white ball. For the first 10 overs the white lacquer makes it swing all over the place which makes it very difficult to control when you're running in hard to bowl fast, and I find that I have to bowl wider of the crease to get the ball to pitch in line. After 10 overs the lacquer comes off, you can't shine the ball, and it goes soft like a tennis ball. It seems crazy to play such an important tournament with equipment that is only ever used under floodlights. Again it's all for the benefit of TV and making money, not for the players. It's not only the bowlers who would rather be playing with the red ball; certainly all our batsmen find the white ball hard to sight.'

Wasim's first spell from the pavilion end confirmed his fears, as he mixed the unplayable with the untouchable, bowling 7 wides in the process. He ran in faster than for a couple of years, bowling wide of the crease in an attempt to control the extravagant swing, but with no luck. Aaqib found himself bowling into a strong head wind from the Southern Stand end and was erratic in line and length, and from the moment that he and Wasim finished their opening spells wicketless there was not too much doubt about the result. There was perhaps a flicker of a chance when Aamir Sohail had Haynes dropped behind off his first ball when the score was 95, and dropped him off a dolly caught and bowled in his next, but Haynes and Lara soon snuffed out the Pakistani hopes as they began to take the bowling apart. Indeed, it was only an inswinging yorker from Wasim that landed on Brian Lara's foot, causing him to retire hurt, that prevented him and Haynes from breaking the World Cup first wicket partnership of 182 scored by the Australians McCosker and Turner against Sri Lanka in 1975. Richie Richardson came out to continue where Lara left off, and he and Haynes saw the West Indies through to a comfortable 10-wicket victory with more than 3 overs to spare.

After the game Wasim's legs rebelled against the heavy Melbourne outfield by going into spasms of cramp, but even so he was not particularly down-hearted by the defeat. 'We had a team meeting after the game which was very helpful.

Rameez said that he had gone slowly against the spinners because it had been so long since he had played that kind of bowling on a bouncy wicket, but that he would know how to handle it from now on. Besides the Pakistan side always starts tournaments badly. We did in India for the Nehru Cup and we did in Sharjah. I don't know why it is, but it must be something in our temperament.'

Early the next morning the Pakistan team flew to the Tasmanian capital of Hobart for the match against Zimbabwe. Hobart is only an hour's flying time across the Bass Strait from Melbourne, but it could easily be decades away in terms of the pace of life. It has the cosy, sleepy feel of Eastbourne in winter in the nineteen fifties. Hobart is a charming, friendly place, but in the evening it is a comparative rarity to see a car on the streets; come to think of it, there isn't much traffic in the day-time either. For the players such a venue is deadly; there is no time to go sightseeing, and there is nowhere to go out in the evening, unless they fancy a flutter in the casino.

For Wasim, the four days in Tasmania were spent either at the cricket ground or in the hotel. At the hotel, Wasim spent most of the time in his room. He slept, watched TV, and even had his meals there. 'It does get boring, even though the company is good,' he said. 'All the hotels have the same in-house movies on the video channels, and you end up mindlessly watching them again and again. I've already seen "Backdraft" and "Naked Gun $2\frac{1}{2}$" four times each, and I dread to think how many times I'll have seen them by the end of the tour.'

The Bellerive Oval, Hobart's cricket ground, is situated some ten minutes' drive out of town, on the other side of the River Derwent to Hobart proper. It is one of the most attractive grounds in the world; the members' pavilion is framed by Mount Wellington in the background, and from the Church Street end you can look straight down the pitch to the river and sea beyond. A crowd of little more than a thousand gathered to see Zimbabwe take on Pakistan, and the whole game had the feel of a first round Nat West tie, with Dorset taking on Lancashire, rather than a World Cup clash.

The result may have been a foregone conclusion to all the pundits, but Wasim was concerned before the game. 'Our team isn't playing well, and games that you are supposed to win easily always worry me. The Zimbabweans are an unknown quantity; Moin Khan, the wicket-keeper, went on tour there last year and so he has been able to fill us in a bit, but basically we know next to nothing about them. Anything can happen in a one-day game, and the pressure will very much be on us.'

Imran declared himself available before the start, a statement more of the need for Pakistan to settle down and play a full strength side, than of his fitness, and he was clearly hoping to get through the game without having to bowl unless absolutely necessary. If he managed to achieve this, it would mean that Pakistan would have got by with the most extraordinary complement of bowlers. After the opening burst by Wasim and Aaqib, the bulk of the overs would have to come from the two main leg-spin bowlers, Mushtaq Ahmed and Iqbal Sikander, the seldom used leg-spin of Salim Malik and the left arm off-spin of Aamir Sohail.

Zimbabwe won the toss and chose to field, which is what Pakistan would have done had they won. The wicket had a lot of early bounce, and batting was never easy for Rameez and Sohail, even against the likes of Eddo Brandes and Malcolm Jarvis. Rameez was given out early on, caught behind off

Jarvis, to a ball he didn't touch, and just over 10 overs later Inzamam-Ul-Haq was caught at square leg off one of his few aggressive shots. Inzamam had come to the World Cup with a reputation for being a fine striker of the ball, but looked out of sorts. 'I don't think it's just a matter of confidence with Inzy,' said Wasim. 'He's playing in a completely different style to how he did in Pakistan. It's almost as though someone has said to him, "You've got to play cautiously because it's the World Cup." He should be getting after the bowling like he does back home.'

Javed Miandad joined Aamir Sohail at the fall of the second wicket and together they put the game all but beyond Zimbabwe's reach with a partnership of 145. Zimbabwe did not help their cause by dropping Sohail three times as he compiled a century, and although he and Miandad were out before the end chasing quick runs, Pakistan closed their innings comfortably placed on 254–4.

The Zimbabwe openers, Kevin Arnott and Andy Flower, had no answer to the pace of Wasim and Aaqib. They had only taken 14 off the first 8 overs, when to the first ball of Wasim's 5th over, Flower edged to Inzamam at slip to give Wasim his 150th one-day international wicket, and later in the same over Wasim celebrated by yorking Andy Pycroft for 0. Wasim showed his respect for Dave Houghton by giving him a short-pitched delivery first up, that reared uncomfortably close to the Zimbabwean skipper's nose. It had the desired effect, and Houghton later said, 'When I got that first ball from Akram, I thought it was my last day at the office.'

Zimbabwe got further into trouble when Wasim took a neat, tumbling catch to dismiss Arnott off Iqbal Sikander, and although they managed not to lose any more early wickets, they steadily fell further and further behind the run rate.

Their inexperience showed in their inability to put pressure on the fielders and on many occasions the opportunity to turn ones into twos, and twos into threes, was lost. Wasim returned to bowl at the end, and immediately yorked Andy Waller, to give him the impressive return of 10-2-21-3, and Pakistan ran out easy, if far from convincing winners, by 53 runs as Zimbabwe finished their innings on 201-7.

Dave Houghton was the first to admit the gulf between the two sides. 'You spend a lot of your time just trying to survive against that sort of bowling, which makes keeping up with the run-rate very difficult. They give you so little to hit. Likewise, when you're bowling at them you have a tiny margin of error, as anything fractionally off line will be hit.' Imran was delighted with the way the game went. 'It was the perfect day's cricket for me; no batting, no bowling, and no catching. It's the sort of day that Aamir Malik would have loved.' On a more serious note he continued that, 'We still don't have the right balance, but I'm the eternal optimist. Without Waqar, I think that my bowling is the key. If I can perform as I think I can, we'll be a hard side to beat.'

Back in the hotel, Wasim was pleased with the two points that victory brought, but was not overwhelmed by the umpiring or the Pakistani team effort. 'The umpiring is still so inconsistent. Brandes bowled a ball that bounced straight over the keeper's head and went for four, but it wasn't even given as a no ball or wide. Likewise, Mushtaq had a batsman trapped leg before with his flipper, but the umpire read it no better than the batsman. Also we didn't show that killer instinct. We had the game won, and we relaxed rather than finishing them off. Aaqib tried to experiment with yorkers and slower balls, when he should have just been concentrating on bowling length balls.'

Australia had lost their second match in a row the previous night when they went down to the South Africans at Sydney, a result that again gave immense pleasure to the Pakistanis. However, England, Pakistan's next opponents, defeated the West Indians in imposing fashion at Melbourne that night, showing that they, along with New Zealand who had also won two on the trot, were the form teams of the tournament. 'England are going to be very tough to beat,' said Wasim, adding prophetically that, 'a lot will depend on the wicket. The Adelaide pitch used to be ideal for batting, but it's been relaid recently, so anything could happen.'

16

The World Cup: And The Rains Came

Adelaide is the most conservative of Australia's mainland state capitals with its many churches and the heavy stone architecture of the early colonists dominating the city centre. Even so, it still came as a rude awakening after Hobart, for the Pakistan team were staying in a hotel on Hindley Street, the city's epicentre for nightlife, which reverberates around the clock to the sound of discos and all night bars.

The match against England provided the opportunity for those of the team who had played county cricket to see familiar faces. Salim Malik met up with Graham Gooch and Derek Pringle, and Aaqib with Robin Smith. For Wasim it was a mixed blessing, because Bob Bennett, the Lancashire manager was now England's manager. It could have been a sticky moment for both parties, but it passed without incident. 'He said hello to me,' said Wasim, 'and I said hello back. We were both polite to one another, but there was no big rapprochement..'

Much happier was Wasim's reacquaintance with Neil Fairbrother and Phillip DeFreitas, his Lancashire team mates.

'I spend more time each year with the Lancashire boys than I do with the Pakistan guys,' said Wasim, 'and so in many ways I know a few of them better than I do some of the Pakistanis. When I go out with some of the younger Pakistan players, I sometimes have to watch what I say because I'm a senior team member and I have to be careful to set a good example. I think it is very important for the senior players to socialize with the young players, because I remember what it was like to be ignored when I was a newcomer to the team. All the younger players want to feel valued, and they won't feel like that unless the older players make time to talk to them and help them to feel comfortable within the team. However, when I go out with someone like Harvey, as here in Adelaide, I can totally relax and be myself, because we know that we are both equals.'

The Adelaide Oval has a timeless quality, and is the most English of the Australian grounds. It is steeped in tradition, and portraits of Don Bradman, Vic Richardson, Clarrie Grimmett, the Chappell brothers, and many other greats of South Australian cricket adorn the Members' Area. From the back of the pavilion, with ivy growing up the brickwork, the tennis courts nearby, and the tables and chairs laid out for afternoon tea, you could almost be at Wimbledon. The ground itself is only half enclosed, and the scoreboard, with the cathedral in the background, is almost worth the entrance fee alone. The gently sloping grass banks of the open sections make an ideal spot to park a deckchair and have a picnic, whilst watching the game; except when it's raining.

It hadn't rained in Adelaide for over three months, and so when rain interrupted net practice on the morning before the game, it was generally assumed to be little more than a passing shower. Instead, the rain grew steadily heavier and by tea-time, a full scale storm was in progress. The pitch had remained sweating under covers in the hot, wet atmosphere for all but half an hour that day, and the wicket was almost bound to favour seam bowling.

The morning of Sunday 1 March was warm and sunny, but the weather was far from settled as the two captains, Graham Gooch and Javed Miandad went out to the middle for the toss. Imran had exacerbated his shoulder whilst practising and had decided against playing, which meant a return for Ijaz, whilst the young medium pacer Wasim Haider replaced Iqbal Sikander. For England, there was only one change to the side that had beaten the West Indies, with Gladstone Small coming in for Phil Tufnell, and with Allan Lamb still unfit and unavailable for selection.

Graham Gooch won the toss and had no hesitation in putting the Pakistanis into bat. Within minutes Pakistan were in all kinds of trouble, as the ball moved around alarmingly. Rameez played a tame shot to Reeve at point off DeFreitas, and the next ball Inzamam received the ball of the day which was brilliantly caught by Alec Stewart behind the stumps on the rebound, after Hick had initially fumbled the chance at slip. Miandad chopped on to Pringle, who then picked up an astonishing caught and bowled, when Aamir Sohail attempted a flat-batted pull to a ball that was slightly slower and shorter than he expected. Ijaz was caught behind, Wasim played on, and Malik, seemingly undecided as to whether he should play safe or get whatever runs he could, edged to slip.

After Moin had departed in similar fashion it was left to Mushtaq and Wasim Haider to shore up the innings. They didn't put on that many runs, but in the light of later events, the time they spent at the wicket together was critical. When Haider fell to another good Stewart catch, Mushtaq and Aaqib held up England for a few more minutes. Not that Aaqib would be able to say how; Dermot Reeve managed to bowl an entire over that beat his outside edge. Pakistan were eventually all out for 74 in the 41st over. It was their lowest ever score in a one-day game, and the lowest ever by a Test playing country in the World Cup.

'It was an appalling wicket for a one-day game,' said Wasim, 'but even so none of our team showed the right attitude. It was as if they all gave up when we lost the toss and had to bat first. Even if it's not a fair wicket, you still have to get on with it, and battle it out. We should have made up our minds right from the start that 150 would have been a good score, and batted cautiously to make certain we got that many. I played a stupid shot; on a seaming wicket you should always play straight, but I tried to play across the line to a slower ball.'

There was time for Pakistan to bowl a few overs before lunch, and clearly Wasim and Aaqib would be a difficult proposition on that wicket, though as Gooch conceded, 'Once you've got a side out cheaply you hold the psychological advantage, and you should make the runs.' In a hostile 6 over spell Pakistan picked up just the 1 wicket, when Wasim got a ball through Gooch's defence to have him caught behind, and England went into the interval at 17–1.

Rain began to fall during the lunch break. At first it was an almost imperceptibly fine drizzle, but it gradually gathered in intensity, and as it dawned on everyone that the weather was set in, the despondency in the Pakistani dressing-room began to give way to smiles. When it was still raining some two and a half hours later, it seemed a foregone conclusion that the game would be abandoned, regardless of whether it stopped raining or not; the outfield was saturated, and the bowlers' run ups had been left largely uncovered, since, because it so seldom rains in Adelaide, the covering for the wicket was less than extensive.

The rain stopped at 4.45 and the two umpires Bucknoor and McConnell declared the pitch fit for play to restart immediately. One could understand the umpire's anxiety to get a finish to a game in which one side so clearly held the upper hand, but it was hard to imagine that the ground could have been fit so soon after so much rain. Wasim had another point of view. 'There were about 7,500 people in the ground, and only about 50 of them were supporting Pakistan. I'm not convinced that everyone would have been quite so keen to get on with it if the positions were reversed. It was a sensitive situation for the umpires, and I'm sure they felt under pressure. Play had to end at 5.45pm regardless of the weather, and they had to be certain that they could squeeze another nine overs in to get a result.' Under the playing conditions no result could be declared unless both teams had batted for at least 15 overs.

At 4.55pm the players came out to finish the game. Under a new law brought in for the World Cup, England's revised target was 67 in 19 overs, or effectively 50 from 13. The new law stipulated that in a reduced over game the side batting second had to chase the total that the side batting first achieved in their most productive similar number of overs. The law had been introduced to redress the balance that had always favoured the side batting second, when such calculations were determined by run rate, but no one seemed to have given much thought to how it might work in practice. Instead of an asking rate of 1.48, England were now being asked to score at nearly 4 an over, a figure that was easily attainable, but by no means certain on an unpredictable wicket. What might have seemed a better system to decide rain-affected games in theory, was proving to give a far greater advantage to the side batting first, than the previous system ever gave to the side batting second.

As if to heighten the tension, no sooner had the players come out on to the field, than the rain came again to halt the proceedings. At 5.12pm a final attempt was made to resolve the game with England chasing a revised target of 64 off 16 overs, but after 2 overs had been completed with England advancing their score by 6, the heavens opened for the final time, and the game was abandoned, with both teams awarded a point each.

It was a bitter disappointment for England, who could justifiably look on the game as a point lost rather than a point won, but the match did serve as a harsh reminder to the organizers that the rules for the competition were poorly considered, and unfair to players and spectators alike. After the game, Graham Gooch appeared bemused by the turn of events. 'What took place today takes some understanding. It seems strange that when you bowl a side out for 74, you end up having to chase 60. I suppose it doesn't matter in the end though, because the rain beat us anyway.'

Perhaps, even, in some ways justice was done. The wicket was wholly unsuitable for a one-day game. Graham Gooch found it hard to remember any one-day wicket apart from one at Headingley that had so favoured the bowlers, and it is not improbable that had Pakistan bowled first it would have been England who welcomed the rain. A Pakistan side that was playing with little confidence and way below its potential would have been hard pushed to beat an in-form England even on a fair wicket, but it did not deserve to lose to what amounted to a toss of the coin.

While confusion was reigning in Adelaide, a similar debacle

was unfolding in Brisbane. India had already suffered once at the hands of the weather in the tournament, when their match against Sri Lanka which was scheduled to take place in Mackay, North Queensland, was abandoned with just two balls bowled, but this time the consequences were even more severe. Rain interrupted India's pursuit of Australia's 237, and their target was reduced by only 3 runs with a loss of a similar number of overs. In the event, India lost a game they would have won easily by just one run.

Three points from three games was hardly the start that Pakistan would have wanted at the beginning of the tournament. But with New Zealand and England continuing, weather permitting, to beat all comers, and with the rest of the teams highly inconsistent, and producing convenient results, Pakistan found itself in fourth place in the qualifying table, even given its current state of dishevelment.

Wasim wasn't fooled by Pakistan's position in the table, but he remained optimistic. 'I still think we're going to qualify for the semis. At this stage I would back England, New Zealand, West Indies and Pakistan to get through, but we've got to start getting our act together. I think a lot of our players have this attitude that, because a lot of our domestic cricket is so bad, if they can get into the team and perform for three or four games then they are in the side for good, and that they can do whatever they want. This has got to change. Our next two games, against India and South Africa, are vital. We must win both these to have a chance.'

A day–night game in Sydney was the venue for the encounter with India. Sydney is the most beautiful modern city in the southern hemisphere, and perhaps in the world. The bridge and opera house take centre stage, but the harbour itself creates a myriad of inlets and beaches, every one of which has something to recommend it. With its climate and sense of freedom, it's almost like being on the West Coast of America, except there isn't a self-satisfied and self-obsessed population to go with it. In such an attractive city, it was unfortunate that the team were staying in a hotel, albeit with every amenity on the inside, that was cunningly disguised as a building site from the outside.

There was plenty for Wasim to worry about, without having to contend with the sort of distractions that a visit to Sydney brings. 'Imran, Malik, Rameez, Aaqib, and myself, had to attend a lunch at the Pakistan Embassy,' he said. 'I hate that kind of function where you have to dress up, and talk to people who all ask you the same questions about cricket. Normally, the players end up talking to each other, and that's exactly what happened here.'

'I'm still concerned about my bowling. The white ball does create problems, and I'm bowling a lot of wides. It's not just me; look at Allan Donald. Two years ago I'd bowl a couple of overs at half to three-quarters pace to start with, but because it's the World Cup, and we don't have Waqar, I'm running in hard from the word go, to try and get a breakthrough. I don't know whether I should try that again or not. At the moment my rhythm is upset, because I'm worried about bowling wides.'

Any Pakistan v India game has an extra edge, and for a World Cup game even more so. Certainly the players were feeling the pressure, and the net sessions and fielding practices were undertaken with extra effort, although the side was still far from looking a finely-tuned unit. For the first time Imran sat his players down at the ground in a semi-circle in an attempt to foster those missing elements of cohesion and will to win.

Playing under lights brings problems of its own, and is very different from the ordinary game, as Wasim explained. 'If you're not used to the lights, it's undoubtedly a benefit to bat first. The ball tends to swing more when the night mist comes across the ground, and the wicket gets a little damp which makes the ball skid. The only disadvantage to the fielding side is that high catches coming out of the lights can be difficult to pick up.'

Pakistan went into the India game with a catalogue of injuries. Rameez had again damaged his shoulder which had twice been dislocated previously, Javed Miandad had been struck down with a stomach bug which had caused him to pass blood, and Imran had still not recovered from his shoulder injury, but had decided that for such a crucial game he would play with the aid of a pain-killing injection.

The Members' and Ladies' pavilions, with their distinctive green corrugated iron roofs, are all that remain of the original Sydney Cricket ground, now that the last remaining grass areas of the Hill has given way to seating, but for all that the SCG still has an atmosphere that is unique. Sydney has a large Asian community, and a crowd of over 10,000, making enough noise for double that, saw Pakistan denied the opportunity to bat first, as they lost the toss for the fourth game in a row. Wasim ran in hard, but without much luck. In his first over, he almost cut Jadeja in half with a ball that nipped back over the stumps, and with his next delivery Jadeja fine-glanced perilously close to the keeper. Srikkanth edged a simpler chance to Moin in Wasim's second over, but the chance was again missed though this was not to prove costly, as he soon fell caught behind off Aaqib.

Thereafter the scoring progressed quite freely until Jadeja fell to a smart catch at square leg off Wasim Haider, and Azharuddin was taken behind the stumps off Mushtaq. Kambli played an entertaining knock of 24, and Tendulkar and Kapil Dev both timed the ball well, but neither played the decisive innings that could have taken the game away from Pakistan. Kapil holed out to Imran off Aaqib, and Wasim ran out More with a brilliant piece of fielding off his own bowling, as India reached a final total of 216-7, off the 49 overs that Pakistan managed to bowl in the time allowed.

It was a score that should have been well within Pakistan's grasp. They made their usual shaky start; Inzamam, being asked to play out of position and open in Rameez's absence, looked at odds with the moving ball and was trapped in front of his stumps for 2, and Zahid Fazal, who had been unable to come to terms with the bounce of Australian pitches after such a successful season in Pakistan was soon caught behind. Out of such unpromising beginnings, a partnership developed between Aamir Sohail and Javed that seemed to have settled the game. Sohail had been one of the successes of the tour; he is a very self-possessed left-hander, who takes his batting very seriously, and is not afraid to take the bowlers on early in his innings. It was Sohail who dominated the scoring in the partnership of 88, but when he departed for 62, the rot set in.

Batting in the middle order is a different proposition in a one-day game, when you're out of form, as Wasim describes. 'Most of our middle order simply hasn't had any practice in match conditions on this tour. When you're just playing one-day games the first four batsmen get the majority of the time at the crease, and if the next three batsmen are needed it invariably means there is some pressure. Either the top order has failed and we have to rebuild the innings, or else we're chasing quick runs and we have to slog. Either way, it's not the ideal way to have to find one's form.'

'Against India, Salim Malik decided to try and hit his way back into form against Prabhakar, which wasn't the most intelligent thing to do, as Prabhakar had been brought on specifically to get rid of him; Imran hesitated over a single and was run out, I tried a stupid shot against Raju and was stumped, and we collapsed to 173 all out. It was a big disappointment; we should have been able to get the runs. Even though we were behind the asking rate, 6 an over is nothing at the end of the innings.'

Imran retained his customary up-beat line in optimism after the game, insisting that the Pakistan performance had not been that bad, and that he was still confident of qualifying for the semis, but his face was beginning to show the tell-tale signs of stress so familiar to losing captains.

Failure is not tolerated lightly in Pakistan, and the knives were already being sharpened in the press and media for the team's return, and so it was a depressed Pakistan side that left Sydney the next day. Even losing to India assumed less importance in the face of the wider consequences to Pakistan's World Cup hopes. In fact the only solace to be gained was that many of their rivals for a semi-final spot were playing as indifferently as they were, and results elsewhere were continuing to go in their favour, as South Africa lost to Sri Lanka, and Australia to England.

Thanks to the tourist boom along the Queensland coast, Brisbane has blossomed into Australia's third largest city, but the Gabba, Brisbane's cricket ground, still has the slightly country feel of the city of ten years ago. It looks as though it was either built without reference to an architect, or with the help of too many, and there aren't that many Test match grounds that have a dog track around the perimeter of the oval.

The Gabba was the scene for the match between Pakistan and South Africa, a game that was vital to both teams' chances, as it was generally felt by players and pundits alike that whoever lost might as well pack their bags for home. It had become axiomatic in this competition that, if there was the slightest hint of rain, whichever team won the toss batted first regardless of what it might have planned, because the rule-book penalised the side batting second so heavily. Under these circumstances it was surprising that Imran elected to field first.

It was a decision that mystified Wasim. 'The weather was very unsettled, and so I asked the captain and coach if they had consulted a weather forecast. They said they had, and that it was clear. I thought it would rain, and so did most of the other players; the reception desk at the hotel had even told me it would rain.'

The South African innings was a curious affair. They only achieved the very modest total of 211, but of that score at least 30 were donated by the generosity of the Pakistani fielding. 'I don't really know what happened,' said Wasim. 'Our nerve just seemed to go. The game wasn't running away from us, but we just panicked. No one bowled really badly; I didn't bowl that well to start with, but I came back OK to take a couple of late wickets. But our fielding was worse than that of a schoolboy team. There were a couple of showers, and the ball got damp, but that's no real excuse. We dropped catches, let the ball go through our legs, and forgot to back up; it was just pathetic.'

Even so 212 was an easily attainable target. Aamir Sohail

and Zahid Fazal, aided by some wayward bowling from Allan Donald, put on 50 for the first wicket before they both fell at that figure. All afternoon the rain clouds had been gathering, and when Sohail and Fazal were dismissed it seemed as though they were caught in two minds as to whether they should slog to increase the run rate, or to play a normal innings. Inzamam and Imran upped the tempo slightly as they realized that rain was inevitable, but with the score at 74–2 in the 22nd over the downpour arrived.

The Gabba has an excellent drainage system, but even so, play was held up for more than an hour. 14 overs were lost, but Pakistan's target was only reduced by 18, and they were required to score another 120 in 14.3 overs at a rate of 8.64 to win the game. For a while it seemed as though Pakistan might achieve the impossible as Inzamam blazed away with solid support from Imran. However, when Inzamam was superbly run out by Jonty Rhodes, and Imran was caught behind off McMillan in the same over, the match was effectively lost. Malik, Wasim, and Ijaz, with no time to play themselves in, all fell trying to hit out, and the Pakistan innings closed 20 runs short of the revised total.

The weather and the rules had wrecked another game, and Wasim was inconsolable afterwards. 'I know we didn't play very well, but 212 was always getable; when the rain came I felt we were walking it. We may have got a point we otherwise wouldn't have done in Adelaide, but we've lost two today, and it's as good as put an end to our World Cup hopes.'

Kepler Wessels, the South African Captain, was gracious enough to admit that his side was fortunate. 'I didn't think we had made enough runs in our innings,' he said. 'It became a completely different game when the rain came, and it was undoubtedly to our advantage.' The two points that South

Africa gained kept them well on course for a semi-final berth, but for Pakistan only the prospect of three meaningless games in Perth and Christchurch beckoned.

17

The World Cup: A Ray of Sunshine

An outside mathematical chance, as much dependent on other teams producing favourable results as on Pakistan winning their last three games, was all that remained for Pakistan to reach the semi-finals, but most of the players weren't even aware of this, as the team flew west to Perth for matches against Australia and Sri Lanka. Indeed most team members were so fed up, that they would have far rather hijacked the aircraft home to Lahore than spend the week in Perth.

For Wasim, this highlighted part of what had gone wrong with the Pakistan side. 'Sometimes you have to just play for your own pride and self-respect. Even when the team is out of the running, you have to turn up and do your best. You have to look inside yourself for your motivation, when there are no outside reasons to go on. Some of the team seem to have lost that battling, aggressive attitude, and are almost resigned to defeat. Performing well in a World Cup should be all the driving force that anyone needs, but anyway, in this case, we do still have a chance, however remote. Some of the younger players don't seem capable of working this out for themselves.

'I think there's a big communication problem in the team at the moment. For instance, Imran was talking to me about how we still had a chance, and all the youngsters hung back, but after he had left they were asking me what he had said. It seemed to come as a complete surprise to them to discover that we could still possibly make it.

'It's as if the team is scared of Imran. We have team meetings, and everyone's invited to say what they feel, but no one says anything. Imran has been unapproachable on this tour; usually he's with the boys a lot of the time, but for some reason he's withdrawn, and spending a lot of time on his own. I think it must be because he's under a lot of pressure; the team isn't playing well, and he's concerned about his own form and fitness, but it feels as though he's passing the pressure on to the players rather than absorbing it himself as he used to.

'Injuries and results haven't been going our way, but what we desperately need is a settled side. At the moment, we are changing the team and the strategy for almost every game as we look for a winning combination, and it's hard for a player to perform at his best if he doesn't know what is going on. How can you prepare yourself if you don't know whether you are going to be batting at number 3 or number 5? Likewise, we should be trying to build up each other's confidence, but people are shouting at each other. I know I've lost form with my batting, but it doesn't help when others openly lose faith in you as well. In Sharjah recently, I was all set to go in when Malik was out and India had two left-arm spinners bowling, and the captain said, "No Waz, you shouldn't go in now because you're out of form." What sort of thing is that to say to someone who's about to go out to bat? It's important to me that at least the captain should have faith in me.'

Wasim was also critical of the Pakistan set-up. 'The game

against South Africa was vital, and yet our net sessions were hopeless. We didn't even have any balls to practice with, apart from a few old ones that had gone soft. The Manager told us that the new balls were very expensive at $43 each, and that we couldn't afford to replace them that often. How can you run an international team like that? The Pakistan Board can't be so broke that it can't afford a few cricket balls. Also, our batsmen aren't getting the right practice. By the time Inzy batted in the nets, there were only Moin and Inti bowling at him, which is hardly the way to prepare for Allan Donald. We are just so amateurish. Look at England: Micky Stewart goes out of his way to find good local bowlers to give the batsmen practice, and he pays them by giving them match tickets. That's what we should be doing.

'Our Board is so tight with money that we have a manager but no coach. England has Bob Bennett and Micky Stewart, South Africa has Alan Jordaan and Mike Procter; in fact, it's only India, West Indies, and ourselves that don't have a coach. It means that we don't really have anyone running our net sessions. A coach is so important when things are going wrong, because he can rebuild your confidence and can point out errors in technique. As it is, we often don't even know when our net sessions are going to happen. The Manager might tell us the night before that we will be practising at 10am, but it doesn't mean that much, as we are just as likely to get another call saying that practice will be at 12pm. It's all so haphazard, and it's not the way to prepare for any game, let alone the World Cup.'

Pakistan were now in a situation where every game amounted to a final; if they lost, they were out of the tournament, but even if they won the remaining three games there was no guarantee of qualifying. Australia, Pakistan's next opponents, found themselves in a very similar position. Both teams had been widely fancied before the start of the competition, but now the round-robin nature of the tournament ensured that one team would almost certainly be eliminated.

The tension in both teams was self-evident as they practised at the WACA, Perth's cricket ground, the day before the game. Perth used to be something of a backwater in cricket terms, separated by the Nullarbor Plain from the nearest Test centre in Adelaide. However the exploits of Lillee and Marsh, among others, for Western Australia helped put the city on the map, and the WACA became a regular Test match venue in the early seventies. It is one of the fastest wickets in the world, and understandably Wasim was one of Allan Border's main concerns. 'He's as good as any fast bowler going around. When he hits his straps he's a real handful. If Pakistan had had Waqar Younis to bowl with him from the start of the tournament, I'm sure they would have gone all the way.'

Imran was quite clear about the terms of the contest. 'The side that wins will be the side who can best survive the pressure,' he said. 'It's hard not to feel the pressure; for me the pressure hasn't mounted as the tournament progressed, I've felt it throughout.' However, while Australia still seemed confused about what their best team was, with Allan Border and Bobby Simpson, the coach apparently in disagreement, Pakistan had a team meeting which helped to clear the air, and rekindled that missing spark. 'Everyone was more forthcoming,' said Wasim. 'Malik and myself told the captain that we thought he wasn't with the team as much as in the past, and he acknowledged that.' Such openness received a quick and public declaration of faith in Wasim's abilities by Imran. 'A lot of the time Wasim has been more worried about controlling the white ball, than with getting people out. From now on I want him to fire in from the word go, and not worry about no balls and wides.'

The Pakistan v Australia game was a day/night match, and with the evening mist from the nearby Swan river swirling in after dark making the ball liable to swing, the toss would be all important. Fortunately for Pakistan, Imran called correctly and as a matter of course decided to bat. The pitch allowed some movement for the bowlers, and although it had some bounce, it wasn't as quick as some WACA wickets, and Sohail and Rameez found it very much to their liking as they raced along at nearly 4 an over, until Rameez was caught at short mid-wicket for 34 off the bowling of Mike Whitney. Almost immediately a second wicket fell when Salim Malik, elevated to number 3 for the first time in the tournament, and on a pitch that was the least suitable for such a promotion, was bowled for 0 as he drove over the top of a full length ball from Tom Moody.

For a while the innings lost momentum, as Sohail and Javed sought to restore order, but gradually they began to dominate. Javed had made runs throughout the tournament without ever having found his best form. Here he battled for singles, settling for only the odd boundary shot, and was content to play a supporting role as Aamir Sohail carried the attack to the Australians. When Sohail was caught by Healy, top-edging a pull for 76, Pakistan were 157-3 with 13 overs to go, and poised for a total in excess of 250.

Some credit must go to the Australians, in particular Steve Waugh who bowled a tight containing spell, for restricting Pakistan to 220, but the main reason for such a poor total was that the batting completely lost its way. Imran stayed in for 8 overs but could only make 13, including one huge six into the members' pavilion, Ijaz was run out for 0 attempting a suicidal single off a dropped catch, Wasim went first ball as he failed to pick a slower ball, Inzamam was deemed to be run out, and it was left to Moin and Mushtaq to scrape together what runs they could in the final over.

The moisture in the air was visible from the stands as Wasim and Aaqib opened the bowling for Pakistan. They both ran in hard, and there was significantly more movement than there had been earlier in the day. Aaqib began to get his outswinger working perfectly, and with the first ball of his third over found the edge of Moody's bat, and Malik took a good low catch at first slip. Shortly afterwards Wasim was certain he had Boon caught down the leg side. 'It was a definite nick, and the ball didn't go near his pad, but the umpire gave it not out,' he said. Aamir Sohail found the decision so unbelievable that he appealed twice, a course of action that was reported by the umpire, and earned Sohail a $250 fine for dissent. In the event, the decision was not costly for Pakistan, for in the tenth over Aaqib again found the outside edge, and Mushtaq picked up the catch at third slip. It was just reward for a fine spell of bowling, and for the attacking captaincy of Imran for posting three slips, and Australia were in trouble at 31–2.

Thereafter, Marsh and Jones consolidated the innings. Marsh, as ever, was laborious in his stroke play, but Jones was in good touch, and his running between the wickets was in a class of its own. Together they had added 82, and things were beginning to look ominous for Pakistan when Jones tried to hit Mushtaq over the top. 'It was a terrible moment waiting for Aaqib to catch the ball,' said Wasim. 'We knew that Jones was the key wicket, and Aaqib isn't the best catcher in the side. Everyone was praying, "Don't drop it Aaqib." When he took the catch, I felt quite confident that we would win, because the pressure was now back on them.'

From then on the innings self-immolated. Marsh edged Imran to Moin, Border flicked a Mushtaq leg-break to Ijaz at square-leg, Steven Waugh was well taken by Moin down the leg side, and Healy pulled Aaqib to deep mid-wicket where Ijaz took another fine catch. Wasim returned to trap McDermott leg before for 0, and Mark Waugh became the third batsman to hole out to Ijaz on the leg side.

A sour note was introduced before the end when Mushtaq clearly had Mike Whitney caught behind, and the decision was not given. In the ensuing contretemps, Moin and Whitney had words with one another, and Whitney struck the keeper with a back hander. Both players were later fined $250, but the Pakistan side was very upset that Whitney later spoke to the press, alleging that Moin had called him a cheat. 'Considering that the Australians had been abusing us throughout the game, it was just too much,' said Moin. 'Besides, it didn't happen like that. I was appealing, and couldn't believe the decision hadn't been given. Whitney turned round and asked me why I was appealing. I said that he had nicked it and was out, and he then called me a cheat. After that, I certainly told him that it wasn't me, but him, that was cheating.'

Again it wasn't a crucial decision, because in the next over Wasim beat Whitney for pace, causing him to play on, and Australia were all out for 172, leaving Pakistan easy winners by a margin of 48 runs. For Pakistan, victory still left them with a ghost of a chance, but more importantly it was the first step in the rediscovery of their self-belief and self-respect.

Unbelievably, Australia still had in theory a glimmer of a chance, albeit an even smaller one than Pakistan, but after the game Allan Border conceded that it was almost inevitably the end of the road for his team. 'I think that's it. I don't think there's any chance we can get through now,' he said. It was a sad end to the season for Allan Border; on paper the Australian side was one of the strongest in the competition and should have been good enough for at least a semi-final spot, but it couldn't deliver the goods when it mattered. Ironically, in the end the Australians were probably undone by the greed of the TV companies and their own Board in the end, having played the World Cup at the end of a season that had included five Test matches, a triangular World Series against the West Indies and India, as well as a full Sheffield Shield programme. 'I get the feeling that we've just played too much cricket,' said Border. 'I don't want to make excuses when we've played badly, but there's been a flatness in our preparation, and everyone's a little bit jaded. There was no respite after a long hard season, and we didn't go into the World Cup full of beans.'

There were three free days for Pakistan before the Sri Lanka game, and for the first time on tour the players began to unwind. It was as though the pressure had temporarily evaporated, and smiles began to cross faces that had only previously appeared hunted. Spirits were further lifted as other results continued to work in their favour. On the day after the Pakistan and Australia game New Zealand maintained their winning ways and eliminated India from the competition in the process.

On the same day in Melbourne, England took on South Africa in a game which had Wasim glued to the TV set. 'England hadn't bowled that well, but they were cruising it when Stewart and Botham were going so well,' said Wasim. 'Then it started raining, and not only did they have to score at a ridiculous rate, but the ball began to bounce and swing as well. The rain rule is so stupid, and it's ruining the tournament. It was only some wonderful batting by Stewart, Harvey, and Lewis, that saw England through. England are suffering with injuries, but if they can play as professionally as that, they must be favourites for the cup.'

South Africa's defeat ensured that there were still two semi-final places up for grabs, as Pakistan continued their mixture of practice and relaxation. Unexpected rain interrupted nets the day before the game, and with the forecast for the following day predicting further showers, there was a real danger of another contrived result. All this, though, was academic to Sri Lanka who had been knocked out of the running by the West Indies the previous day in Berri, and who, because of the demands of their itinerary, would arrive in Perth too late to even fit in one training session at the ground.

Mercifully, the weather held on the Sunday and the match was played through to a fair conclusion. All the indications were that Pakistan would sweep to a convincing victory over a demoralized side that had nothing to play for, but instead crept to an unsteady 4 wicket last over win. Gone was the slickness in the field, and the aggression of the early order batsmen that had characterized the Australia game, and back came the tentativeness that had marked their earlier games, and it was hard to know whether to put this down to over-confidence or an attack of nerves.

Sri Lanka won the toss and batted. Wasim removed Mahanama, the danger man, early on with an unswinging yorker, and soon after Mushtaq clean bowled Hathurusinghe, but Pakistan never looked like running through the Sri Lankans cheaply. It was almost a repeat of the South African innings, in that catches were dropped, and overthrows conceded, but even with that help the Sri Lankans only compiled 212.

'We were determined to try and play positively,' said Wasim, 'but some of our snappiness was missing. In our side, you have to be strict with the players, and remind them to back up, because the standard of fielding in Pakistan cricket is not that high. I think we were lucky in that Sri Lanka had no strategy for their innings; they never worked out what was a good score on that wicket, and they let things drift. Against their mediocre medium pace attack we always fancied getting the runs.'

On such a good one-day wicket the target should have presented no problems, but Pakistan made heavy weather getting there. When Sohail was out early on slicing Rama-nayake to gully, there was little aggression shown, and the innings crawled along, with Imran, who had come in at the fall of the first wicket, remaining runless for long periods of time. Rameez skied a catch just as he was beginning to get going, and when Imran was third out with the score on 84, Pakistan were in a spot of trouble and significantly behind the run rate.

Fortunately, Salim Malik chose this moment to find some form, and together with Javed Miandad he took Pakistan to within sight of victory. It wasn't a partnership of great strokeplay, but the way they systematically made inroads into the target and the run rate, without ever appearing to rush, was professionalism of the highest order. There was still time for a mini collapse at the end, when Javed, Malik, and Inzamam, were out in quick succession, but Ijaz and Wasim kept their heads, and Ijaz finished the match with a straight driven four off the first ball of the last over.

It was far from an impressive victory, but they had survived another game, and were still in the competition. Indeed there was even some comfort in the knowledge that they could still win, even when playing badly. Elsewhere, the news was not quite so good. South Africa had defeated India in yet another rain-affected game, and had secured the third semi-final spot. The final place would be decided by the last two qualifying games of the tournament. If Pakistan were to reach the semi-finals they would have to become the first team to beat New Zealand, and they would have to rely on Australia defeating the West Indies in Melbourne.

18

World Champions At Last

After thirty-three League games, with only three still to be played, there was an astonishingly wide variety of permutations to determine who would meet whom and where in the semis. New Zealand had already qualified by finishing top of the round-robin tournament, and were due to meet whoever finished fourth. England had qualified in second place and would play whoever finished third. South Africa had qualified, but whether it was in third or fourth place would only be determined after the last round of matches. The last place was to be decided on Wednesday 18 March between Pakistan, Australia, and the West Indies. If the West Indies beat Australia then they would qualify in third place, and New Zealand would meet South Africa in the semis; if Pakistan beat New Zealand, and Australia defeated West Indies, then Pakistan would qualify in fourth place; and if Pakistan lost, and Australia beat the West Indies by more than 33 runs, then they would qualify in fourth place. If either Pakistan or West Indies qualified then New Zealand's semi would be played at Auckland, but thanks to another arcane piece of World Cup legislation, if Australia qualified then it would receive home advantage in Sydney, regardless of having qualified in last place.

New Zealand had confounded the predictions of the experts, and indeed of their most loyal supporters, by remaining the only unbeaten side in the competition after seven matches, having crushed a jaded and injury-hit England in their previous game. New Zealand had had the advantage of playing all their games at home on slow, lifeless wickets, but even so, under the captaincy of Martin Crowe, they had played some inspired and imaginative cricket. Crowe himself had led from the front with his batting, which was to win him the award for the player of the tournament, and the Kiwi renaissance had thrown up some unlikely heroes in the shape of Mark Greatbatch, Dipak Patel, Chris Harris, and Gavin Larsen, from whom little had been expected.

A full day's travelling through four time zones, from Perth on Australia's west coast to Christchurch on the east coast of the south island of New Zealand, with only one free day to practise and recover, was far from the ideal way to prepare to meet the form team of the competition for one of the most important one-day games in Pakistan's history. 'We're all shattered, but there's nothing we can do about it so we've got to put up with it,' said Wasim as he arrived in Christchurch at midnight two days before the game. 'It's another absurd piece of scheduling, but I guess that nobody ever imagined that this would be a critical game, and thought that it wouldn't matter too much if we were tired.'

Much play was being made in the New Zealand media of how the only way the Kiwis could ensure a home semi-final was by deliberately losing to Pakistan, and thereby eliminating Australia. Even allowing for the antipathy between the

Aussies and the New Zealanders, for whom the Trevor Chappell underarm delivery is still not forgotten, this was an extremely fanciful notion, and one that Wasim was quick to dismiss. 'No one would throw a game. The New Zealanders have got into a winning rhythm and they won't want to disrupt it. Besides, if they did lose to us, they would have a 50–50 chance of meeting us in the semis, and they wouldn't want to give us that psychological edge. In any case, the Kiwis have a point to prove against us; when we last played them we hammered them in the Tests and the one-day games, and Imran refused to play against them because so many of their best players didn't tour.'

Christchurch could almost be a film set for an American black-and-white film about England in the post-war years. There is the cathedral, the river Avon, friendly helmeted policemen, and fifteen-year-old schoolboys in blazers and shorts. However, as in so many seemingly ideal locations, there is a darker undercurrent of passion that can go unnoticed. Only the previous week a long standing history of child abuse had been discovered in one of the city's day care centres.

Lancaster Park, Christchurch's cricket ground, is situated to the south of the city, and like all New Zealand's Test grounds, except for the Basin Reserve in Wellington, it doubles as a rugby ground in winter. However, unlike most New Zealand grounds, the pitch is quite quick and has a fair amount of bounce. Wasim was looking forward to bowling on it. 'The wicket should be ideal for me, and I'm feeling more confident than at any time on tour. Viv Richards suggested to me in Perth that if I was getting too much movement early on, and was bowling too many wides, then I should immediately bowl from around the wicket. I think that was good advice; I feel that in the earlier games I have delayed doing that for a couple of overs and in the process have got frustrated about being erratic.'

There was a cold antarctic wind, and yet again there was rain in the air, with more forecast, as the Pakistan side gathered at Lancaster Park for practice, the day before the game. The training was now suffused with an infectious air of enthusiasm that had been absent earlier in the tour, and even Imran, who had previously always left net practice to get treatment for his shoulder, stayed behind to bowl. It was as though the team had found unity in having survived the despair of Brisbane, and now believed that they were destined to win the competition.

'I know I've said it before, but it's just like the Nehru Cup and Sharjah, and I'm sure the end result will be the same,' said Wasim. 'We've just begun to click, and the players have started to enjoy being with each other, and to do things for one another. For instance, a few of us, including myself, find inspiration in the music of Nusrat Sateh Ali Khan, who sings Qawali (religious utterances) to a background of a mixture of eastern and western music. So we decided to take a tape recorder with us and listen to the music in the coach and in the dressing-room. We all sing along, and it's a wonderful way of unifying the team. Likewise here in Christchurch most of us went to the local go-kart track after practice, and spent the afternoon racing each other. We all spent a lot of money, but apart from the fact that it was good fun and very relaxing, the important thing is that we were together.'

Much to everyone's surprise the morning of March 18 brought clear skies, though the snow-capped peaks of the southern alps to the east of the ground and the bitingly cold wind lent an appropriately autumnal flavour to the proceedings. With the prospect of an uninterrupted day's cricket, Pakistan put New Zealand into bat. 'At the team meeting the day before, we had decided that this would be our best chance,' said Wasim. 'New Zealand had looked strongest when they were chasing a target, so we wanted to throw them off their stride. We had also decided to take a leaf out of Martin Crowe's book and get Mushtaq on early. Greatbatch had been in superb form against the quickies and the medium pacers, but we felt that he wouldn't have a clue against leg-spin.'

Pakistan got off to the worst possible start. After Wasim had bowled the first over for just one run, Greatbatch laid into Aaqib with great effect, taking two fours and a six over wide mid-wicket in his first over, and after just two overs New Zealand had raced to 17–0. Despite his age, Aaqib is a seasoned campaigner, and to his credit he kept his line and length and was rewarded with the wicket of Rod Latham who touched an outswinger to Inzamam at slip in his next over.

The very next ball Andrew Jones set off for a risky single to get off the mark and the television replay clearly showed that Greatbatch had failed to make his ground when Moin took the bails off. The decision went in New Zealand's favour, and earlier in the tour such a reversal might well have been the signal for heads to go down, but now was merely a spring-board for greater effort. Wasim was living up to his promise of charging in; he was still bowling a lot of wides, but he was also bowling some gems, and he was soon rewarded with 2 wickets. 'I knew that Jones and Martin Crowe were the key batsmen, and I was determined to get them out. Jones was leg before to an inswinging yorker that hit him full on the foot; I could see that Crowe was having problems picking the same delivery so I decided to work on this. One attempted yorker ended up as a leg stump half-volley and he just flicked it to Aamir at square-leg.'

Greatbatch and Ken Rutherford revived the innings, though not without a considerable amount of good fortune. As the Pakistanis had anticipated, Greatbatch could not pick Mushtaq and had resorted to trying to sweep his way out of trouble, and Rutherford had been dropped behind the wicket off Imran. Just when it seemed that the threatened break-through would never come, Wasim and Moin combined to dismiss Rutherford. Rutherford had been struggling to get Mushtaq away, and when he nudged a ball wide of Wasim at cover he set off for a sharp single. By the time he realized that the run was never on, Wasim had rifled the ball back to the keeper, who completed a brilliant piece of fielding by taking the return on the half-volley and breaking the stumps with Rutherford still short of the crease.

The fall of this wicket opened the floodgates for Pakistan. Harris was completely baffled by Mushtaq and was stumped, Greatbatch top-edged a sweep to Malik, Ian Smith was bowled by Imran, Patel hit Sohail to Mushtaq at point, and New Zealand were on the ropes at 106–8. However, sensible batting from Larsen, Morrison, and Watson carried the Kiwis through to a score of 166, with Wasim taking the final 2 wickets, to finish with figures of 9.2–0–32–4.

A total of 166, augmented by the usual Pakistani generosity of 42 extras, was substantially more than New Zealand had any right to expect at one point. Even so, it was never likely to be a challenging score on what was a reasonable batting track, and as Rameez and Sohail walked out to open the innings, the result appeared to be a foregone conclusion. The first ball of the innings put paid to that notion. Danny Morrison had been recalled to the New Zealand side and was determined to prove that he had the pace and aggression to spearhead the attack. His first delivery to Sohail was a bouncer which the batsman pulled to Patel at fine-leg and Pakistan were 0–1.

Sohail was furious. 'It was clearly a no-ball; I even played it deliberately uppishly because I thought there would be no risk. At first I had thought about leaving it, but then I said to myself, "Why waste the opportunity to get off the mark from a free hit?" I couldn't believe the square leg umpire didn't give it.' The Pakistani camp was just as angry. 'It probably wasn't the best shot to play first up,' said Wasim, 'but anyone could see the ball was over shoulder height. I don't know what Steve Randell was doing; I can only imagine that he wasn't concentrating properly. You could tell that Steve Bucknor at the bowler's end thought it was a no ball by the way he stared at Randell. Later on, both Inzamam and Javed received balls well above shoulder height that weren't called either. It's ridiculous – a batsman has got to know where he stands, but in this game it seemed quite arbitrary.'

Things got worse for Pakistan almost immediately. Inzamam had again been promoted to number 3, a position to which he was quite unsuited as his technique is suspect against the moving ball, and after one pull for 4, he went neither forward nor back to a ball from Morrison and was bowled. Pakistan were in difficulties at 9–2, when Miandad joined Rameez. Miandad was not in the best of form; he was unsettled by Morrison and bemused by Patel, and could have been out any time. However he battled through, and provided the perfect foil to Rameez as together they turned the innings around. Rameez completely belied his reputation as a plodder, as he drove and pulled his way to an unbeaten 119. Miandad departed for 30 with the score on 124, but Salim Malik took over where he left off, and in the end Pakistan cruised to victory with 7 wickets and 5 overs to spare.

The Pakistan side was jubilant. 'We were all pumped up for this one,' said Wasim. 'We were determined to play aggressively, and it's paid off. The Kiwis are no longer the mild-mannered types they used to be, and one or two of our boys had verbal confrontations with them. When Danny Morrison came to Pakistan he was really quiet, but now he struts around like some kind of god. He was swearing at Sohail and Inzamam when he got them out. If we do qualify for the semis I can promise you that our batsmen are going to try and murder his bowling.'

The joy was tempered by the fact that all Pakistan could do now was sit back and wait for the result of the Australia and West Indies game. The time difference between New Zealand and Australia, and the fact that the West Indies game in Melbourne was a day/nighter meant that there was an agonizing seven hours to endure to discover whether they would be returning to Lahore the next day, or flying on to Auckland for the semi-final.

Generally speaking the organization of the competition and its TV coverage had been far superior in New Zealand than on the Australian mainland, and the Pakistan team were able to watch their fate unfold ball by ball before their eyes. 'I found it almost unbearable,' said Wasim. 'At one stage Australia looked like they would make a huge total, but when they subsided to 216 I thought we were finished. Then, when Haynes and Lara started so well Ijaz, Mushtaq and I got so depressed that we decided to go out to dinner and just keep an eye on the score.'

'We couldn't believe it when wickets began to fall; I think that the West Indies have paid dearly for not taking the experienced players like Greenidge, Richards, and Dujon. Mike Whitney bowled really well for his 4 wickets, and after the game our team sent him a message offering to pay the Australian the $250 fine that he picked up against us! By the time the 8th wicket fell I knew we would qualify, and that we would go on to win the competition; I even signed a note for the cab driver saying that Pakistan would win the World Cup. When we got back to the hotel, everyone was shouting and hugging each other. We'd all been under such pressure for so long that it almost felt as though we had already won the Cup. It was a very emotional moment, and I couldn't get to sleep for hours. For so long it's been a personal goal to do well in the World Cup, and I thought I had lost my chance; to get it back is just unbelievable.'

There was no such thing as a lie-in for the World Cup semi-finalists as they had to be up at 8am to fly on to Auckland for their re-match with New Zealand. Many of the team were exhausted on arrival and chose to skip the optional practice in favour of a few hours extra sleep. By now the confidence in the side was unshakeable. 'It seems odd to say so, but we are now the team in form,' said Wasim. 'England have gone off the rails with injury and tiredness, South Africa have always been a bit up and down, and New Zealand are going to be wary of us now that we have beaten them. Also, if any team can beat them at Eden Park it's us, because we're used to slow wickets.'

Martin Crowe confirmed that Pakistan were the last side his team wanted to meet. 'You never know quite where you are with the Pakistanis. Akram can bowl three bad balls an over, but you've also got to be prepared for the three that are almost unplayable. I would rather be playing the South

Africans because their bowling attack is so much more predictable.'

At nets on the day before the semi-final it was the Pakistanis who were relaxed and joking, and the New Zealanders who were under pressure, with the spotlight of the home media firmly fixed upon them. 'I know just what they're going through,' said Wasim. 'Four years ago in Lahore we were the local favourites. We had been the first team to qualify for the semis, and everyone just assumed we would win the competition. In the end through a mixture of over-confidence and pressure we cracked. I think the same thing will happen to the Kiwis.'

Auckland is the most densely populated of New Zealand's cities. Viewed from the water of one of its harbours it looks very pleasant, but the city centre where the Pakistani team was staying is unprepossessing and many of the players found Auckland a forbidding town and the local people unfriendly. Such impressions are never helped when New Zealand lives up to its nick-name of 'The Land of the Long White Cloud', or in this case 'The Land of the Long Black Cloud'. Throughout the three days that Pakistan spent on the north island, it was either raining or threatening to rain.

The organizers had made provision for a spare day in case of rain, that ought to have ensured that a fair result could have been achieved, but once again the rule book defied logic. If the rain that was forecast for Saturday 21 March arrived on time there was every possibility of another contrived result. Instead of using the second day as an overspill to complete any overs that couldn't be completed on the first day as is the case in most other one-day competitions, it had been decreed that the second day would only be used if a result could not be forced on the first. If this was the case the first game would be declared null and void, and a new one begun. The same discredited system for the deduction of overs that had been used in the earlier games would again be in operation, with the one concession for the semi-finals that at least 25 rather than 15 overs must be bowled by each side to get a result.

There was no rain on the morning of the 21 March as Martin Crowe and Imran went out to the middle for the toss, but there couldn't have been anyone in the crowd of 40,000 who did not think it would do so later in the day. Martin Crowe won and elected to bat, a decision that he would almost certainly have reversed if the forecast had been better. Eden Park is primarily a rugby ground and the wicket is positioned diagonally across the field, and many teams batting first had found it difficult to pace an innings on the slow pitch, while Martin Crowe was a master at placing his field to defend the short boundaries.

Pakistan had made one change to the side that had defeated New Zealand earlier in the week, with Iqbal Sikander coming in for Ijaz. On paper this had looked a clever move because none of the New Zealanders had been happy against leg spin, but Sikander was not in the same class as Mushtaq, and batsmen could attack the spinners at Eden Park with relative impunity, safe in the knowledge that even a mishit would carry the boundary.

Mark Greatbatch seemed overawed by the occasion at first, being beaten three times outside the off-stump in Wasim's first over, but he soon found his six hitting form; his first was a slice to the short boundary off Wasim, but there was nothing tentative about his towering on drive into the South Stand off Aaqib. Aaqib put an end to Greatbatch with the perfect slower ball, which was no more than a gentle off-break, and when

John Wright mishit Mushtaq into the wind to Rameez at long on, Pakistan were firmly in control with the Kiwis on 39–2.

Andrew Jones and Martin Crowe took the score along to 87, but the real acceleration in the innings came with the partnership between Rutherford and Crowe. Rutherford had a slow start, taking 21 balls to get off the mark, and was very fortunate that an Akram yorker which trapped him in front of his stumps when he was 0 was ruled a no ball, but as his confidence increased so did his strokeplay. Yet it was Crowe's innings that was the masterpiece; so good was his timing, and so accurate his placement that his shots seemed effortless, and he never had to resort to any measures other than orthodox cricket strokes.

By the time that Rutherford top-edged Wasim to Moin for an even 50, New Zealand had moved on to 194. Shortly after, Crowe, who was using a runner after pulling a hamstring, was run out by Salim Malik, but Harris, Smith, Patel, and Larsen all played attacking cameos as New Zealand reached a total of 262–7 from their 50 overs. An astonishing 132 runs had come off the final 15 overs as Pakistan seemed powerless to stop the flow of boundaries. Only Wasim and Mushtaq could take any pleasure in their bowling analyses, both taking 2–40, and a target of well over 5 an over seemed a forlorn hope.

'Oddly enough, we always thought we could do it,' said Wasim. 'Even when wickets were falling we were very confident, because we knew just how hard it was to defend those short boundaries when the batsmen start to get after the bowling. Our only worry was the weather, but that was out of our hands. We knew that if it rained we would lose on run-rate, so we just had to play normally and hope for the best.

Luckily for us the expected rain came two hours after the end of the match.'

Rameez and Sohail got the innings off to a brisk start taking 20 off the first 4 overs from Patel and Morrison, but the impetus died when Sohail mistimed a sweep to Jones. Imran found it almost impossible to get the ball away in what he later described as one of his worst ever innings, and Rameez was caught on the boundary as he was beginning to get the scoreboard moving again. Javed came in to join his captain, but although he had no trouble in taking the singles, he too could not dominate, and when Imran and Malik were out in quick succession Pakistan were floundering at 140–4 with only 15 overs to go.

Inzamam looked relaxed to the point of being laid-back as he meandered out to the wicket. Still only twenty-two, and yet to make his Test début, he was utterly composed as he began to play the innings which transformed the match; from his very first ball he timed the ball sweetly and found the gaps in the field that everyone else had found so elusive. Yet it was only on Wasim's insistence that Inzamam had played. 'Inzy had suffered from a stomach upset the night before the game, and had hardly slept,' said Wasim. 'That morning he had told me he was thinking of making himself unavailable. I told him that the team needed him, and that there were times when you had to have faith in your own talent and back yourself to pull through.'

At first it seemed as though Inzamam's innings could only be a brief, bright interlude before New Zealand reasserted its authority, but as his assault on the bowling continued so the body language of the Kiwi fielders betrayed their panic. Unfortunately for New Zealand, Martin Crowe was not on hand to calm his side as his hamstring injury had prevented him from fielding. John Wright, the acting captain, had neither the on-field presence nor the tactical awareness of Crowe; Crowe might have shuffled his bowlers to disrupt the batsmen, but Wright elected to give his bowlers longish spells and Inzamam and Javed began to do as they pleased.

The fifth wicket partnership had realized 87 runs of which Inzamam had scored 60 in just 48 balls, and victory was well within reach when Inzamam was run out at 227. Javed was still finding run making difficult, but he used his experience to inspire his colleagues to make the runs. Wasim came and went for a quick-fire 9, and Moin smashed 20 in next to no time, including a six over mid-off with a shot that resembled a short-arm jab with a nine iron, and Pakistan cantered home with an over to spare.

As Moin swept Harris to the boundary for the winning runs, the whole Pakistan side ran on to the pitch to congratulate Javed and Moin, and the celebrations continued in the dressing-room as the players sung and danced to the sound of 'Allah Hoo' by Nusrat Sateh Ali Khan. It had been a game worthy of the occasion; the umpiring of David Shepherd and Steve Bucknor had been excellent, and for sheer excitement, tension, and artistry it transcended all the earlier games of the competition. Pakistan, who had been written off only ten days earlier, had won a World Cup semi-final for the first time in five attempts.

The Eden Park crowd was stunned; for six hours it had enjoyed the cricket, certain in the knowledge of a home victory, only to see it snatched away in the final overs. 'While they thought they were winning some of the crowd started racially abusing us as we sat on the players' balcony,' said Aamir Sohail. 'We were all furious at the time, but we couldn't help noticing that the same spectators went home crying in silence.'

Martin Crowe himself was close to tears as he described his feelings after the game. '262 should have been an easy total to defend. In the end it comes down to a matter of spirit. We wanted to win the World Cup, but if someone else wants it that bit more they'll get it, and perhaps Imran and his team wanted it more than we did. Pakistan showed just how desperate they are to win this cup; it's clearly worth being that desperate.'

The Pakistan players were too exhausted, both mentally and physically for any formal celebrations. Some went back to the hotel to watch TV, while others did some last minute late-night shopping. Wasim went out for a quick meal, but then retired to his room to unwind. 'Imran said that he wanted us to fight like cornered tigers,' he said, 'and we've done just that; with the spirit we showed today we could have got 300 if we had needed to. The very Pakistani newspapers that were vilifying us a short while ago, are now treating us like heroes. I think it was the fear of going home in disgrace that has given the team its will to win. It's so difficult to explain how much cricket means to the people of Pakistan. The whole country has been at a standstill for our games; even the streets of Lahore and Karachi have been quiet. Various government ministers and judges have flown in for the semi, and more will be arriving for the final. If we win, the government has even pledged to take the whole team to Mecca for Umra, a pilgrimage of thanksgiving.'

For Pakistan the World Cup odyssey had come full circle; the campaign that had begun in Melbourne would find its conclusion in the same stadium four weeks later. Imran had joked that 'the team would rather meet England in the final, because then the whole crowd would be behind Pakistan', but by now none of the players could have cared less whom they met so sure were they of winning. Nevertheless, keen interest was taken in the England and South Africa semi-final in Sydney.

'It was just a farce,' said Wasim, after England had won through after a rain interruption had left South Africa with a revised target of 22 runs in one ball. 'Before the rain came we all thought that South Africa would do it, because 22 runs in 13 balls wasn't that difficult. The rain rule has spoiled so many games in this tournament, and I feel so sorry for South Africa. How can you have a rule that makes a mockery of the semi-final of the World Cup? It will have to be changed next time; rather than just deduct the least profitable overs, why don't they deduct the overs in which the most and the fewest runs were scored? At least that way the system would be fair.'

It wasn't just the rain rule that was at fault in the semi-final. South Africa only bowled 45 overs; for this they merely received a fine, which to a country of South Africa's wealth was insignificant, while England was denied the opportunity to benefit from the 'slog overs'. Perhaps then justice was done, but it would have been far better for players and spectators alike if the game had been played to a natural conclusion. Two days had been set aside for the semi-final, ample time for both teams to receive their full allotment of overs. Television's desire to see a result on the day, without disrupting later programmes, did immeasurable damage to the game of cricket on Sunday 22 March.

The pressure on both the Pakistan and England teams was immense in the build-up to the final, and the players tended to keep a low profile inside their hotel, away from the barrage of pressmen and the attention of well-wishers. The only public function they had to attend was the pre-match dinner where Botham and Gooch walked out in protest at a royal insult. 'I saw them get up and go,' said Wasim, 'but I didn't give it too much thought. All of us thought the whole evening was fairly dreadful, and we left at 9pm, ten minutes after they did. The dinner was really just another excuse to make some more money out of the World Cup.'

Wasim got up late on the morning of the final; some of the players took advantage of the beautiful sunny weather to savour the atmosphere outside, but he preferred to prepare himself for the game alone in his room. 'It's a day/night final which might cause us some problems if we have to bat second,' he said, 'but I'm very confident that we'll handle the tension better. All of our last four games have been sudden death and we're on a roll. England have lost key players, like Robin Smith, through injury, and they're looking exhausted. They're a great team if they are allowed to dictate the pace of the game, but we feel that if they are put under pressure, then they'll crack.'

Pakistan won the toss, and Sohail and Rameez walked out to bat in front of a crowd that would build up to become a world record one-day attendance of 87,182. After their usual breezy start, Sohail and Rameez were dismissed within minutes of one another, both falling to Derek Pringle, who despite injury, was bowling a tight, controlled spell with the new ball. Had the openers survived the first ten overs then Malik would have come in at number 3, but the fall of two early wickets meant that Imran and Javed, the stalwarts of Pakistan cricket, and the only two men to have played in all five World Cups, were left in charge of the innings.

In previous matches the Pakistan batting had become

bogged down when Imran had come to the crease; he had stemmed the fall of wickets, but had been unable to increase the tempo of the innings. At first it seemed that the same pattern might be repeating itself, as the run-rate seemed to be fatally short of an adequate total at the half-way stage. Yet gradually, and inexorably, Imran found his form, and if it wasn't the vintage form of his prime, it was a fair imitation. Javed, who is never averse to a battle, kept good company for his captain, and together they took the score to 163 before tiredness induced Javed to reverse sweep Illingworth to Botham.

Once again Inzamam wandered to the wicket as if the game was of no more importance than a game in the park, and once again he did not disappoint, as he unleashed a formidable array of strokes. He was joined by Wasim, when Imran hit Botham to long-on. Wasim had struggled to find his touch with the bat throughout the tournament, but like his captain, he chose the big occasion to come good. Aided by some English bowling that was too wide and too full, the two batsmen plundered the attack as Inzamam took 42 runs from 35 balls, and Wasim raced to 33 in just 19, to see Pakistan through to a total of 249.

It was a target that was by no means out of reach, but England were under pressure from the start as Botham and Stewart fell cheaply. Botham received a ball from Wasim that bounced more than he expected and took the outside edge. Botham indicated that he had not got a touch, but Wasim was in no doubt. However if there was a question mark about Botham's dismissal, there should have been none when Stewart got a big deflection to an Akram outswinger, but the batsman was given not out. The decision did not cost Pakistan dearly; Stewart, who had played some vital World Cup innings, looked out of sorts, and it wasn't long before he edged another outswinger, this time off Aaqib.

Wasim almost claimed a second wicket as Moin leapt to grab an edge from Gooch, but the end of his five over spell was no signal for Hick or his captain to relax. Mushtaq, who replaced Wasim at the Member's end, is a worthy successor to Abdul Qadir, and although only twenty-one years old, he has already acquired the full repertory of the leg-spinners art. He may not be able to command a regular place for United Bank, his department side in Pakistan, but he teased and tested the English batsmen to the limits. Hick was unable to pick the googly, and there was an inevitability about his dismissal leg before; 10 runs later, Gooch tried to sweep a ball that turned and bounced, and Aaqib took a sprawling catch half-way in from the boundary.

From the low point of 69–4, the game took yet another turn. With Pakistan's three front line bowlers having completed their first spells, Fairbrother and Lamb rebuilt the innings against the lesser threats of Imran, Ijaz, and Sohail. They started slowly, but as they gained in confidence, so the scoring rate increased, and by the time the second drinks break came after 34 overs, England were the marginal favourites.

Imran decided to recall his main strike bowler, and Wasim responded with an over that swung the match irrevocably. Running in from around the wicket, he bowled Allan Lamb with a near unplayable delivery that pitched off and hit off, and with his next ball bowled Chris Lewis with a fast inswinger. 'The ball that got rid of Allan Lamb was the better ball,' said Wasim later. 'It went like a fast leg-break and I don't think he ever saw it. It was one of the best balls I've ever bowled. Chris Lewis was just beaten for pace as much as by the inswing.'

Wasim's double strike left England floundering at 141–6, and from then on there was only one winner. Fairbrother made a brave attempt to go for the runs, and the tail-enders had a whole-hearted slog but only divine intervention could have saved England, and God was very much on Pakistan's side. At 10.18pm it was all over; Illingworth lofted the second ball of the final over, bowled by Imran, to Rameez at mid-off and Pakistan had won by 22 runs.

Immediately the celebrations began; players hugged each other and kissed the turf, and it was an emotional Imran who stepped on to the podium to receive the World Cup. Wasim was nominated Man of the Match for an all-round display that was touched with cricketing genius. 'It's the best day of my cricket life,' he said. 'It's always been my dream to perform at my best on the big occasion, and there's no bigger occasion than a World Cup final.'

After the obligatory lap of honour, the players returned to the dressing-room for a rousing chorus of 'Allah Hoo'. Yet the excitement and joy was tinged with a sense of stunned bewilderment at the enormity of what they had achieved. After an endless round of interviews Wasim slumped into a corner to collect his thoughts and to pack up his gear. 'I feel sorry for England; they've played great cricket but they just went off the boil at the end. But this win will mean the world to the Pakistani people. For many of them cricket is a way of life, and their reaction will be unbelievable. Even now the streets of Lahore will be packed with people singing and dancing.'

There was just one more hurdle for the Pakistan team, as they had to run the gauntlet of their admirers from the ground back to the hotel. Safely back on the sixteenth floor of the Hilton, the players began to unwind away from the throng that besieged the lobby downstairs, and enjoyed a hastily prepared alfresco meal cooked by local Pakistani friends. This was liable to be their last moment of privacy for quite some time. Reaction from Pakistan had begun to filter through, and already promises of money both for the Cancer Hospital and for the players has been made. All the early defeats on the tour had been forgotten, and after a brief stop-over in Singapore for some shopping, and a short trip to Mecca, the players would return home as heroes.

So, against all the odds, Pakistan had won the World Cup, and in so doing had broken all the unwritten rules of one-day cricket. They had played two leg-spinners when most teams are reluctant to play one; they had got through the entire tournament without a proper fifth bowler; and they had given away literally hundreds of runs in extras; one can only imagine how they would have done if Waqar had been fit. It was a victory for talent over professionalism, but the key to the Pakistan success lay in the attitude of the players who rediscovered their faith in themselves, their captain, and each other.

19

Pakistan in England: The Sting in the Tail

Throughout Pakistan's tour of England in 1992 the atmosphere was heavy with bad feeling on the field and innuendo off it. Yet, given the friction between the two sides when they last met in Pakistan in 1987, officials from both countries might well have breathed a sigh of relief as the dust settled on the final Test that the series had passed without a major diplomatic incident. True, there had been unsavoury moments at Old Trafford and Headingley, but nothing on the scale of the Mike Gatting–Shakoor Rana affair. With only a few one-day internationals and a three day county game remaining, the most taxing problem for the TCCB would surely be to count the profits from what had been a highly lucrative tour.

What followed was completely unexpected, and provided the tabloid press with the headlines for which they had been praying all season, and cricket's administrators with a headache that steadfastly refused to respond to placebos. England had easily won the third one-day game at Trent Bridge to take an invincible 3–0 lead in the series, and the venue moved to

Lord's for the fourth match in the series. This game, reduced to 50 overs a side and stretching to two days because of bad weather, was won in a tense finish by Pakistan. Yet the result was soon rendered almost irrelevant by the news, delivered at the post match press conference, that during the lunch interval of the England innings the match ball had been changed. What is more, an official source 'off the record', said it had been changed under Law 42.5 concerning 'unfair play'.

In the course of the morning session, Allan Lamb had apparently suspected that the Pakistanis were tampering with the ball, and alerted the two umpires, Jack Hampshire and Ken Palmer. During the lunch interval, they informed the match referee, Deryck Murray, who advised both teams of what he was proposing to do, and summarily ordered the ball to be changed. There has still been no official clarification from the TCCB or the ICC as to why the ball was changed, and the lips of the umpires and the referees are, as is customary, sealed. In the meantime, the Pakistani management confused the issue still further by releasing a statement that the ball had been changed under Law 5, because it had gone out of shape.

There the matter might have rested, albeit in the face of stiff resistance from the press who were clamouring for a straight answer to the simple question, 'Under what law was the ball changed?' Yet even the most hardened hack will eventually give up in the face of a repeated wall of silence from officialdom, and although the ICC might be shown up as ineffectual, it would have achieved its ends of political and legal expediency. Yet three days after the incident Allan Lamb burst into print in the Daily Mirror with the subtlety of a claymore mine, and ensured that all the participants in the affair, officials and players alike, would be showered with debris, most of it highly-adhesive mud.

Lamb accused the Pakistanis, and Wasim and Waqar in particular, of gouging the ball with their fingernails and then hiding the marks with sweat, in order to obtain the late swing that had proved so lethal in the Test series. He went on to say that the secret of their swing was in fact well-known on the county circuit and had been ever since Sarfraz played for Northamptonshire in the seventies.

Suspicion of ball tampering had never been far from Wasim and Waqar since their performance against New Zealand in Pakistan in 1990. Nothing was ever proved, but unsurprisingly, the mutterings grew louder in this country as the Pakistan tour to England got under way. The first hints were rumours that the Pakistanis had doctored the ball in their victory over England in the World Cup final in Melbourne. This was highly improbable. Traditionally, the Pakistanis achieved their reverse swing after 50 overs or so; in a match limited to that number of overs, any advantage they might gain would be very marginal. In addition, the tournament was being played with white balls, and under the rules of the competition a different ball was to be used from each end during an innings. This meant that not only would each ball be used for a maximum of 25 overs in an innings, it would also be returned to an umpire at the end of each over, who would be able to keep a close eye on any deterioration.

In an early Tetley Challenge game against Somerset speculation grew that Pakistan had been warned for ball tampering, and by the time Wasim and Waqar had, on three separate occasions in the Lord's, Headingley, and Oval Tests, sunk the English middle order and tail, it had reached fever pitch. Consequently, Allan Lamb's statement after the Lord's game was seen by many as the voice of truth.

Putting aside the accuracy of Lamb's statement for the

moment, he raises some interesting moral questions. It he had known that Sarfraz was tampering with the ball, should he not have spoken out then, rather than keep quiet and enjoy the success that they shared with Northampton? Likewise, if it was well known on the county circuit that Wasim and Waqar were gouging the ball, should not someone have said so? Wasim had played for Lancashire since 1988 and Waqar for Surrey since 1990, and there must have been ample opportunity to expose them.

The inescapable conclusion must be, that if the Pakistani pacemen were interfering illegally with the ball, then their county team mates and opponents must have been willing to condone it. Yet when Wasim and Waqar represented their country the offence became indictable. In which case, there is one morality for the county game, and another for Test cricket.

Law 42.5 states that 'no-one shall rub the ball on the ground or use any artificial substance or take any other action to alter the condition of the ball'. Taken literally this means that any action other than polishing the ball is illegal. Roughing up the ball, or interfering with the seam, is illegal. Yet many a bowler the world over tries to raise the seam to extract more movement from the ball. As Mike Selvey pointed out in the Guardian, 'If Pakistan have cheated, then so has virtually every seam bowler who played first-class cricket, and a good few spinners too. Lifting the seam is common practice and always has been. Ironically no one knows this better than Ken Palmer, a seam bowler for Somerset and England.'

'Ethically there is no difference between a scuffed-up ball that swings into a batsman at 90 mph and one which jags back at the same pace off a seam lifted to the consistency of razor wire. If one is cheating, so is the other.'

'Nor does common practice stop at seam-picking. Polishing agents have always been used – from running fingers through brylcreemed hair and applying them to the ball, to using lip salve and sunscreen. One of my former playing colleagues was so open with his use of Lip Ice he did not care that the ball reeked of mint, while I tried pure lanolin once, and the ball looped the loop. Next time you are at a county ground observe the red marks on bowlers' trousers: grease leaves a dark red stain immediately, while normal shining leaves a much softer mark.'

Just how widespread such contraventions are became apparent last September when Surrey were fined £1000 after being reported by the TCCB for ball tampering for the third time. Waqar had to be innocent of at least one of these incidents, because he was playing for Pakistan at the time. The Surrey administration has expressed embarrassment at being reported, especially as it had no knowledge of the first two incidents, which went no further than the cricket management committee. Surrey investigated these matters promptly. They set up a board of enquiry, which submitted proposals to the TCCB which will be implemented this season.

Yet if ball tampering is common practice within the game, one could be forgiven for thinking that if everyone else was at it, why shouldn't Wasim and Waqar? Wasim and Waqar have always insisted on their innocence of all allegations of ball tampering, and such insistence is understandable given the abuse and opprobrium that has been heaped upon them. It is perhaps with good reason that the two Pakistanis feel they have become the victims of their own success.

This feeling was reinforced by the Pakistanis' belief that the incident at the one-day game at Lord's was handled in a different way to which similar suspicions of ball tampering have been handled in other international games in this country. During the final Test against the West Indies at the Oval in 1990 the England captain was spoken to severely by umpire John Holder about the condition of the ball. No further action was taken either during or after the game, and the only discernible repercussion is that John Holder has been dropped from the TCCB panel of umpires. David Gower mentioned in his autobiography that the Indians were similarly warned by Nigel Plews during the Oval Test of 1991. The Indians have denied this, but the official scorecard backs Gower. Again no action was taken. Yet at the one-day game at Lord's in 1992 it appears as if the Pakistanis received no warning as to the state of the ball before it was changed.

Amid the accusations it is often overlooked that Wasim and Waqar are the finest fast bowlers in the world at the moment. Whatever they may or may not do to a cricket ball would be completely incidental but for their prodigious talent. If they had taken only a handful of wickets during the summer, and had England won the series, then no-one would have really cared what they did to the ball. Aaqib Javed had exactly the same opportunities to exploit the late reverse swing, and significantly failed to achieve it. Likewise, when Wasim and Waqar represent their counties, why don't Phillip DeFreitas and Martin Bicknell get the same movement?

It is clearly hypocritical to pillory the Pakistanis for their success. If ball tampering is now seen as a threat to the structure of the game then it must be eradicated at all levels. A county pace bowler, with match figures of 1–140, who fiddles with the seam must expect to be reported and receive the same punishment as an overseas Test player who has just picked up a 10 wicket haul.

The ball tampering furore raised another important question – Why have so many series between England and Pakistan been contested in such acrimony? It is true that in recent years Test cricket has become a tougher battleground. Sledging and accusations of home team bias from umpires have become rife, and Pakistan has been involved in its fair share of series that have been less than harmonious. Yet Pakistan and India have been virtually at war over Kashmir ever since partition, and whilst some tours have been cancelled because the safety of the players could not be guaranteed, they have managed a number of enjoyable series against one another. But in recent years Pakistan and England have been unable to contest a series without an added edge of animosity.

The blame for this is hard to attribute. The Pakistanis claim there is still a colonial hangover, that a bad decision in Pakistan is seen as bias whilst a bad decision in England is regarded as human error, and that they are treated in an underhand manner by the tabloid press. In response, the English assert that they act towards the Pakistanis as even-handedly as they do to the other Test playing nations; the press reply that they report as they find. In other words, both sides are keen to apportion the responsibility for the hostility to the other. In this instance, though, the search for the originator of the problem, and the allocation of blame is not just unhelpful but futile. Pakistan and England have a symbiotic cricketing relationship; it has grown over years of Test cricket, and responsibility for any misunderstandings and misconceptions must be shared.

Ever since the beginning of the 1980s whenever Pakistan have toured this country they have done so with a siege mentality; they expected to get the wrong end of decisions, and to get vilified in the press. 1992 was no different, and county colleagues of Wasim, Waqar, and Aaqib, noted a marked difference from the carefree, open attitude they had shown the year before. The danger of going on tour with such expectations are obvious. You may sense bias where none existed, with the result that you engender the very responses you first feared. Mike Brearley pointed out that Mervyn Kitchen and Ken Palmer's refusal to uphold any of Pakistan's repeated appeals in the early stages of England's first innings at Headingley may have been because they took against the tone. The vociferousness implied that the umpires would have to be fools, biased, or both if the batsman was not given out, and subconsciously they decided to dig their heels in. The further the umpires dug their heels in, the more frequent and more insistent became the Pakistani appeals as their belief in the partiality of the umpires grew.

Of course, explanations may lead to greater understanding, but they will cannot excuse bad behaviour. Extreme petulance and dissent, even with what may seem at the time good cause, are contrary to the spirit of the game and should be treated accordingly. It was right that Aaqib Javed and Rashid Latif should be reported and fined for their conduct at Old Trafford and Headingley respectively. Even here, there is a double standard in their treatment by the British press. When Mike Gatting had his run-in with Shakoor Rana in Faisalabad in 1987 certain papers held him up as the defender of the truth; when Chris Broad refused to walk on the same tour, his dissent became understandable, and what's more was seen to be rewarded with a bonus of a £1000 hardship allowance that was given to every member of the touring party.

Relations between the Pakistanis and some parts of the English press have always been strained. The English cricket press is regarded by the Pakistanis as the most influential in the world; what is written about them in England is likely to become the basis of fact and opinion for cricket fans the world over. Equally the Pakistanis are aware that their own press has no voice outside its own country. Thus they are wary of an institution that appears to have so much power.

This distrust is fuelled by what many Pakistanis feel are inherent attitudes of bias in the tabloid press. Deliberate or not, many papers adopt an attitude of racial stereotyping towards England's international opponents. The Australians are 'tough and uncompromising', the Indians are 'gentle and mysterious', and the West Indies are 'brutal and aggressive'. The epithet for the Pakistanis has been 'devious and untrust-worthy'. As with the Pakistanis seeking bias in the English umpiring and finding it, so the English press have sought untrustworthiness and found it. When the ball tampering story broke, up went the cry of 'cheat', a highly emotive word to describe what has been shown to be commonplace. Yet when ball tampering is mentioned with England or a county as the culprit, the language used is far more morally neutral.

The way forward is far from clear; indeed attitudes may be so deeply entrenched on both sides that there may be no solution. The 1992 England and Pakistan series saw a further deterioration in relations between the two countries. Indeed the only people to gain much satisfaction from the tour were the lawyers, whose eyes lit up at the number of writs. If amends are not made the logical conclusion is that the two sides will meet less and less frequently, and that would be very sad for a public that was gripped by some enthralling cricket from both sides throughout the summer.

There are positive signs, however. The ICC has found a sponsor for an independent panel of umpires and referees for Test matches involving Zimbabwe, India, New Zealand, and South Africa for the winter of 1992–3. There were real hopes that independent umpires would also be appointed for the series between India and England in 1993. Pakistan has been a staunch advocate of such a move for many years, and there is no doubt that the presence of independent umpires in all matches, and particularly those involving England and Pakistan, would have a calming influence on cricket's international diplomatic relations. As Sir Colin Cowdrey, chairman of the ICC said, 'Cricket is the last sport to turn to independent officials. If there is one thing causing hassle around the cricketing world, it is the question of umpires.'

The omens were distinctly unpromising as the Pakistan touring side arrived in England on a grey, dank day in late April. Imran Khan, who had led Pakistan to some of its greatest triumphs, had decided not to tour, and Javed Miandad was appointed captain in his stead. Javed had a reasonable track record as skipper, but it was widely felt that he lacked Imran's inspirational qualities, and that over the course of an arduous four month tour he would find it difficult to maintain the respect and cohesion of the team.

The reason that Imran had given for his non-appearance was the shoulder injury that he had sustained in the World Cup. While Imran was still suffering from this condition, there were other factors in his decision. The anti-Imran feeling that had been growing amongst the team during the World Cup had not dissipated in victory. Indeed the speech he made whilst accepting the trophy was received by his teammates with the sort of enthusiasm that David Gower reserves for Mickey Stewart. For a long time Imran had made no secret of the fact that his prime motivation for continuing to play cricket was to raise money for his Cancer Project in Lahore, and there is no doubt that certain senior players felt that he was no longer sufficiently involved with the team to remain as captain.

Money, as ever, exacerbated the situation. Pakistani cricketers are not well-paid by their Board of Control, and they have come to rely on the munificence of grateful compatriots to supplement their income. Obviously the greater the success the greater the abundance of gifts, and so the World Cup was seen by many players as the ideal opportunity to cash in. A conflict of interest arose as Imran regarded the World Cup victory as an ideal vehicle to raise funds for his hospital. The depth of the rift between the team and Imran was highlighted by their inability to negotiate an amicable compromise, whereby certain functions would be for the Hospital Appeal and others for the players.

Another concern for Pakistan was the fitness of Waqar. He was a passenger on the plane to London, and given the serious nature of his injury, there was a distinct possibility that he would remain a passenger for much of the tour. 'I had taken no exercise at all for three months,' said Waqar. 'The doctors had told me to get as much hard bed rest as possible, and to do nothing more strenuous than walking. It was a very demoralizing time; it was exciting to see Pakistan win the World Cup, but it was desperately disappointing to miss it, especially as I was so unsure of my future. The tour management had hopes of me being fit by the third Test; I secretly entertained hopes of being fit by the first Test, but with a stress fracture of the lower back you couldn't predict anything.'

Waqar was packed off to the Oval for some intensive physiotherapy and fitness work under the supervision of John Deary, while the rest of the team toured the country playing side games against the counties, and he only rejoined the other players when they gathered in London for the first two one-day internationals. There was no question of Waqar playing in either of these games, and Pakistan's worries centred on the fitness of Wasim, their other strike bowler, who was complaining of pain in his right foot.

Wasim declared himself fit to play in the first game at Lord's, and, although he bowled eleven tidy overs, he was clearly below par. With no other bowler capable of containing the batsmen, England cruised to 278, with half-centuries from Stewart, Smith, and Lamb, a score which Pakistan never remotely threatened. Wasim's injury worsened overnight and an X-ray revealed a stress fracture. The furrows in Pakistani brows as Wasim was taken to hospital to have his foot encased in plaster were etched deeper as England piled on the agony against an anaemic bowling attack and achieved a second easy victory at the Oval.

Wasim was particularly depressed about his new injury. 'I'd worked so hard at building up my strength and fitness to ensure I wouldn't break down, and then I got another stress fracture. It couldn't have happened at a worse time with Waqar still unfit and a five match Test series against England about to begin.' Yet there was some heartening news on the horizon for the Pakistanis. Waqar was included in the team to play Middlesex prior to the first Test at Edgbaston, and although far from match fit, he came through the ordeal unscathed and in good spirits.

Waqar's decision to play in the first Test was greeted with amazement by almost everyone, and there was general concern that such an early return to five day cricket could severely damage his back. However Waqar was well aware of the risks he was taking. 'Our bowling had been really struggling without Wasim or myself, and I wanted to give the side a lift. I knew that I was going to bowl well within myself.

I didn't bowl very quickly in that game, but it all helped to restore me to match fitness.' It speaks volumes for Waqar's importance to the side that he could be allowed to use a Test match as a prolonged fitness test.

The Edgbaston Test was dominated by the weather and the docile nature of the pitch, and a draw was always the only likely result. Only two balls were bowled on the first two days, both of them on the first. The TCCB stuck to their principle of not offering spectators a refund if any play was possible, thereby proving that some principles are not worth sticking to, and losing a lot of friends in the process. Thereafter the game became the preserve of the batsmen. Salim Malik and Javed Miandad notched hundreds for Pakistan, which were matched by centuries from Alec Stewart and Robin Smith for England, as the game petered out without recourse to a second innings.

Waqar's strength gradually returned in side games against Nottingham and Northampton, and with Wasim also fit once more, it was a full strength Pakistan side that met England at Lord's for the second Test, in a match that will go down in cricket history as one of the classics. England won the toss and chose to bat, and there was no hint of the drama to come as Gooch and Stewart compiled chanceless half centuries, and put on 123 for the first wicket. Early in the afternoon Wasim bowled Gooch for 69, and thereafter wickets tumbled steadily. Hick pulled Waqar to mid-on, Smith fenced at Wasim outside the off-stump, and off the last ball before tea Stewart hit the occasional bowler Asif Mujtaba to cover.

Yet it was after tea that the pyrotechnics began as England collapsed from 197-4 to 247 all out, in the face of hostile swing bowling from Waqar and Mushtaq's beguiling leg spin. Waqar takes up the story. 'Before tea I had been bowling downhill from the pavilion end, as I thought that would give me a bit of extra pace. When I switched to the nursery end I felt more settled, found my rhythm, and the ball began to swing.' For Botham, Lewis and Lamb, this was something of an under-statement as they were all three bewitched by inswinging yorkers in a matter of minutes, and Waqar finished with figures of 5–91 as he completed his eighth five wicket haul in his 18th Test.

Pakistan were 31–0 by stumps, and by lunch the next day had cantered to 123 for the loss of Ramiz, with Aamir Sohail scoring his maiden Test fifty. Rain washed out the rest of the second day, and the following day saw England fight back bravely. Malcolm took 4 wickets on his return to the England side, DeFreitas 3, and Ian Salisbury, the leg spinner, made a promising debut with a couple, as Pakistan were restricted to a first innings lead of 38. Graham Gooch fell leg before to Aaqib as England edged to 14 ahead by the close of play on Saturday.

Tense as the cricket had been, the first three days proved to be merely an appetizer for what was to come. Stewart and Salisbury, who had come in as night watchman the previous evening, held firm for an hour before Salisbury was trapped in front by Wasim. Thereafter, England were dismantled by the spin of Mushtaq in the pre-lunch session, and destroyed by the pace of Wasim and Waqar in the afternoon. The last three wickets fell to Wasim in the space of four balls and England were all out for 175.

Pakistan were left with a target of 138, with four and a half sessions to get the runs. 'We thought it was going to be a doddle,' said Waqar. 'I and the other bowlers had showered and changed out of our whites, as we expected to get the runs for the loss of a couple of wickets at the most. Everyone was relaxed in the dressing-room. Perhaps the early batsmen were too relaxed, because Chris Lewis bowled brilliantly and suddenly the pressure was on.' Comatose would be a better word to describe the performances of Ramiz, Javed, and Asif Mujtaba, who left a prial of 0s at the top of the scoreboard, and Pakistan in trouble at 18–3. It required a firm, calming influence to steady the Pakistani innings, but panic was all that was at hand as batsman after batsman succumbed to the pressure. By the time Waqar joined Wasim at the crease the score was 95–8 and the game had been as good as handed back to England.

Waqar was not noted for his batting prowess, though he had produced the odd cameo in the past, but here he was a model of correctness and determination. 'I wasn't trying to play any flashy shots, I was just concentrating on not getting out,' said Waqar. Gradually the runs began to come as the two batsmen grew in confidence; they were aided by Gooch's curious decision to replace Salisbury with Lewis and some aerial shots that evaded the fielders, and shortly before the close of play Wasim hit Salisbury through the covers to hit the winning runs. Wasim finished with 45 and Waqar with 20 as they shared an unbeaten partnership of 46 to secure a memorable 2 wicket victory for Pakistan. Wasim was named Man of the Match and after the game he commented, 'It's a dream come true to win a Test match like this; to do it against England at Lord's, the home of cricket, makes it all the more special. Winning the World Cup was great, but this is even better.'

The weather and some stout-hearted resistance from the England tail prevented a result in the third Test at Old Trafford. Sadly, this game will be remembered more for the petulant behaviour of Aaqib, than for some sparkling individual performances. The sight of either Palmer brother in a white coat seems to send the Pakistanis into fits of apoplexy, and on this occasion Aaqib, aided and abetted by Javed, mistakenly imagined that Roy Palmer had handed him his sweater in a less than gracious manner at the end of the over in which he had been warned for short-pitched bowling at Devon Malcolm. There was a gentle irony in this, for if there is a worse number 11 in Test cricket than Malcolm it is Aaqib. The net result of the incident was that Conrad Hunte, the match referee, imposed a fine on Aaqib, issued a warning to Pakistan and inexplicably to England too, and the long history of bad relations between the two sides continued.

All this was a pity, as on the first day Aamir Sohail had raced to a double century against some friendly English bowling, and after a day's play had been lost to the rain, Pakistan were able to declare at 505–9 shortly before tea on the third day. Bad light restricted England's reply to 72–2 by stumps, with Wasim taking both wickets, but England could have been in a much worse position had all the chances offered been accepted by the slip fielders. The greasy hand syndrome continued on the Monday, and with David Gower making 73 on his welcome return to the side, thus passing Geoff Boycott's record of most runs scored for England in the process, and with both Lewis and Salisbury also making half centuries, England saved the follow-on and killed off the match.

The fourth Test at Headingley was played for the most part in the overcast stygian gloom which has become as integral to cricket at Leeds, as champagne and strawberries are to Lord's. Wasim and Waqar were not expected to find conditions to their liking, and Headingley was widely regarded as England's best chance to square the series. As such they paid meticulous care to selection, so there was a first Test cap for the accurate seamer, Neil Mallender, and a recall for Derek Pringle. The cloud cover was as low as the bounce of the ball on the first morning, and the only person who appeared to be unsurprised at Javed's decision to bat first was Graham Gooch, who announced that he would have done likewise. Pakistan were always likely to struggle on a pitch that offered movement coupled with uneven bounce, and they were duly dismissed early on the second morning for 197, with the only significant contribution coming from Salim Malik, who remained unbeaten on 82.

Conditions were much improved for batting on the second day, which was more than could be said for the Pakistanis' humour as appeal after appeal was turned down, and play ended with England in the commanding position of 216–1. The next morning Gooch and Smith resumed the attack; Gooch powered his way to a century, and it was something of a shock when Smith flat-batted a short ball from Aaqib to depart for 42. Shortly afterwards, Aaqib sustained an injury and Waqar was summoned from mid-off to bowl in tandem with Mushtaq. In next to no time England had slumped from 292–2 to 320 all out; Mushtaq had three wickets, Waqar five, and a bemused David Gower was stranded on 18 not out.

It still needed a disciplined batting performance from Pakistan to salvage the game, but despite a half-century from Ramiz, and another unbeaten 80 from Malik, they succumbed to the accuracy of Neil Mallender who took five wickets on his debut, and England were left to make 98 for victory. They made the runs with six wickets in hand, with a little help from the umpires, but mainly thanks to the steadying influence of David Gower, and the series were squared with one match to play.

Pakistan were disappointed at losing the game, but Wasim

was not particularly distraught. 'I hate losing when we've played badly, but all our supporters have made a point of telling us that they don't blame us for the defeat. Even so, you can't excuse younger players like Rashid Latif for losing their temper, though you can certainly understand it.'

If the Lord's Test had proved to a wider audience that Wasim and Waqar were the finest pace bowling double act in international cricket at the present moment, their efforts at the Oval invited comparison with the greats of cricket history. The Oval wicket was not at its quickest, but even so Pakistan cruised to victory with over a day and a half to spare. England were dismissed for 207 in their first innings; as so often the English batsmen made a dogged start, reaching 190–4, only for the tail to be swept aside by Wasim who collected figures of 6–67. The Pakistani reply was never authoritative, but it was sufficient to establish a first innings lead of 173. England got off to a poor start in their second innings; there may have been question marks raised about Wasim and Waqar's ability to swing the old ball, but here Waqar swept aside Stewart, Atherton, Gooch, and Gower, with the new ball. After this, it was merely a question of whether Pakistan would have to bat again. Thanks to a fighting 84 not out from Robin Smith, England did get their noses in front, but only by one run, and Pakistan duly completed a 10 wicket victory to take the match and the series.

All that remained of the tour was for Pakistan to collect their £50,000 bonus for defeating eight of the English counties which they accomplished with a match to spare, and to play the last three Texaco one-day games that had been scheduled by someone who was cartographically dyslexic. In the first of these at Trent Bridge, Pakistan resembled a bunch of jaded amateurs and lost easily, and in the second at Lord's the result was overshadowed by the ball controversy. By the time the final game at Old Trafford began both sides were heartily sick of one another. England forced a fourth convincing victory, but the presentations on the balcony at the end of the game said it all. There was no sadness that a hard fought series was over, only relief that all the ill-feeling and mutual suspicion was at an end for the time being. The quickest run that the Pakistanis took all summer was from the departure lounge at Heathrow to the plane taking them home.

Despite the doubts raised about the protean nature of a cricket ball in Pakistani hands, few independent observers would challenge Wasim and Waqar's right to be seen as the two greatest fast bowlers in the world. Even David Gower and Robin Smith, who had suffered at their hands during the summer, were generous enough to admit this. In a straight contest between Wasim and Waqar and their rivals, one would always back the two Pakistanis; their variation, length and line, and sheer pace and accuracy would be more than a match for any opponent.

After the Oval Test, Mickey Stewart rightly nominated Wasim and Waqar as Pakistan's joint Men of the Series. Wasim had twice taken five wickets in an innings, and Waqar three times, and they finished the series with 21 and 22 wickets respectively. Indeed one could conclude that the main difference between the two sides was Wasim and Waqar. On paper England had the stronger batting line-up, and had the English batsmen been confronted by their own bowlers it is likely they would have fared even better than the Pakistanis.

Certainly, allegations of cheating have done no financial harm to Wasim and Waqar. They have signed new contracts with Lancashire and Surrey respectively which make them among the highest paid cricketers in the county game. Lancashire and Surrey are no mugs; they know how devastating the two Ws can be with a cricket ball in their hand, and they are prepared to pay for it.

If the series between Pakistan and England proved nothing else, it did show that international sportsmen need to retain a sense of humour. After all, what is on-field bickering and a row over ball tampering compared to 3 million unemployed in Britain, and thousands killed and homeless from floods in Pakistan? A Test cricketer who took what was written too personally would soon be a candidate for a psychiatric hospital or an intensive care unit. In early September, at the height of the speculation over ball-tampering, Wasim could still raise a smile. He was opening a new betting shop in Southall, and a local photographer asked him to pose holding a cricket ball. With a wide grin, he picked up the ball with his finger nails, dug them in, and said, 'Is this how you would like me to hold it?'

CAREER TEST MATCH RECORDS

BATTING AND FIELDING

	M	I	NO	HS	Runs	Avge	100	50	Ct
Waqar Younis	20	23	6	20*	144	8.47	–	–	1
Wasim Akram	45	58	9	123	1013	20.67	1	4	12

BOWLING

	Overs	Runs	Wkts	Avge	Best	5wI	10wM
Waqar Younis	665.4	1989	102	19.50	7–76	11	2
Wasim Akram	1661.1	4211	177	23.79	6–62	12	2

CAREER LIMITED OVER INTERNATIONAL RECORDS
BATTING AND FIELDING

	M	I	NO	HS	Runs	Avge	100	50	Ct
Waqar Younis	74	32	14	37	237	13.16	–	–	8
Wasim Akram	153	118	22	86	1327	13.82	–	1	29

BOWLING

	Overs	Runs	Wkts	Avge	Best	5wI	R/Over
Waqar Younis	606.1	2526	127	19.88	6–26	11	4.16
Wasim Akram	1306.1	4995	215	23.23	5–16	11	3.82

Statistics supplied courtesy of Bill Frindall and include matches played to 6.4.93.

PAKISTAN V WEST INDIES
MELBOURNE CRICKET GROUND, 23 FEBRUARY 1992

PAKISTAN

RAMEEZ	not out	102
SOHAIL	c Logie b Benjamin	23
INZAMAM	c Hooper by Harper	27
MIANDAD	not out	57
EXTRAS (1b, 31b, 5w, 2nb)		11

FALL: 45, 97

BOWLING

	O	m	r	w
MARSHALL	10	1	53	0
AMBROSE	10	0	40	0
BENJAMIN	10	0	49	1
HOOPER	10	0	41	0
HARPER	10	0	33	1

WEST INDIES

HAYNES	not out	93
LARA	ret hurt	88
RICHARDSON	not out	20
EXTRAS (2b, 81b, 7w, 3nb)		20
TOTAL (for no wicket)		221

BOWLING

	O	m	r	w
AKRAM	10	0	37	0
AAQIB	8.5	0	42	0
HAIDER	8	0	42	0
IJAZ	6	1	29	0
SIKANDER	8	1	26	0
SOHAIL	6	0	35	0

MAN OF THE MATCH: BRIAN LARA

WEST INDIES WON BY 10 WICKETS

PAKISTAN V ZIMBABWE
BELLERIVE OVAL, HOBART, 27 FEBRUARY 1992

PAKISTAN

RAMEEZ	c Flower b Jarvis	9
SOHAIL	c Pycroft b Butchart	114
INZAMAM	c Brandes b Butchart	14
MIANDAD	lbw b Butchart	89
MALIK	not out	14
AKRAM	not out	1
	EXTRAS (91b, 4nb)	13
	TOTAL (for 4 wickets)	254

FALL: 29, 63, 208, 253

BOWLING

	O	m	r	w
BRANDES	10	1	49	0
JARVIS	10	1	52	1
SHAH	10	1	24	0
BUTCHART	10	0	57	3
TRAICOS	10	0	63	0

ZIMBABWE

ARNOTT	c Akram b Sikander	7
FLOWER	c Inzamam b Akram	6
PYCROFT	b Akram	0
HOUGHTON	c Rameez b Sohail	44
SHAH	b Sohail	33
WALLER	b Akram	44
BUTCHART	c Miandad b Aaqib	33
BRANDES	not out	2
TRAICOS	not out	8
	EXTRAS (3b, 151b, 6w)	24
	TOTAL (for 7 wickets)	201

FALL: 14, 14, 33, 103, 108, 187, 190

BOWLING

	O	m	r	w
AKRAM	10	2	21	3
AAQIB	10	1	49	1
SIKANDER	10	1	35	1
MUSHTAQ	10	1	34	0
SOHAIL	6	1	26	2
MALIK	4	0	18	0

MAN OF THE MATCH: AAMIR SOHAIL

PAKISTAN WON BY 53 RUNS

PAKISTAN V ENGLAND
ADELAIDE OVAL, 1 MARCH 1992

PAKISTAN

RAMEEZ	c Reeve b DeFreitas	1
SOHAIL	c & b Pringle	9
INZAMAM	c Stewart b DeFreitas	0
MIANDAD	b Pringle	3
MALIK	c Reeve b Botham	17
IJAZ	c Stewart b Small	0
AKRAM	b Botham	1
MOIN	c Hick b Small	2
HAIDER	c Stewart b Reeve	13
MUSHTAQ	c Reeve b Pringle	17
AAQIB	not out	1
EXTRAS (11b, 1nb, 8w)		10
TOTAL		74

FALL: 5, 5, 14, 20, 32, 35, 42, 47, 62, 74

BOWLING

	O	m	r	w
PRINGLE	8.2	5	8	3
De FREITAS	7	1	22	2
SMALL	10	1	29	2
BOTHAM	10	4	12	2
REEVE	5	3	2	1

ENGLAND

GOOCH	c Moin b Akram	3
BOTHAM	not out	6
SMITH	not out	5
EXTRAS (1b, 31b, 1nb, 5w)		10
TOTAL (for 1 wicket)		24

FALL: 14

BOWLING

	O	m	r	w
AKRAM	3	0	7	1
AAQIB	3	1	7	0
HAIDER	1	0	1	0
IJAZ	1	0	5	0

MATCH ABANDONED

PAKISTAN V INDIA
SYDNEY CRICKET GROUND, 4 MARCH 1992

INDIA

JADEJA	c Fazal b Haider	46
SRIKKANTH	c Moin b Aaqib	5
AZHARUDDIN	c Moin b Mushtaq	32
KAMBLI	c Inzamam b Mushtaq	24
TENDULKAR	not out	54
MANJREKAR	b Mushtaq	0
KAPIL DEV	c Imran b Aaqib	35
MORE	run out	4
PRABHAKAR	not out	2
	EXTRAS (31b, 9w, 2nb)	14
	TOTAL (for 7 wickets)	216

Fall: 25, 86, 101, 147, 148, 208, 213

BOWLING

	o	m	r	w
AKRAM	10	0	45	0
AAQIB	8	2	28	2
IMRAN	8	0	25	0
HAIDER	10	11	36	1
MUSHTAQ	10	0	59	3
SOHAIL	3	0	20	0

PAKISTAN

SOHAIL	c Srikkanth b Tendulkar	62
INZAMAM	lbw b Kapil Dev	2
FAZAL	c More b Prabhakar	2
MIANDAD	b Srinath	40
MALIK	c More b Prabhakar	12
IMRAN	run out	0
AKRAM	st More b Raju	4
HAIDER	b Srinath	13
MOIN	c Manjrekar b Kapil Dev	12
MUSHTAQ	run out	3
AAQIB	not out	1
	EXTRAS (61b, 15w, 1nb)	22
	TOTAL	173

FALL: 8, 17, 105, 127, 130, 141, 141, 161, 166, 173

BOWLING

	o	m	r	w
KAPIL DEV	10	0	30	2
PRABHAKAR	10	1	22	2
SRINATH	8.1	0	37	2
TENDULKAR	10	0	37	1
RAJU	10	1	41	1

MAN OF THE MATCH: SACHIN TENDULKAR

INDIA WON BY 43 RUNS

PAKISTAN V SOUTH AFRICA
THE GABBA, BRISBANE, 8 MARCH 1992

SOUTH AFRICA

HUDSON	c Ijaz b Imran	54
WESSELS	c Moin b Aaqib	7
RUSHMERE	c Sohail b Mushtaq	35
KUIPER	c Moin b Imran	5
RHODES	lbw b Sikander	5
CRONJE	not out	47
McMILLAN	b Akram	33
RICHARDSON	b Akram	5
SNELL	not out	1
EXTRAS (8lb, 9w, 2nb)		19
TOTAL (for 7 wickets)		211

FALL: 31, 98, 110, 111, 127, 198, 207

BOWLING

	O	m	r	w
AKRAM	10	0	42	2
AAQIB	7	1	36	1
IMRAN	10	0	34	2
SIKANDER	8	0	30	1
IJAZ	7	0	26	0
MUSHTAQ	8	1	35	1

PAKISTAN

SOHAIL	b Snell	23
FAZAL	c Richardson b McMillan	11
INZAMAM	run out	48
IMRAN	Richardson b McMillan	34
MALIK	c Donald b Kuiper	12
AKRAM	b Kuiper	9
IJAZ	c Rhodes by Kuiper	6
MUSHTAQ	run out	4
MOIN	not out	5
SIKANDER	not out	1
EXTRAS (2lb, 17w, 1nb)		20
TOTAL (for 8 wickets)		173

FALL: 50, 50, 135, 136, 156, 157, 163, 171

BOWLING

	O	m	r	w
DONALD	7	1	31	0
PRINGLE	7	0	31	0
SNELL	8	2	26	1
McMILLAN	7	0	34	2
KUIPER	6	0	40	3
CRONJE	1	0	9	0

MAN OF THE MATCH: ANDREW HUDSON

SOUTH AFRICA WON BY 20 RUNS

PAKISTAN V AUSTRALIA
THE WACA, PERTH, 11 MARCH 1992

PAKISTAN

SOHAIL	c Healy b Moody	76
RAMEEZ	c Border b Whitney	34
MALIK	b Moody	0
MIANDAD	c Healy b S Waugh	46
IMRAN	c Moody b S Waugh	13
INZAMAM	run out	16
IJAZ	run out	0
AKRAM	c M Waugh b S Waugh	0
MOIN	c Healy b McDermott	5
MUSHTAQ	not out	3
	EXTRAS (9lb, 16w, 2nb)	27
	TOTAL (for 9 wickets)	220

FALL: 78, 80, 157, 193, 194, 205, 205, 214, 220

BOWLING

	O	m	r	w
McDERMOTT	10	0	33	1
REID	9	0	37	0
S WAUGH	10	0	36	3
WHITNEY	10	1	50	1
MOODY	10	0	42	2
M WAUGH	1	0	13	0

AUSTRALIA

MOODY	c Malik b Aaqib	4
MARSH	c Moin b Imran	39
BOON	c Mushtaq b Aaqib	5
JONES	c Aaqib b Mushtaq	47
M WAUGH	c Ijaz b Mushtaq	30
BORDER	c Ijaz b Mushtaq	1
S WAUGH	c Moin b Imran	5
HEALY	c Ijaz b Aaqib	8
McDERMOTT	lbw b Akram	0
WHITNEY	b Akram	5
REID	not out	0
	EXTRAS (71b, 14w, 7nb)	28
	TOTAL	172

FALL: 13, 31, 116, 122, 123, 130, 156, 162, 167, 172

BOWLING

	O	m	r	w
AKRAM	7.2	0	28	2
AAQIB	8	1	21	3
IMRAN	10	1	32	2
IJAZ	10	0	43	0
MUSHTAQ	10	0	41	3

MAN OF THE MATCH: AAMIR SOHAIL

PAKISTAN WON BY 48 RUNS

PAKISTAN V SRI LANKA
THE WACA, PERTH, 15 MARCH 1992

SRI LANKA

MAHANAMA	b Akram	12
SAMARASEKERA	st Moin b Mushtaq	38
HATHURUSINGHE	b Mushtaq	5
DE SILVA	c Sohail b Ijaz	43
GURUSINHA	c Malik b Imran	37
RANATUNGA	c Sub b Sohail	7
TILLEKARATNE	not out	25
KALPAGE	not out	13
EXTRAS (15lb, 6nb, 11w)		32
TOTAL (for 6 wickets)		212

FALL: 29, 48, 99, 132, 158, 187

BOWLING

	O	m	r	w
AKRAM	10	0	37	1
AAQIB	10	0	39	0
IMRAN	8	1	36	1
MUSHTAQ	10	0	43	2
IJAZ	8	0	28	1
SOHAIL	4	0	14	1

PAKISTAN

SOHAIL	c Mahanama b Ramanayake	1
RAMEEZ	c Gurusinha b Wickremasinghe	32
IMRAN	c De Silva b Hathurusinghe	22
MIANDAD	c Wickremasinghe b Gurusinha	57
MALIK	c Kalpage b Ramanayake	51
INZAMAM	run out	11
IJAZ	not out	8
AKRAM	not out	5
EXTRAS (12lb, 9w, 8nb)		29
TOTAL (for 6 wickets)		216

FALL: 7, 68, 84, 185, 201, 205

BOWLING

	O	m	r	w
WIJEGUNAWARDENA	10	1	34	0
RAMANAYAKE	10	1	37	2
WICKREMASINGHE	9.1	0	41	1
GURUSINHA	9	0	38	1
HATHURUSINGHE	9	0	40	1
KALPAGE	2	0	14	0

MAN OF THE MATCH: JAVED MIANDAD

PAKISTAN WON BY 4 WICKETS

1992 WORLD CUP SCORECARDS

PAKISTAN V NEW ZEALAND
LANCASTER PARK, CHRISTCHURCH, 18 MARCH 1992

NEW ZEALAND

GREATBATCH	c Malik b Mushtaq	42
LATHAM	c Inzamam b Aaqib	6
JONES	lbw b Akram	2
CROWE	c Sohail b Akram	3
RUTHERFORD	run out	8
HARRIS	st Moin b Mushtaq	1
PATEL	c Mushtaq b Sohail	7
SMITH	b Imran	1
LARSEN	b Akram	37
MORRISON	c Inzamam b Akram	12
WATSON	not out	5
EXTRAS (3b, 23lb, 12w, 4nb)		42
TOTAL		166

FALL: 23, 26, 39, 85, 87, 93, 96, 106, 150, 166

BOWLING

	O	m	r	w
AKRAM	9.2	0	32	4
AAQIB	10	1	34	1
MUSHTAQ	10	2	18	2
IMRAN	8	0	22	1
SOHAIL	10	1	29	1
IJAZ	1	0	5	0

PAKISTAN

SOHAIL	c Patel b Morrison	0
RAMEEZ	not out	119
INZAMAM	b Morrison	5
MIANDAD	lbw b Morrison	30
MALIK	not out	9
EXTRAS (11b, 1w, 2nb)		4
TOTAL (for 3 wickets)		167

FALL: 0, 9, 124

BOWLING

	O	m	r	w
MORRISON	10	0	42	3
PATEL	10	2	25	0
WATSON	10	3	26	0
HARRIS	4	0	18	0
LARSEN	3	0	16	0
JONES	3	0	10	0
LATHAM	2	0	13	0
RUTHERFORD	1.4	0	11	0
GREATBATCH	1	0	5	0

MAN OF THE MATCH: MUSHTAQ AHMED

PAKISTAN WON BY 7 WICKETS

PAKISTAN V NEW ZEALAND
EDEN PARK, AUCKLAND, 22 MARCH 1992
WORLD CUP SEMI-FINAL

NEW ZEALAND

GREATBATCH	b Aaqib	17
WRIGHT	c Rameez b Mushtaq	13
JONES	lbw b Mushtaq	21
CROWE	run out	91
RUTHERFORD	c Moin b Akram	50
HARRIS	st Moin b Sikander	13
SMITH	not out	18
PATEL	lbw b Akram	8
LARSEN	not out	8
	EXTRAS (4b, 7lb, 8w, 4nb)	23
	TOTAL (for 7 wickets)	262

FALL: 35, 39, 87, 194, 214, 221, 244

BOWLING

	O	m	r	w
AKRAM	10	0	40	2
AAQIB	10	2	45	1
MUSHTAQ	10	0	40	2
IMRAN	10	0	59	0
SIKANDER	9	0	56	1
SOHAIL	1	0	11	0

PAKISTAN

SOHAIL	c Jones b Patel	14
RAMEEZ	c Morrison b Watson	44
IMRAN	c Larsen b Harris	44
MIANDAD	not out	57
MALIK	c Sub b Larsen	1
INZAMAM	run out	60
AKRAM	b Watson	9
MOIN	not out	20
	EXTRAS (4b, 10lb, 1w)	15
	TOTAL (for 6 wickets)	264

FALL: 30, 84, 134, 140, 227, 238

BOWLING

	O	m	r	w
PATEL	10	1	50	1
MORRISON	9	0	55	0
WATSON	10	2	39	2
LARSEN	10	1	34	1
HARRIS	10	0	72	1

MAN OF THE MATCH: INZAMAM-UL-HAQ

PAKISTAN WON BY 4 WICKETS

PAKISTAN V ENGLAND
MELBOURNE CRICKET GROUND, 25 MARCH 1992
WORLD CUP FINAL

PAKISTAN

SOHAIL	c Stewart b Pringle	4
RAMEEZ	lbw b Pringle	8
IMRAN	c Illingworth b Botham	72
MIANDAD	c Botham b Illingworth	58
INZAMAM	b Pringle	42
AKRAM	run out	33
MALIK	not out	0
EXTRAS (19lb, 6w, 7nb)		32
TOTAL (for 6 wickets)		249

FALL: 20, 24, 163, 197, 249, 249

BOWLING

	O	m	r	w
PRINGLE	10	2	22	3
LEWIS	10	2	52	0
DeFREITAS	10	1	42	0
BOTHAM	7	0	42	1
ILLINGWORTH	10	0	50	1
REEVE	3	0	22	0

ENGLAND

GOOCH	c Aaqib b Mushtaq	29
BOTHAM	c Moin b Akram	0
STEWART	c Moin b Aaqib	7
HICK	lbw b Mushtaq	17
FAIRBROTHER	c Moin b Aaqib	62
LAMB	b Akram	31
LEWIS	b Akram	0
REEVE	c Rameez b Mushtaq	15
PRINGLE	not out	18
DeFREITAS	run out	10
ILLINGWORTH	c Rameez b Imran	14
EXTRAS (5lb, 13w, 6nb)		24
TOTAL		227

FALL: 6, 21, 59, 69, 141, 141, 180, 183, 208, 227

BOWLING

	O	m	r	w
AKRAM	10	0	49	3
AAQIB	10	2	27	2
MUSHTAQ	10	1	41	3
IJAZ	3	0	13	0
IMRAN	6.2	0	43	1
SOHAIL	10	0	49	0

MAN OF THE MATCH: WASIM AKRAM

PAKISTAN WON BY 22 RUNS